A Good Woman

a novel

Dorothy Weil

Plain View Press
P. O. 42255
Austin, TX 78704

plainviewpress.net
sb@plainviewpress.net
512-441-2452 (phone/fax)

Cover Art: Detail of *Letter from the Shadows* © CB Follett, 2006, photograph by Duff Axsom.

Thanks to those who read this work in manuscript, for their encouragement, praise, and helpful suggestions: Ceil Cleveland, editor and author, Stephen Birmingham, novelist and social historian, Dr. Ed Lahniers, Rex and Bruce Weil who gave their usual honest critiques, and Sidney Weil, who read the work at least ten times. Thanks also to Susan Bright, editor, for her multifarious efforts on behalf of literature that addresses serious themes.

To My Family With Love

A Good Woman

October 1, 1904

Lancaster Ohio County Register : "Melissa Bromen of RR 82 gave birth to a baby girl on Friday. Welcome Mary Lou Bromen!"

Mary Lou's Children

The century is almost at an end. Frederic thinks: time to leave all its sorrow and tragedy behind and concentrate on the present. At his age, he might not see much of the new century, but his children and grandchildren will. He looks forward to vacationing with them next week in Aspen. He has given them good lives, better than his and that of his parents, whom he always wonders about this time of the year.

The significance of the month of March cannot be ignored, even though Helen tries. She talks about the past often, mostly about her mother's neglect. She looks forward to the millennium. Armageddon will come: the unsaved will be punished and the anointed raised.

Although Sylvia predicts the future through tarot cards for her customers, it is the past she would like to see into. For all she has of them, her parents are like those fairytale characters (usually wicked) struck dead, imploding into a heap of garments, a hat, shoes, an umbrella. Was there blood on any other hands? In the eight years since it occurred, she has never stopped trying to understand the terrible thing that happened at her childhood home.

March 15, 1991

"This is murder pure and simple, and will be pursued and prosecuted like any other case."
Hamilton County Prosecutor, *Cincinnati Times*

MARY LOU

Mary Lou awoke shuddering: she dreamed Don's doctor beckoned her and Don into the dark basement of a hospital. All they could see was his white hair and white coat, a milky wisp as he whirled around slowly and disappeared. They groped their way through the blackness to an open elevator and entered, but there were no buttons to push.

Death was stalking them, relentless as a cat slinking toward its prey. The only question was: where would it come from? From inside the house or out?

Mary Lou thought of the old couple several houses down the street, about her and Don's age, both ill. Recently an ambulance had pulled up and several men in white carried the woman down the steps wrapped like a mummy. On Halloween a year ago, two teenagers pushed their way into the house of an old couple who were giving out dimes, and killed the man.

Mary Lou had to pee. She got out of bed and headed for the bathroom. Her back and legs hurt. Her knee was swollen. She thought of Elaine. Her daughter's name would be on her lips in her dying moment, she was sure. But she reminded herself once again not to dwell on the inevitable, the unchangeable, not to let loss and the fear of death take over. She came from strong people. Country people. People who farmed the land around Lancaster, where General William T. Sherman was born.

As she returned to bed, Mary Lou thought, *Old people are always peeing, and we're gassy as cows.* She slid back into bed carefully so as not to wake Don, and went back to sleep.

She awoke to an old radio jingle running through her head:

Pepsi Cola hits the spot
Twelve full ounces that's a lot
Twice as much for a nickel too
Pepsi Cola is the drink for you

Now where did that come from? It popped into her mind like one of those unwanted ads on the Mac. Back in the thirties she and Don had heard that song constantly on the radio, and they *had* shifted to Pepsi because it was cheaper than coke. *Sixty years ago.*

She and Don were young parents then. Now her hands were covered with liver spots and her skin was wrinkled as a poppy. When Billy was little, he looked at her arms once and said, "Grandma, did someone let all the air out of you?"

She had to laugh, the image was so apt.

Mary Lou went downstairs and fixed breakfast: cereal and skimmed milk, no sugar, for Don. She glanced out the window over the sink: looked like a good day. The kids would be coming for trick or treat in spite of the decay of the neighborhood and the crime.

Don appeared at the doorway, just clearing the lintel, a big man even now, though his face was wrinkled beneath his heavy white hair. He walked slowly, pitching slightly from side to side. When Mary Lou first met him he was built like a prizefighter—and was loading hundred pound sacks of meal and flour at her father's mill. . . .

"Did you sleep OK?" she asked. He wouldn't complain even if he hadn't.

"Pretty good."

She handed him the newspaper.

"I have to go buy stuff for the kids coming around tonight," she said. "I'm going to do a little work in the garden first."

"Do you think we should hand out stuff this year with all the problems?"

"I'll close up early." She wished she were as sure as she sounded.

Last year's shooting had been in the worst part of the neighborhood, she told herself, where the boys selling drugs hung about the entrance to the expressway that sliced the community in half.

"The little kids would be disappointed," she said.

Mary Lou was glad to be outdoors. The air was balmy, and the earth she dug into was warm. The cosmos were still blooming though their legs were gray and ugly like those of an old woman (hers were still young looking except for her bad knee; she had what Sylvia called "great legs"). As she put the bulbs in beds, she marveled at what wonderful things they were: onion-shaped, drab, but in spring suddenly popping up like children in the morning. Colorful as the children who would be coming for trick or treat: red devils and white angels, scaly green monsters.

As Mary Lou covered the last few bulbs, she thought of all the mothers helping their kids get their costumes together. Up and down the street, even all over the country. Did her own children remember the outfits she had made for them? On her old treadle when Helen and Frederick were little, then on an electric. She made a silver dress and tiara for Helen who wanted to be a princess, a pirate's outfit for Frederick. Sylvia went one year as Alice in Wonderland; Elaine, who never grew old enough to go alone, was adorable as a white rabbit. Billy was Superman. The children were always so excited on Halloween, loving their vivid new selves, trading good for bad, plain for beautiful, timid for brave.

Mary Lou as a child once dressed as a gypsy, in a swingy skirt, red and blue kerchief, and bangles and beads from her mother's "jewelry" box. She loved it. The neighborhood kids shouldn't be deprived of their fun because of a few rotten apples.

Mary Lou stood and brushed her muddy hands on her apron, then went indoors and got dressed to go on errands. As she pulled on her skirt, she tucked it tightly around her hips and swung them to the tune of "The Stripper," watching herself in the mirror (*was that silly?*). But it was Halloween, the night to be something different, to let yourself go. And inside her body there was still a young girl.

Before she left the house, Mary Lou made sure Don was comfortable, his pack of lifesavers nearby and the phone handy. She laid out his medicine: he had a regular pharmacy in his bathroom closet. So did she for that matter, though she was basically well, but keeping up an old body, like keeping up their eighty-year old house—a Victorian with a big porch and a peaked roof—required constant care. There was stuff for her bones, her blood, her skin, for something was always wearing out, and though the house was one of the nicest on the street, there was always something coming loose, springing a leak, parting company with the walls, tiles slipping off the roof. Well, Mary Lou thought, her philosophy did not allow giving in to illness and age or crying over problems (that was for Helen, who acted as though she were the only one whose dishwasher broke down or whose bathtub leaked). She had to be strong. Don had always been the strong one, unchanging as the seven hills of Cincinnati. Now she was the one who had to be strong.

Even as she worked, she noticed out the window the squirrels getting into the bird feeder. They or some other creatures were skittering around the attic, too. But then often, from the woods behind the house that made the squirrels so plenteous, a buck deer would push through the trees and stand majestically in the yard, or a bright red tree in the gloomy fall weather would blaze like a god reminding her that life was worth living.

The supermarket where Mary Lou shopped was situated just off an expressway in a No-Man's-Land of discount stores. Its shelves of bright cans and shiny boxes, its labyrinth of aisles, were dazzling and confusing. There were always new and different clerks, so from week to week she saw no one there she knew. When she was a child, the butcher at the small country store where her father bought meat was a neighbor and would talk over local news with her father, and he would give Mary Lou a wiener for free which she would eat right there in the store. Well, she reminded herself, even Mr. Jaeger, her local butcher, had been gone for fifteen years. Was he dead or in Florida?

When the neighborhood was still nice, she could walk to the grocery store, the library, the hardware store and the five and dime. There was a shoe shop (where she bought Frederick boots with a pocket knife attached), a clothing store, several restaurants, a gas station, a beauty parlor, and a drugstore with a soda fountain (marble-topped, smelling of vanilla and nectar syrup). Now there was only the bank and one bar, a fast-food place and a grimy newsstand. The neighborhood grocery had long since closed, the windows still strewn with signs for Lestoil detergent and an ashtray full of cigarette butts, as if the owners had just stepped out for the afternoon.

The movie house was boarded up; in the window was a faded poster for *West Side Story*.

When Mary Lou and Don first bought their house, some forty years ago, the streets were clean as Mary Lou's kitchen (so she liked to say). Now the sidewalks were full of paper cups and cigarette filters, and an occasional plastic bag hung in a tree like a nest of tent caterpillars.

In the old days, people gathered on their front porches on summer evenings. Walking by, you could see the white of summer shoes and the red glow of cigarettes. You would hear the creak of porch swings and the kids singing "In the Gloaming," and "You are My Sunshine"—and the newer songs like "Deep Purple" and "I Hear a Rhapsody." Families would send one of the children up to the drug store to get a quart of ice cream. There was nothing to fear in the dark.

The changes had come, like old age, slowly, one at a time. After the war, fire-escapes appeared on some of the nice old houses, and the stores closed and disappeared, until all of a sudden there were groups of empty buildings. The streetcars gave way to buses and then the buses cut their routes, and cars took over and families moved out to the suburbs. New people moved in whose kids hung out in the street.

Don's lawn mower was stolen by kids—the ones who cut through the yard, trampling her flowers, she was sure.

There were still a few long-established families in the neighborhood who didn't want to move—like Mary Lou and Don. The houses were well-built, made to last by the old-time German workmen, and in spite of much neglect were good places. Families who couldn't afford the suburbs came into the area for its cheaper prices.

So many new faces. The only person Mary Lou knew to say hello to now was Mrs. Wong, who always said good morning and thank you in one sentence and not much else. She was a nice woman with her newspaper covered with Chinese writing stuffed in her string bag. Penny and Stan, with whom she and Don had gone on boat rides—and the Miller family—it seemed everyone Mary Lou knew was gone, died or moved away. She sometimes felt like she was up past her bedtime.

At six that evening, Mary Lou served dinner and cleared away quickly. The children would be coming to the door before dark. Too bad they couldn't tear around at night like they used to. Of course when Mary Lou was a girl the kids did naughty things like putting the neighbor's trash cans on their roof or a bucket of water against a door—ringing the bell and running. But no one ever heard of razor blades in candy or big kids grabbing the little ones' treats. Or a man getting shot for a dish of dimes.

Mary Lou turned on the porch light and stationed herself inside the screen door with a large bag of candy bars and waited for the children to show up. They came in small groups, many with a parent herding them along.

Batman and ballerinas were the thing this year along with the usual clowns and princesses. Some were so tiny they had to be told to say "Happy Halloween" and "Trick or Treat" by a parent. They were cute as always. Mary Lou invited them into the hallway so Don could see them and help dump candy bars into their plastic bags. He gave them too many, but Mary Lou loved seeing him smile.

As the evening grew darker, the visitors thinned out, and the sound of young voices calling "trick or treat" died away. Don waited for a few more stragglers, then went to bed. When it was all the way dark, Mary Lou figured it would be safe to put the leftover candy away: no more little Batmen or monsters would be coming by.

She stared at the ghost made of a twisted bed sheet on the Wongs' porch; it swung spookily and their pumpkin jack o'lantern was lit up with a candle smile. By morning it would be smashed on the sidewalk.

Reaching for the porch light switch, Mary Lou jumped at the sound of heavy footsteps. Two tall boys were coming up the stairs. There were usually a few kids too old for trick or treat, some not even from the neighborhood. She quickly locked the screen.

The two were barely made up. One was a good foot taller than Mary Lou, with a few streaks of dirt on his face, a bum's derby hat and a patched shirt. The other wore a football helmet and a black T-shirt. She was sure these were the boys who were always cutting through her yard. Mary Lou had complained to the kids' mothers many times that they had trampled her flowers and were trespassing, but the mothers had not seemed to care and the two boys just did worse things. She knew their names because she had reported them to the police, and the police had shown her their pictures with their names on them. Harold, the one done up as a bum, had been in juvenile detention; the other, Byron, was always getting in fights at school.

"Trick or Treat!" they said.

They held their plastic grocery sacks wide.

"You boys are too old to go Halloweening."

Mary Lou prepared to close the door.

"Aw—c'mon," Byron said.

"I'm all out of candy."

"We're safe," Harold said. "We don't go around hasslin' old ladies like some guys."

Mary Lou's hands on the door frame trembled. Why did they say that? What if they pushed through the screen and grabbed her?

Mary Lou slammed the door in their faces and leaned against it. She switched off the porch light.

"Go away!"

She waited a second, breathing heavily, worried they would go around to the kitchen where she couldn't remember if she'd locked the door. In a moment she heard them going down the porch stairs, then their voices raised loud on purpose.

"My cock itches!"

"Fuckin' A!"

Mary Lou held her ears. The boys around here talked like that all the time. What happened to the little kids who came to the door so polite and sweet?

She went to the kitchen quickly: the back door was locked, and the windows too. Did they know that Don couldn't help? Mary Lou

returned to the living room. Maybe she should turn the porch light
back on. She switched it on, then went to the window to pull down the
blind.

"Hi!"

Harold stood there with a flashlight making his features look eerie.

"You get away!"

"I just want a treat. Give me one Snicker and I'll go away."

"I'm calling the police."

"You done called 'em. "

"Said we stold your lawnmower."

"Why'd you lock that door the minute you saw us?" Byron said.
"What do you think we're gonna do?"

"Get away. Don—my husband—is in the next room and he's got a
rifle."

The boys laughed and stomped up and down on the porch. Mary
Lou was afraid they'd push through the window screen. Harold imitated
Don's unsteady walk. Mary Lou slammed down the window. She pulled
the blind down and did the same with the others.

"Aw!"

"Trick or Treat!"

"We got no treat—we got to trick."

"Trick my dick!"

"Tricky dicky."

Mary Lou went over to the phone. She should call the police.
But the boys quieted down and she thought maybe they had left. She
listened, trembling. She heard a splattering noise. What on earth? She
went to the window and peeked around the blind: they were peeing on
the porch, laughing. She went back to the phone, but put down the
receiver when she heard a thump and the boys running down the steps.

"We'll be back!" they called.

Her heart wouldn't stop pounding; she wondered what they would
have done if she'd opened the screen door. She was dumb to open her
house after last year.

What did they mean, they'd be back? When?

Mary Lou went over to the fireplace and sat on the sofa. She should
keep watch for awhile. But they were probably just bluffing.

When she heard nothing more from outside, she dozed. Her mind
drifted back to earlier days as it did so often: Halloween in her gypsy
costume, then riding across the alfalfa field on her horse Tim—the wind
blowing through her hair, nothing on her mind, nothing in her world

but the sound of Tim's breathing, the smell of the fields. When the sky and earth began to turn gray and blue, she would take him to the barn, and follow the light from the kitchen window to the warm oil-lit kitchen where her mother and grandmother would be cooking, and the smell of ham and cornbread, green beans and fried apples would fill her with a happy mix of hunger and tiredness.

"Get washed up," her mother would say. And Mary Lou would pump water at the sink, water that tasted faintly metallic—iron-y.

In the evening, she would cuddle by the fireplace with her mother while her grandmother read from *One Hundred and One Great Poems* and the Bible. She read the gentler passages—"judge not lest ye be judged," "do unto others as you would have others do unto you."

Each night her grandmother sat by Mary Lou's bed while Mary Lou said the little German prayer she'd taught her: "Ich bin klein (I am little), mein herz ist rein (my heart is pure). . . ." She prayed for her mother who was "sickly."

Those early years in the country were her best memories, though there was death and cruelty then too. In bed she could hear the shriek of the rabbits caught by owls and there was the pig slaughtering she was not allowed to go to, where her father and the neighborhood men got drunk and drank the pig blood as they butchered the meat. There were roughnecks—boys who got rid of unwanted kittens by throwing them at the barn, laughing as they watched their bloody bodies slide down the siding. But she had never been afraid.

She awoke stiff from sitting. How long had she been here in the living room? The clock said quarter of twelve—almost midnight. She stood and stretched, her back aching.

She peeked out the front window. The street was quiet, a silver moonlit stretch of macadam, blackened here and there by the shadows of trees moving in slow motion. Mary Lou crept upstairs to her and Don's bedroom, changed into her nightgown in the dark and slid under the covers. Don stirred and looked at the clock radio.

"What are you doing up so late?"

"Nothing. Couldn't sleep."

"I heard something. Was it those boys again?" Don said.

"They're just neighborhood kids."

She knew he wanted to believe her.

Don rolled over, making room for Mary Lou in the bed.

"You're shaking," he said.

"No I'm not."

Mary Lou put her arms around Don. His big ropey muscles had slackened. But she hung on to him tightly, as though he were still the strong young man who had carried her off in his sleigh.

2

When Mary Lou awoke in the morning and went to the back yard to feed the birds, she saw that the garage had been broken into.

"What now?" She walked gingerly over to it and peeked in. Don's truck was parked next to her car, a second-hand Mercedes convertible Don had bought her some twenty years ago that he and Billy had spent hours keeping in good shape, replacing some parts and touching up its sporty cream color. She had once loved whizzing around with the top down. (No more, too dangerous).

She entered and looked around. The truck seemed OK, but her driver's side window was smashed and the radio gone.

Mary Lou looked up toward her and Don's bedroom. Could he see from the window that the garage door was off its hinges? He did not need this. She went into the kitchen and called the police. Not that they would do anything.

She fixed Don's breakfast and called him to the table.

"Did we have many more Halloweeners last night?" he asked.

"Not many."

The police came while Don was in the bathroom. They asked a few questions, tramped around the garage, and took down her name (like they hadn't been there before). She told them it was Harold and Byron, she was sure, and they said they would check them out, but if she hadn't actually seen them. . . .

Billy arrived later that afternoon. The sight of him lifted Mary Lou's spirits like the deer or the red tree or a spring bulb pushing its way up through the earth. So young and alive and with his dreams still intact. He gave her a kiss, then when she pointed out the garage, he said, "I'm gonna nuke 'em."

Billy wore a varsity football letter on his sweat shirt, but Mary Lou worried that he was no match for the trespassers.

"No fighting," she said.

"I'll get you a new radio soon's I can."

Billy inspected the damage to the garage door. His face got red just the way Don's did when he was angry.

"I'm gonna get those two, I swear."

He spent the next few hours putting a new lock on the door.

It did Mary Lou good to hear the sound of a hammer and see a man at work. Don always kept the place in order until he got sick. When he complained, it was about being unable to work, not about his pain.

When Billy had the garage door fixed, he said, "I think this'll do it. If they so much as come in the yard, call the police, Grandma."

"I did and all they did was poke around. Didn't believe I knew who broke in, but I'm sure. Those boys came up on the porch last night and threatened me."

"They came up on the porch?"

"Yes, dressed up for trick or treat—"

Billy slammed his fist into his palm.

"What did they do?"

Mary Lou hadn't meant to tell Billy what the boys did, but now it was too late.

"Just acted crazy, wanted candy they said and they—"

"What?"

"Never mind—"

"Tell me."

"Well, they peed on the porch."

"If I get my hands on them—"

"They're not worth it, Billy."

"You keep your door locked, Grandma. Damn."

"There goes Harold now."

A car screeched out of the driveway three doors down, Harold at the wheel. Billy ran into the street.

"Hey! Hey!"

The car kept on going, around the corner and out of sight. Billy ran to his motorcycle parked in the driveway, jumped on and gunned it, and flew off in pursuit of Harold. Mary Lou listened for the sound of the bike, trying to follow Billy's path. In a few minutes, he was back.

"I'm going to get him, I swear. I know that kid from school. Him and his buddy are totally vicious."

"I don't understand these boys," Mary Lou said.

"They're punks."

"His mother never puts their garbage cans away," Mary Lou said.

"Figures."

Billy caught his breath, then he and Mary Lou walked around to the side yard and he picked up Mary Lou's cans to carry to the curb.

"And she tosses everything in them without bags, leaves them out for days—orange peels and plastic junk all over the sidewalk."

Not only Harold's mother, but a lot of the newer people did the same, except for Mrs. Wong, whose garbage was as neat as Mary Lou's.

"Maybe I'm too persnickety," Mary Lou said, "but I'm German and don't know any other way." (*But the right way*).

As she and Billy went toward the house, the yard grew dark. It was getting dark earlier each day. Remembering the night before, she shivered.

"Don't mention the break-in or anything to Don," Mary Lou said.

Billy sat at the kitchen table drinking a can of beer, and he poured one into a glass for Mary Lou while she fried chicken. This was like the days when he had lived with her and Don—only then it had been milk and cookies while she talked about her childhood on the farm, and they laughed together about little daily happenings.

She dipped the chicken in the skillet of deep fat, and tested the boiling potatoes with a fork.

"I thought about Tim last night and all the fun I used to have riding through the fields and over the hills," Mary Lou said. "And how we would sit by the creek and talk. He understood everything I told him."

"I feel that same way about my Harley," Billy said.

Mary Lou slapped his arm.

"Hat in the house," she said. He was wearing his baseball cap backward as usual.

He told her the latest joke going around at school.

How I miss him being here every day, she thought.

He had been such a quiet child when he first came to her and Don. His eyes were full of doubt, and for weeks he had followed Mary Lou from room to room like a lonesome puppy. He had come to them at three when Sylvia left him and his father, and went off to "find herself."

He must have felt the way she did when her father moved from the farm to the grist mill in the basin of Cincinnati. Her mother and grandmother were left behind in the country graveyard. Her father's new wife, Mother Nina, and *her* mother, took their places. Mother Nina spent her time reading religious pamphlets and the strange new grandmother sat all day at her card table, made chairs rise at "séances," and put people in contact with the dead. They spoke to each other in German when Mary Lou was around.

Mary Lou took the rolls from the oven, the little soft kind that came in a tube you whacked open at the seam. She put the salad on the table. She loved the smell of fresh vegetables; in spring on the farm the first green onions and radishes and cucumbers promised good things to eat after a winter of canned food.

"So what's been happenin' around here, besides break-ins?" Billy said.

"The other night, one of those pesky salesmen called me, the ones who call right at dinner time? As usual he called me Mrs. *Fried*-man like fried chicken instead of Freed-man and asked me how I was doing, though I know that's just a pitch, so I said 'my bad knee is the size of a grapefruit; how are you?'"

"Grandma, you are a trip and a half."

"I felt bad after. It wasn't the salesman's fault I'd had a rough day. But I did take the air out of him."

Mary Lou loved Billy's laugh.

Billy was the child she and Don should have had for their own. Helen and she were so different that Mary Lou sometimes wondered if they were truly mother and daughter. When Frederick was born she was so happy: a boy for Don! But Frederick was not the typical boy: he loved school and reading, not the active things Don liked. He was a good kid, almost super-good, the most intelligent of her children. He never got less than an "A" in school, and worked his own way through college. Now he was a vice-president of a food distributing company in California.

Mary Lou was very proud of Frederick, but Billy was her darling.

Well, each child was different. Her grandmother always said there were no two alike and she'd had ten. Elaine was the sweetest of all Mary Lou and Don's children, but that was not to be. Sylvia was the family problem, probably Don's favorite, but always off somewhere on some new quest for perfect happiness.

She had spent years starting and quitting school, going from one dead-end job and one dead-beat boyfriend to another, and was still rootless, working as a waitress though she was a talented actress.

Maybe Helen was right: Mary Lou and Don had treated Sylvia more like a grandchild than a child—as Helen often said. Well, maybe Mary Lou shouldn't have had a baby so late—she was in her forties—but she didn't think about getting pregnant that late.

"What do you hear from Mom?" Billy said.

His devotion to Sylvia was heartbreaking. Every one of the nine years he had lived with Mary Lou and Don, he had made Sylvia a Mother's Day card, covering it with paper hearts and sprinkles. On her occasional visits, he was so good it was painful to watch. As Sylvia always forgot to send Billy gifts, Mary Lou bought birthday and Christmas presents for him and signed them 'with love from Mom.'

"Has she called?" Billy asked.

"Not lately," Mary Lou said.

And not likely.
"How's your Dad?" she said.
"He's OK."
"And Sheri?"
"OK."
Sheri lived with Mike, a woman somewhat younger than Sylvia. Mary Lou didn't like Sheri—because she had little interest in Billy—not because she and Mike weren't married. Mary Lou had reluctantly gotten used to the new sexual freedom. It had appeared in her world suddenly and stealthily, like acconite, the showy yellow weed that came from the woods and took over the farm's vegetable garden and lawns. First, Mr. Pfaltzgraf, her and Don's old house painter, started wearing a toupee and going to "'singles' bars," and next a niece of Don's was moving in with some man (when Mary Lou was young, she would have been called "wayward." Mother Nina would have called her "a scarlet woman"). Then when her friend Penny's daughter was in college, *she* moved in with some boy and Mary Lou certainly couldn't think of Penny's daughter that way. Not too long after, Sylvia—the first child she and Don could afford to send to college (they were planning to finance Billy when he was ready)—lived with her boyfriend for a while, in a messy apartment with posters of Timothy Leary and other sixties drug people all over the walls.

When they came to visit at Christmas she and Mary Lou had a big fuss over where the boyfriend would sleep. Sylvia said her room.

What would her grandmother and Mother Nina say?

"I can't allow that," Mary Lou told Sylvia.

"That is so hypocritical."

"OK, bring it up with your father," Mary Lou said.

The young man ended up on the couch.

"What are you thinking about, Grandma?" Billy said.

"Oh, nothing."

Mary Lou slid the chicken onto a platter and surveyed the table.

"Go get Grandpa," she said.

Don looked better tonight, as he always did when Billy was around.

"Smells good. I even believe I could eat," Don said.

When they were seated, everyone in his old place, Mary Lou passed the platter of chicken; Don helped himself to a thigh and leg.

"Here, let me take the skin off," Mary Lou said.

"Oh the hell with it." Don bit into his chicken letting the forbidden grease run down his chin.

"Man's gotta have some fun," Billy said, seeing Mary Lou's concern.

Mary Lou was so glad to see Don smile, she didn't interfere; anyway in spite of his piled-up plate, he still didn't eat much.

"What were you and Grandma doing out by the garage this afternoon?" he said.

Billy, luckily, was biting into a second drumstick, and Mary Lou nudged him under the table.

"Old lock and hinges were rusted through," she said. She turned to Billy and passed him the chicken again.

"Where does it all go?" she asked.

Billy pulled up his T-shirt and pushed his stomach out, imitating a gluttonous good ole boy.

"Maybe with the six pack I just drunk."

"Oh stop that."

After dinner Billy put up the card table in the living room, just as when he lived with her and Don. It had been awhile since he'd stayed this late, and he was pleased to find the cards in the same place they'd always been, tucked in the drawer under a lamp table.

"How about some rummy, Grandpa?"

Don nodded and the three took seats around the table. Mary Lou felt good with her two men beside her. She forgot about the threats to herself and her home from the darkening street. She loved this room with its Rookwood fireplace and bookshelves where she kept the row of green-jacketed Dickens novels her father once bought from a door to door salesman. Helen was always trying to get her to move to a safer neighborhood, closer to the mall, into an apartment, but Mary Lou pictured a sterile, soulless place with none of the good solid workmanship and trim of this place: the carved pineapple on the banister of the staircase, the solid plaster walls (not like these new places with walls you could put your fist through). The big windows brought in the sunlight and it moved around the house all day like a busy housewife.

The card game went on until 10 o'clock when Mary Lou served the threesome's traditional glasses of ginger ale (orange juice for Don), and Ritz crackers and cheese. Gulping down his drink, Billy announced that he would have to go soon.

Of course, Billy had his own life, Mary Lou thought, one she and Don knew little about. Signs of this other life occasionally appeared, just as evidence of overnight garden visits by squirrels and rabbits appeared in Mary Lou's garden by way of torn up mulch and nibbled leaves. There was the sticker on his bike: "sex, drugs and rock n' roll," and the hand-rolled cigarette that fell out of his leather jacket one time when she hung it up for him, which she supposed was marijuana.

Still, to Mary Lou, Billy would always be the kid she and Don watched tv with and read stories to, him in his blue pajamas, his little cold feet just fitting in a hand. He would always be the boy who made her a dried macaroni necklace in school and made her close her eyes while he slipped it around her neck—the boy she and Don took to the Grand Canyon and Yellowstone Park, snapping pictures with the Polaroid camera they bought him, and licking a red and white striped lollipop the size of a dinner plate.

Billy helped Mary Lou gather up the glasses and plates. Don looked at his watch. "Have you got a girl friend?" he asked.

Billy blushed and Don said, "I hope she's as pretty as your grandmother."

"Pooh," Mary Lou said. She never thought she was pretty. Both mother and grandmother said, "pretty is as pretty does." But a photo of her in a frame on the tv did show a slim young girl she had to admit was attractive.

"Just hangin' out with some guys," Billy said.

"Drive carefully," Mary Lou told him. "My cousin. . . ."

"I know—has a steel plate in his head from a motorcycle wreck." Billy grinned.

"And he has two little children."

Billy kissed Don and Mary Lou, and went to the door. Mary Lou followed.

"Have you and Grandpa got a gun?" he whispered.

"No, of course not."

"You need one in this neighborhood."

"Your grandfather doesn't believe in guns."

"I'll get one for you. I'll show you how to use it."

"My father taught me when we lived on the farm. But—"

She had not touched a gun since the night Tim came limping, bleeding into the yard: her father got his rifle and made her hold it and told her she must shoot, "to put him out of his misery."

"Those sons of b's come back here again, blow them away."

"No, Billy, don't even think about guns."

"Those no-good punks have them. Why shouldn't you?"

Billy gave her another quick kiss and ran down the steps. Mary Lou watched him mount his motorcycle. He was off in a noisy blast, leaving gas fumes rising off the macadam. Where was he going? *Did he have a gun? Did those other kids?* What if he ran into Byron and Harold and got into a fight?

Why had she told him about the boys coming up on the porch? She should have kept it to herself. As a kid he had often had stomach aches from worry, and she noticed his fingernails were still bitten to the quick. He had a temper.

When Mary Lou returned to the living room, it looked dim and no longer cozy. Long shadows darkened the corners, and Don looked awfully old and sad.

"What's wrong?" she said.

"Nothing."

But she could tell something was bothering Don. She had lived with him most of her life, ten times longer than she had been alive before she met him.

He tugged at his pants leg.

"My pants are tight," he said.

Mary Lou kneeled down and rolled up the cloth. The bruises were worse and the leg was very swollen. She felt his calf.

"Does that hurt?" she asked.

"No feeling in it at all."

This was what Mary Lou had been dreading. And what Don refused to think about. She picked up the phone and called the doctor. She knew what the worst would be. She made her voice sound steady though a cold draft passed over the back of her neck, as when she gardened in the sun. Maybe death was *inside* the house, sitting on the edge of her and Don's bed, or waiting on the living room sofa like a gentleman caller.

3

Mary Lou stared at her own feet as she waited in Don's hospital room for him to come back from tests. She noticed she had on two different colors of knee-hi's. She'd been doing that all her life. The colors called 'beige' and 'flesh' were almost identical, but no two shades were ever exactly the same. When one sock tore, you couldn't put the good one together with another extra to make a matching pair. That's how they could sell you so many of these things.

The mismatch didn't mean she was senile the way Helen and the nurse who settled Don in his room seemed to think. Both were getting on Mary Lou's nerves, the nurse for calling her Mary Lou as though she were a three year old instead of a woman of eighty-six, Helen for being so impatient when she couldn't find her Medicare card right off. And then she talked for Mary Lou as though she could not answer questions herself.

Oh God, she thought, don't let them take Don's leg.

She didn't want to even think the word *amputation*.

Never mind what a lot of people thought—that old people were like spent cartridges littering the ground after wars. She and Don were filled with all the feelings other people had, and wanted to be as well and happy as they could.

"Mother, do you want a magazine?" Helen said. She was settling in to wait with Mary Lou, knitting as usual. Why knitting annoyed Mary Lou she couldn't say, maybe because Helen did it so constantly as though just talking to you was a waste of time.

"No thanks."

Mary Lou never knew how to communicate with Helen as she could with Billy or even Sylvia. She wondered sometimes how she had produced her. They even looked different. Helen was tall and big-boned while she was petite and blonde (well, white now) like Sylvia. Helen's hair was dyed black and teased into an impossibly black cloud. She looked a little like Elizabeth Taylor at her fattest.

She began to rattle on about the people at her church as though Mary Lou knew them, in fact, all the world did. Mary Lou had heard it all before: Helen described operations and weddings, champagne fountains and engagement rings, diseases and disasters, in loving detail.

"—and she had to get a colostomy bag," Helen was saying. "I hope I don't live that long."

You'll change your tune on that, Mary Lou thought. And not too long off. Helen had to be near seventy.

Soon she would be into her favorite topic, her own funeral. There would be no visitation at the funeral home. At her church the minister would preach. The choir would sing "Amazing Grace," and the organist would play Pachabel's "Canon." Her grave was to be unmarked except for—

Mary Lou stared out the window. Helen was, she supposed, the "good" daughter and Sylvia the "bad" daughter, but she wished Sylvia were here.

Hours went by, and no news came from Don. Finally, Mary Lou went out to the nurse's station and asked about him. He was still undergoing tests.

"You might as well go home," Mary Lou told Helen when she returned to the room. "It'll be awhile."

"If you're sure," Helen said. "I'll go feed Russell."

Helen always talked about "feeding" her husband as though she simply pitched meat into his cage.

There was something kind of dumb about Russell, Mary Lou thought.

"I'll be back this afternoon. Ask the Lord to save me a parking space."

Now Mary Lou was really annoyed. Helen's insistence that God cared about stuff like parking a car set Mary Lou wild. It was fine that Helen was so religious, she supposed; it was just that she made it seem so personal and paltry and Mary Lou didn't notice church goers being any more compassionate or kind than anyone else. In fact, it seemed, the more avid they were, the less tolerant.

Helen had made it her whole life. She was already stocking up on canned goods and light bulbs and toilet paper to be prepared for the disasters of the millennium, at the same time predicting the end of the world. Mary Lou wasn't worried. She had been born almost at the beginning of the century and the end of the world had been predicted many times—by her Jehovah's Witness stepmother for one—and the dates had come and gone while the earth spun on. Unless mankind blew up the world, she was sure the century would end and a new one begin, though it was hard to think in terms of 2000. She wondered if she would be around to see it.

"You don't need to come back," Mary Lou said.

"How would you get home?"

Oh yes. Helen had brought her. Insisted on driving her, though Mary Lou was perfectly capable of driving herself. She wished Helen would stop treating her and Don like fruits. Maybe their minds weren't working quite as well as when they were younger. They were like the old piano in her parents' parlor with its yellow, chipped ivories: you could still play a tune on it, just every once on awhile you would hit a dead key.

"I'll walk you out," Mary Lou said. She accompanied her daughter as far as the smoking area by the drink machines in the hall, and lit a cigarette.

"You shouldn't smoke, Mother," Helen said.

"I know."

"Especially with Daddy—"

"I never smoke around him."

Was Helen's reminder concern or control? She had a way of being right. She had a point about Mary Lou's driving and she had told her and Don long ago to get out of the neighborhood because it was becoming dangerous. But all that faded away as Mary Lou returned to Don's room and began more hours of waiting.

How did she and Don get to this here and now? To this cutting off. When Mary Lou was young she never thought about getting old or sick. Life was an endless, somewhat frightening path before her. Now it was like a dream she was trying to recall.

The war was almost over when her father bought the mill and they moved to the city. She missed the farm, her mother and grandmother, her darling Tim and the scents of grass and hay and the sounds of crickets and tree frogs, fish flopping in the pond, the breeze over the open fields. The new school was frightening with its long flight of stone steps. Some of the kids threw rocks at her and others with German names. She got into shouting matches with the kids tormenting her. Her father had a limp from his wounds fighting for America. *She wasn't a Hun. She was an American.*

Still, in spite of her losses and new problems, Mary Lou found fresh things to interest her: she discovered the public library and read *Little Women* and *Girl of the Limberlost*. She grew to like the bustle at the mill when the horses and wagons came to load and unload, and she liked the classes and teachers at school (she always got good reports) ; she thought she might go on to college some day, and be a teacher though Mother Nina said a woman's place is in the home and "Whistling girls and crowing hens always come to bad ends."

She was sixteen when she first saw Don. She was standing on the bridge over the stream that powered her father's mill.

She could still feel the trembling of the metal grate, the rushing water dangerous and exciting beneath her. Mr. Neiderhelman's wagon, which would carry flour and cornmeal to market, pulled into the cobblestone yard, the horses neighing and snorting, their metal shoes ringing against the stone. The crew of four men who hoisted the heavy bags onto their shoulders and slung them onto the wagon had been joined by a new man. He lifted the bags with ease, smiling as he worked. He was big and handsome with red-gold hair and ruddy skin.

Mary Lou thought, "I will marry him."

"Mary Lou," her father called. "Go and make coffee for the men."

Mary Lou ran to the kitchen and brewed coffee, glancing out the window now and then at the new man. When she took it outside and poured it into the men's tin cups, she could not look up at him. The other men began laughing and the new young man walked away and sat on a big old discarded mill stone.

Mary Lou's father came out in the yard, hearing the guffaws. "What's so funny?"

"Nothin' much," one of the drivers said. "Just Don."

Mary Lou fled into the house, but she ran straight to the upstairs window and watched as the men finished their coffee and then went back to work.

She couldn't wait for Saturday to come again, but she begged her father not to make her take the men their coffee. She wanted to see the new man—Don—again, but she was so embarrassed. Her father wouldn't relent. He was like a stone.

When Mary Lou served Don's coffee this time, she looked up at him. The air was cold and she could see his breath and her own. His oiled leather coat was open, lined with yellow sheepskin. She could reach in and touch his heart.

"Go on, speak up to her," one of the men said.

Don turned red and slapped at his companion.

"Aw—ain't it sweet?" called one of the drivers.

"Don't pay any attention to him," Don said.

Pretty soon, he said thank you Mary Lou. He knew her name!

Mary Lou ran to her grandmother and begged her to tell her fortune. Usually she was a little afraid of this grandmother who sat at her card table all day with her shoulders hunched like an owl's and eyes that seemed to see everything. She nodded her head when Mary Lou came near and began laying out cards without a word. A red king led the pile, then red hearts, red jacks.

"A great change is coming," she said.

The last time she said that, Mary Lou had gotten her monthly, and Mother Nina saw the blood on her pants and silently went and got her some clean cloths and a cotton belt. It was months before Mary Lou had the nerve to ask a school mate what was happening.

"What change?" Mary Lou asked.

"The cards don't say—but it looks like a man. King of Hearts. The red king means love."

Could she be in love?

"Does the man love—like—me?"

Her grandmother stacked her deck of cards and shrugged. Her hands, with their long sharp nails, reminded Mary Lou of talons.

The following Saturday Don asked Mary Lou for a second cup of coffee. While she poured he said, "Would you like to go for a buggy ride?"

"I have to ask my father.'"

At supper time Mary Lou tried to get her father's attention. He ate with his eyes concentrated on his food, shoveling forkfuls of potato and meat into his mouth. Dessert appeared on the table, a peach pie. Mother Nina cut her father a large piece. He poured cream over it, stirred cream into his coffee and dumped sugar in it. Her step-mother offered a piece of pie to Mary Lou, but she shook her head—she could not swallow. Everything in life moved so slow.

Mary Lou's grandmother said, "Your daughter wants to tell you something."

How did she know that? Mary Lou wondered. She had never been able to explain the floating table at the old woman's séances, or the strange other-worldly voices either.

"What is it?"

"Nothing."

"It must be something. What is it?"

"That new one who helps Mr. Neiderhelman—wants to take me for a buggy ride on Sunday."

Mary Lou's father looked as if he'd waked from a bad dream.

"You're just a girl."

Mary Lou didn't dare contradict him. He had never been easy to talk to, and after he came back from his time in the World War, he was even quieter and more distant.

"You're just a little girl. . . . "

"No," said Mother Nina. "She's not."

Mary Lou saw an unspoken signal pass between her father and step-mother. Her father stood up.

"Go then. Be back before dark."

Mary Lou jumped up from the table and ran to her room. She buried her head in her pillow, then popped up and shook the clock. Sunday was hours and hours and hours away.

On Sunday she was ready by noon. At one, when she heard the sound of horse hooves in the cobblestone courtyard she ran down to meet Don.

He spoke little as they drove, concentrating on the horses. When one of the new Model T's on the road broke down, the other wagon drivers jeered at the man cranking away at his Ford. Don joined in the cries of "Get a horse!"

He slowed down at a railroad track, and held his frightened team back as an oncoming train sped by. He tucked Mary Lou's hand under his arm protectively. Mary Lou trembled; she thought of the girls at school, their talk of kissing, giggling about a girl's shoe prints on the buckboard of a wagon. She had a dim idea of what all this meant. She wondered if Don would ever kiss her.

Sundays used to be the dullest days of the week, church and then an endless afternoon until dinner. As Don's visits became regular, Mary Lou looked forward to Sunday as if it were Christmas.

She sneaked into her parents' room where there was a full-length mirror and looked at her body from the front and then the side. She was definitely bigger on top. At first when she noticed this, she had been ashamed and wrapped a cloth around her chest so the swellings wouldn't show.

In early December the Mill Creek iced over and the trees were like glass ornaments. As Mary Lou waited for Don's Sunday visit, she heard them crack and shards fall and shatter. She was terrified that he would not come for her. But at the agreed time, she saw a sleigh pull into the courtyard. Don was bundled up in his leather coat with the warm lining. He lifted her into the seat beside him. The horses were dancing with excitement.

The sleigh made a scraping noise on the cobblestones, then off they went over the white hills, at times barely touching the ground. Mary Lou clung to Don. He made the horses go faster and faster.

Don stopped the sleigh on top of Price Hill and he and Mary Lou looked down at the city, a basin of red brick houses, tall buildings, factories, and churches. The river flowed in the distance, above it clouds of black smoke from the twenty or thirty steamboats at the landing. Across the water was Kentucky. Mary Lou was amazed that they could actually see into another state.

Don said they should get married and Mary Lou felt afraid, *thrilled,* like she was at the top of a Ferris wheel, the car tilting and rocking high above the earth.

She nodded yes and Don lowered his face to hers and kissed her on the lips. Don's lips were cool as her own when she drank from the mill's icy water barrel, and she could feel his teeth through the soft flesh. They warmed as he kissed her again, this time putting his arms around her. His heart beat madly. Mary Lou could feel it beneath his chest. He was so big and strong. Her dream of being a teacher flew right into the air like a hat blowing off her head.

Mary Lou's father said no when she asked him if she could marry. He would not speak to her again if she did, she was too young. But she was pulled by a force strong as gravity. She and Don ran away to a "marriage mill" in Indiana where you didn't have to take a blood test or wait three days for a license.

As they drove along the river (Don had borrowed a Model T), Mary Lou's legs began to shake. She looked back toward her home. What was she doing? She knew nothing of the flesh, only romance. She'd heard so many stories: of pain and blood, of rapture and bliss. Her step-mother had said "it" was like using someone else's toothbrush, that men enjoyed it and women put up with it. She longed for her dead grandmother who would tell her what to do. But it wasn't only wedding night fears. . . . The world seemed to turn as blank as the highway stretching before her and she was rushing into her future without the slightest notion of who she was or what was coming.

4

The screech of a curtain jerked Mary Lou back to the present, to the hospital room, all white. A man was making the bed next to Don's, another was sloshing water on the floor and mopping it.

She looked at her watch. Don had been gone so long. What was happening?

Mary Lou crossed her fingers. She thought, *Don. My husband. All man.* Always very proud of his strength, his ability to work. And he never gave up his determination to support his family. He had done it, too, and done it well. Mary Lou admired him and loved him (and held the opposites in her secret self). As she continued to wait, she retraced the path that led her and Don to this place, remembered moments and years, distinct as photographs, though old and soft around the edges.

The cheap little apartment Don had rented before they met was up three flights of steps and there were mice and roaches to fight off, but Mary Lou liked having a home of her own. She cleaned it and scrubbed it and put up curtains. She would be all finished working by noon, and would look around and wonder what to do with herself until Don got home. Her whole life became planned around him and never changed.

On Sundays Don was hers all day and they would ride all over town on the electric streetcars that had replaced horse-drawn cars. They bought transfers for a dime and rode up and down the inclines and all the way out to the airport on the east and Price Hill to the west, Don pointing out interesting sights (he loved watching the airplanes at Lunken Field, she loved the vast haunted halls of the art museum). Sometimes they had lemonade at the outdoor café at the top of Mt. Adams and she felt pretty and Don looked handsome. Women at the other tables "gave him the eye" as people said then and Mary Lou felt happy and proud to have a man all her own.

Helen was born soon after their marriage. Now with a crib and a buggy and clothes to buy for the baby, there was just enough money for food and rent. Mary Lou felt trapped and lonely in the small apartment. She was tired much of the time, from washing diapers, scrubbing and cleaning and cooking, and hauling Helen's buggy up and down the three flights of steps and battling the mice and roaches. During Helen's naptime, she listened to the radio and read the newspaper (the "Women's Page"). She didn't feel like reading anything more than magazines. She sometimes borrowed "True Romance" and "True

Story" from a neighbor, which were full of tales of women who passed up good men and were seduced by good-looking fast-talkers who "took liberties."

Mary Lou sometimes wished Don would try to move up in life. But he seemed happy in his work. The smell that hung in the basin from the stockyards never bothered him. He was always cheerful and full of hope. Always the one who tried to keep her spirits up when life looked drab. He thought Mary Lou's modest cooking the best food he'd ever tasted. She read movie magazines and daydreamed over Douglas Fairbanks, though she guessed she shouldn't dream about anything more romantic than what she had.

But there was so much going on in the big world: movies, gangsters, bathtub whiskey, flappers, Prohibition, the Lindberghs, jazz, new dances like the Charleston. Mary Lou longed for a cloche hat and a string of pearls, but had to be satisfied making herself a short dress and cutting her hair in the new bob.

The world around Mary Lou and Don changed slowly but constantly, like figures in a magic lantern. New beautiful stores appeared downtown and several tall buildings rose between their apartment and the river. More and more houses crept up the hills from the basin. The city's canals were covered over with cement streets. Slowly the sound of motors and the smell of gasoline replaced the nickering of horses and the odor of hay and manure. People were moving out to the suburbs spreading over the seven hills.

Mary Lou's father (who had bowed to the fact of her marriage and not carried out his threat) sold the mill and moved to a bungalow in a new neighborhood. The constant chattering of his radio was heard instead of the sound of churning creek water. To Mary Lou her parents' new life lacked all charm and romance. But her father didn't seem to miss the old way of life, and her grandmother simply moved her card table and spirits to Mt. Auburn.

1929—the papers were full of the stock market crash. Almost overnight the bustle around Mary Lou seemed to lurch to a halt: the sound of hammers in the city quieted down; the long lineup of steamboats at the public landing thinned out to two or three; the neighborhood bank closed. FOR SALE signs were everywhere. The store to be built on the corner of Mary Lou's block was abandoned, and the vacant lot full of weeds looked lonelier than ever. It would always be Mary Lou's memory of the time: weeds and vacant lots.

Mr. Neidelhelman went out of business and Don was out of work.

Don never weakened or gave up. He went from one warehouse and factory to another every day, looking for work. Mary Lou ached for him as she saw him go off on the hottest summer days in his one decent suit, a heavy scratchy black wool. And she'd see him return in the evening empty-handed and disappointed—but never complaining.

He wouldn't let her ask for help from her father, either. While her father spoke to them, he kept to his warning when they ran off and got married not to look to him for help—and her step-mother kept a strict hand on the family's cash—even keeping the silver Mary Lou's grandmother had promised would be hers when she married.

"Waste not, want not!" With her grandmother's words ringing in her ears, Mary Lou saved the ends of soap bars and tied them in a rag to make a bathtub scrubber. She mended her and Don's socks until they were so lumpy they hurt to walk on; she saved every bit of thread from sewing, every button that came off a shirt that had finally become a dish cloth. She saved box tops from corn flakes and sent away for free samples. She made stews lasting a week from a soup-bone, which the butcher would give a customer if they bought a pound of meat.

The apartment was hot in the summer and cold in the winter because of its leaky windows. There were two children now—Frederick was born along with the Depression—and Helen was no help with the baby. She seemed jealous of him—he was so quick and good while Helen was slow and fretful. She was still wetting the bed while Frederick was in diapers. Mary Lou's life seemed to have shrunk to the length of a clothesline.

She lectured herself constantly to be strong and selfless, but she missed the outdoors, the creek and the fields of the farm, the rushing water and bustle of wagon-loading at the mill. Don seemed to have lost his good spirits and was as let-down as she. Mary Lou yearned to tell Don about her feelings, and have him share his, but he didn't seem to want to talk to her. They spent the evenings listening to the radio. If she asked him what he was thinking, he looked puzzled and said, "nothing."

It seemed the Depression would never end, that they would fall lower and lower. That the world would always be lonely and gray and sad. And hot. The only air-conditioning was in the theaters and Mary Lou went to the movies when she could find an extra dime or a potato on "Feed the Hungry" nights. Before the feature, an image of a crowing cock would announce, "Pathe News!" and Mary Lou saw images of the dust bowl and the people lined up for food at soup kitchens, the long lines of jobless men. The families in broken-down cars heading out west. And there was President Roosevelt and the WPA—the government providing jobs for men—and the farmers were ordered to shovel under their crops and throw away their milk. Mary Lou's father ranted against the government and said Roosevelt was really Rosenfeld and a Jew.

Don refused to work for the WPA; he thought it was demeaning make-work, a hand-out. And eventually he got a job on a construction site. He loaded bricks on his shoulders from truckloads delivered to a building site and took them to the skilled masons. But soon, because of his willingness to work and skillful way of encouraging the other men, he was promoted.

As Helen and Frederick grew and Mary Lou began to put a few dollars in the bank, the movie screen brought talk of war in Europe, reports of Hitler marching into one country after another: tanks and swastikas, strange goose-stepping troops. Mary Lou hated the scenes of bombs and cannons and guns and marching men. She couldn't wait for the features on new hats.

By the late thirties, Mary Lou and Don gathered together enough money to put a small down payment on the house they were dreaming of in Walnut Hills (and take on a large mortgage). It was the house they lived in now, the big Victorian. The walls had not been painted for years, the fine wood floors were covered with ugly brown varnish and the roof needed repair, but Mary Lou and Don could see the good house beneath its age and ailments. They worked for months, Don re-plastering and painting the ceilings and refinishing the floors, Mary Lou painting all the corners, the woodwork, and kitchen cabinets. They smiled at each other, clothes full of paint streaks and dirt, heads full of dreams.

Mary Lou remembered the exact date they moved in because it was the year Elaine was born. Mary Lou spent a week in the hospital when she delivered Elaine, the most perfect and beautiful baby ever, and brought her home to the new house and their new life. . . .

Now they had a yard for the children, flowers and a vegetable garden. Mary Lou planted a magnolia tree, a tiny one that took years to bloom. In spring the family could smell new grass being mowed instead of the fumes of the stockyard and factories. The years were marked by the holidays: Halloween, Thanksgiving, Christmas, Easter, Fourth of July. And like everything in the bigger world, the Depression seemed to ebb away. Helen and Frederick had their adenoids and tonsils out and Fred broke his leg (which one was it?). Helen had Dionne Quintuplet paper dolls (there was such a fuss in the news about these miraculous little girls that Mary Lou could still remember their names, Marie, Yvonne, Annette, Cecile, and Emilie). Mary Lou and Don got the children a dog from the pound, then other pets came along. How many dogs and cats had they had? There was Sandy, their beagle, and the cats Tiny and Whiskers. They bought a Dodge on time. Mary Lou had a favorite memory of the whole family taking the *Island Queen* steamboat to Coney Island and spreading their picnic on a wooden table in the riverside grove. Somewhere there was a snapshot. . . .

Then came the war, America was in it now, and Don had his own business for the first time, and they had money and paid off their mortgage. And then Elaine's sickness took over Mary Lou's life.

"Do you want anything, Mother—a coke—coffee?"

Mary Lou had barely noticed that Helen had come back and was sitting by the window, knitting.

"No thanks."

"Have you heard anything?"

"No. You don't have to sit with me."

"I know." Helen stayed seated.

"Mother, I know you don't believe, but it might help if you prayed."

"It didn't help Elaine."

Helen looked stricken and speeded up her knitting. *Good, now maybe she'll shut up*, Mary Lou thought. Besides, she had been praying—even though she didn't believe it would do any good. Nothing would. Not if God or whatever decided differently. When she was five years old, how she prayed when her mother went into labor and Mary Lou could hear her screams through the door, and the midwife's and her grandmother's soothing voices. When the doctor finally came in his buggy, he saw Mary Lou sitting alone in the dining room of the farmhouse. He gave her a glance that she would never forget: there were no words, just a silent warning to be strong and not cry. When she was about to weep at the graveyard, she felt her grandmother tug on her sleeve: no tears.

The baby, a girl, was buried with Mary Lou's mother, and over the grave was a beautiful stone angel. Mary Lou wanted to crawl into the warm earth with her mother, a child displaced by a new baby.

She had thought, and still did in some way she couldn't fathom, that if only she had been better—more loveable, more obedient—if she didn't pick her nose or bite her fingernails—her mother would not have been taken away. The grown ups of the family were like shadowy giants, gods, seeing everything you did, threatening punishment. Maybe it was the worse things she did, touching herself or soiling her pants or wetting the bed, which made you a bad girl. *Shame.*

And when Elaine died, her favorite child, though you weren't supposed to have a favorite, she felt herself at fault. Had she loved her enough? Too much? Been impatient with her? Denied her in some way? Mary Lou had planned this baby. Helen came along when Mary Lou was too young and unprepared to be a mother, and Frederick when Don was out of job. But Mary Lou had looked forward to Elaine and loved her with nothing held back, touched by her thin little curls plastered to her head when she cried hard, moved to wonder by her pearly fingertips, her tiny nails like new seashells— And "God" took her—gave her a heart that wouldn't last into grown-up life.

Her long hospital stays and operations put her in pain that no child should have to suffer. All they did in the long run was wear her out, and Don and Mary Lou with her— and devour a lot of their savings. Mary Lou never stopped her self-reproach: she didn't eat properly during pregnancy. She smoked. Now they said that could cause so many things; that it was a big factor in Don's illness. Or her own faulty heart, her lack of heart, some emptiness or weakness in her blood. Or her disloyalty to Don— That doctor she—

Mary Lou tried to strike a bargain: leave Don's leg. Take the house and everything they had. Take five years off their lives. But she knew this was childish wishful thinking.

Mary Lou checked her watch again. Would Don never get back? What was happening?

She needed him to be all right. To be young again and whole. The strong ruddy-faced man who could outwork all the others on Mr. Neidelhelman's wagons, who could lift a mill stone or a girl.

5

Why was Helen so irritating? Mary Lou studied her dark head bent over her yarn, the light from the window bringing out the flatness of her hair color.

She had been the kind of kid who, if you took her on a picnic, invariably got poison ivy, chiggers or poison oak. She was forever full of swellings and bumps and complaints. She was afraid of horses, dogs, insects, water—the whole natural world. Mary Lou couldn't understand this hothouse stuff. She'd stepped in many a cow pie on purpose just to feel it ooze up between her toes. She'd tumbled in hay, scratchy, fragrant, full of ticks, and never gotten the awful bites that Helen could acquire from a single mosquito. When Mary Lou and Don finally got to take the trip to Yellowstone Park they'd dreamed of, their first real vacation, Helen managed to come down with an infected boil on her leg, and ruin the entire trip. And—

"It's starting to snow pretty hard," Helen said.

"Why don't you go on home?" Mary Lou said.

She pointed to the window growing cloudy as a cataract. "Earliest I can remember."

"Daddy ought to be brought in soon."

Helen made him sound like a roast or something, Mary Lou thought. She went back to the time Helen spoiled that vacation. . . . From the day she brought Helen home from the hospital they didn't mesh as mother and daughter.

Mary Lou had always wanted to have a baby; she'd pictured a story book cherub, pink and clean and cute. But when she found out she was pregnant ten months after her wedding, she cried all the way down the steps from the doctor's office. *I'm too young. I'm not ready. I haven't had time to grow up myself.* She saw her ambition to become a teacher fade like a dream she wanted to recapture but could not recall fast enough.

If she was like her grandmother, her life would be one child after another. And suddenly having a child was terrifying; she remembered the night her mother gave birth, the doctor's grim and profound expression, the warm lap of her mother claimed by the dead baby, the stone angel marking their place in the earth.

The day Mary Lou brought Helen home from the hospital she felt so alone and ignorant. The birth had hurt terribly. Some doctors were still suspicious of ether (and people too—God wanted you to suffer) and gave only small whiffs of it—you had to cry out for it.

Sitting in the wheelchair, waiting for Helen to be laid in her arms, she almost wished she could stay in the hospital a little longer where there were people around. She watched the baby nurse stride into the room in her lovely blue blouse and crisp white apron, white stockings and shoes and official RN hat, starched and proud as a crown. Oh what a woman. If only she could be like that.

As she was pushed toward the door with Helen in her arms she heard one of the orderlies whisper, "Children having children."

Don picked her up at the hospital door and deposited her at the apartment and then went right back to work. He seemed uneasy to be a father. She and the strange little creature pulled from her body with such pain were all alone in an empty apartment. Mary Lou's stitches hurt so bad she couldn't sit down. The baby began to cry at once and threw a stringy vomit half way across the room. Was it having convulsions? Mary Lou cleaned up the mess, something you never saw in books or ads for baby powder. She quieted Helen's screams by putting her at the breast.

She couldn't look down. She hated breasts, couldn't even say the word. She thought of cow udders, those awful urgent things bursting with hot milk. Helen ate greedily, but then threw up again. Mary Lou soon developed milk fever, and Helen thrived better on the less rich bottled formula.

Mary Lou tried hard to be a good mother, but it was so cramped in the tiny apartment and so hot in the summer. Only a few years ago, she had been a girl, riding her horse across the fields and into the cool shady woods.

Now, she supposed, she was a woman. She was expected to adore the little black-haired baby demanding her every minute.

Mary Lou noticed Helen's ears stuck out at an odd angle. She asked Mother Nina what to do and on her advice, taped them down with adhesive tape.

She was only eighteen herself.

"I wrote Frederick," Helen said. "He'll try to get home."

"Oh you shouldn't have bothered him. He's so busy."

Helen looked as though she had something to say, but swallowed it.

"Have you talked to Sylvia?" she asked. Whenever she mentioned her younger sister her voice took on a special tone.

"I called. Got the machine. She hasn't called back yet."

"She should come and see Daddy."

Mary Lou wished she'd stop calling Don Daddy. It sounded so

inane. But that was Helen: she was like a big retriever or something that fancied itself a lap dog.

"Sylvia will be here. She will."

There was a little stir at the door and Helen got up to move the screen. Several orderlies were trying to get a gurney around the corner of the doorway. When they'd succeeded, they wheeled it over to the bed and dumped Don rather roughly onto the mattress.

"Be careful," Helen said. "He's lost a leg."

Lost it? Mary Lou thought. He didn't lose his leg. It was cut off. She knew what would happen the minute the doctor had come into the room after Don's tests.

"Right," said one orderly. He slapped Don on the cheek. "Mr. Friedman, you're in your room. Your wife's here."

He buckled Don onto the bed.

Mary Lou went over to him. She was afraid to look, just glanced down at the lower half of her husband, briefly noting that the left side of the sheeted legs was flatter than the other.

Don looked as though he were drowning. His eyes pleaded for rescue. Mary Lou wasn't sure she'd not rather die than have a leg cut off, but Don was clinging to life fiercely. He smelled bad, of—well, shit—and something medicinal. Mary Lou took his hand.

"Well," she said.

The orderly was giving last minute instructions about getting to the bathroom and being sure Don got up and around as soon as possible.

Helen stood on the other side of the bed and took Don's other hand. He drew it away and put both his hands in Mary Lou's. Helen looked hurt.

"Never mind," Mary Lou said to her, "He's not himself right now."

6

When the time came to take Don home, Helen bustled about collecting robes, slippers, shaving things; she made the nurse go over Don's medication schedule for the third time.

"Oh stop *fussing*," Mary Lou said.

"Well, we need to get it absolutely straight. Without his medication Daddy's liable to develop cardiac problems or more gangrene." The specter of Don with no legs at all scared Mary Lou into silence.

Russell, he of the meals Helen made sound like zoo feedings, was there to drive Don home. He was a big hulk of a man, as placid as Helen was officious. Helen had married him just a year ago, ten years after her first husband died. Mary Lou never understood why. Helen seemed relieved as a widow, went traveling and redecorated her house. Maybe she needed someone she could boss around.

"I'll bring the car to the front entrance as soon as you're ready, Mom," Russell said.

"Thanks." Mary Lou had to admit that in a pinch her son-in-law could be helpful. He and Helen had been driving her back and forth to the hospital most every day.

Don looked sour about the whole proceeding. He had been agitating to go home ever since his surgery, but the mechanics of it, and the reality of going ahead with his life on one leg suddenly seemed to hit. Dr. Weiss, Don's doctor, came in for last minute instructions.

He was awfully young to be a doctor, Mary Lou thought: full head of hair (though prematurely white), unlined features, manicured nails and scrubbed pink skin. He could be her grandson—or great grandson. He was relentlessly cheerful.

"Daddy's pretty grumpy," Helen said. "Shows he's feeling better."

"Yes, good sign." Dr. Weiss chuckled almost convincingly. Russell laughed with him as though Helen's remark were a fresh and original observation.

The streets were icy and slick, and the snow a sickly blue for lack of light. Mary Lou had been so confined to Don's hospital room, so narrowly focused on his survival, she had not before felt the cold on her trips home and to the hospital. Today it reached her bones.

On the sloping driveway of the house, where Russell parked the car, there was a breathtaking dance as Russell held one of Don's arms and Helen guided his crutch. Like a comic trio, they shuffled for control. Mary Lou watched in horror, gripping Don's overnight bag with his bathroom supplies and pills. All Don needed was a humiliating sprawl in his front yard and a broken hip. Mary Lou got out of the car carefully, protecting her own mobility. The walk up the front steps seemed endless.

"Sit down," Mary Lou commanded when the four had gotten the door unlocked, and had settled Don in his big chair. Russell obediently took off his coat and plopped down on the couch. Helen pushed her coat off her shoulders. It was like coming home from a funeral, Mary Lou thought—someone or something had been left behind. She could tell Don's leg was on everyone's mind. For the first time she wondered where it was. After her grandmother's gall bladder operation, the gray spongy organ had been put in a glass jar and occupied a special place in the farmhouse. But a leg? What had they done with it? Buried it? Pitched it on a pile of other amputated limbs?

Once again Helen repeated the doctor's instructions. Mary Lou took her reminder meekly. She was barely listening, just trying to get used to being back home. The noises of the hospital died away and her familiar sounds took their place: the hum of the refrigerator, the tick of the kitchen clock; birds singing in spite of the weather.

"I'll make some coffee," Mary Lou said. "Don, how about some of that herbal tea or some diet cocoa?"

"Tastes like chalk."

"Don't bother, Mother," Helen said. "We have to go."

She could never get Helen to drink a drop of coffee or tea, Mary Lou's way of making people feel better. Sometimes she thought Helen liked being uncomfortable.

"I'd like a nice hot cup of coffee," Russell said. He rubbed his hands together. "Can I help you, Mom?"

"No thanks."

Mary Lou was glad to get out of the living room and off to herself. Bless Russell for giving her an excuse. She noted for the first time what a nice smile he had. When she returned to the living room, Don had tears welling up in his eyes. Russell was looking miserable and Helen was rooting around for Kleenex. Mary Lou felt like crying herself. She knew how humiliated Don was. In all their years together she had never seen him cry.

How will we get through this? Mary Lou thought.

She and the others sat still in the room, a group portrait of dejection. She tried to think of something cheerful to say but couldn't find words that didn't sound dumb.

Russell commented on the unseasonable snow. "But that's Cincinnati: if you don't like the weather just wait five minutes."

That tired old comment, Mary Lou thought, but it was better than nothing.

"I've already gotten our winter coats out of the dry cleaner," Helen said.

Just then, the doorbell rang, and Billy burst into the room. He was holding a car radio aloft like a trophy.

"I'll put it in tomorrow!" he announced.

"Look, Don." Mary Lou took the radio and patted Billy on the back. "The car will be all fixed now."

The others seemed mystified and Mary Lou realized her mistake.

"What are you talking about?" Helen said.

Billy described what had happened on Halloween. Mary Lou felt stupid and fearful of what effect this news might have on Don. She looked at him for his reaction, but he seemed not to hear Billy's explanation. He was smiling and wiping his eyes.

Billy went over to Don and kissed him on the forehead. Everyone temporarily relaxed.

Mary Lou served the coffee to murmurs of appreciation and there were a few more ineffective attempts at conversation.

Like chalk on a wet blackboard, Mary Lou thought.

"Maybe we should call Mom," Billy said. "You'd like to see Mom, wouldn't you, Grandpa?"

"Go ahead, Billy," Mary Lou said. "That's a good idea."

She had meant to call Sylvia but hadn't followed through.

Billy picked up the phone and they were all surprised when he reached Sylvia instead of a phone machine. Mary Lou was struck at how his face brightened, hearing his mother's voice.

"Are you coming out, Mom? Grandpa's come through the operation pretty good. I know he'd like to see you."

Billy listened to her answer. His face suddenly became blank and he handed the phone to Mary Lou.

"Wants to talk to you, Grandma."

"You better come home. Dad's in pretty bad shape."

"Can I speak to Pop?" Sylvia's voice was still light and girlish, a little breathless. She sounded much younger than her forty-some years.

Mary Lou looked at Don. He shook his head.

"He's tired, Sylvia."

"I really can't get there right now, I'm afraid. Up to my ears in work. I'm having to move out of my apartment."

"But—"

"Besides, I know Pop wouldn't want me to see him like he is now. He said so the last time I was home. He said 'Sylvia if'—"

"I see." Mary Lou hung up. She was so furious she couldn't say another word. Sylvia was Don's favorite child. He'd paid more attention to her than to any of the others. This phony excuse of Sylvia's was sickening.

"What's the scoop?" Billy said.

"She's not coming. Claims her father wouldn't want her to." Mary Lou repeated Sylvia's story.

"Typical Sylvia," Helen said. "There's no one on earth but Sylvia."

"I'm gonna call her back," Billy said. He pressed the redial button. They all watched his expression.

"Mom? Get your butt out here," he said. "Grandpa needs you and so does Grandma. I mean it."

He was quiet a minute, listening. He put down the phone.

The others looked at him expectantly.

"So?" Mary Lou said.

"She'll be here soon as she can get a bus out."

In spite of herself Mary Lou was cheered. Sylvia was never very reliable, irresponsible in handing Billy over to her and Don, but she was always interesting. And good just to look at. And she didn't say "eye-ther" instead of either, like Helen did—who also affected "thank you, no," rather than just saying "no thank you."

"Don, Sylvia will be here soon as she can!" Mary Lou's voice was high and excited.

"We better batten down the hatches," Billy said. "Mom's on her way."

7

Almost a week had gone by since Don came home from the hospital. Don's old boss had called. Frederick wrote (Helen had written him). Mrs. Wong had dropped over with a plate of Chinese dumplings. But no Sylvia.

Mary Lou wished just for once Helen wouldn't be right. Especially about Sylvia. Don needed something to lift his spirits. He never complained, but Mary Lou could see how hard it was for him to watch her folding his left trouser leg and pinning it under and see the ugly stump each time she changed the dressing.

It wasn't easy for Mary Lou either, seeing the unnatural limb, trying to help Don to the bathroom, helping turn his big heavy body in the bed, watching breathless as he clumsily made his daily trip up and down the stairs. She was on the run all day making sure Don had the right food at the right time, that he took his medicine. And he was little company for her, sleeping so much. She guessed Don just didn't have the energy to talk but it made her feel lonely anyway and she'd have to go out on the porch and smoke a cigarette. This was the year they were going to take a trip with Billy to the Wisconsin Dells. Billy was going to drive!

Well, it was typical of Sylvia to make a promise to come home on the next bus and then not show up.

Mary Lou wondered what she would look like now. She changed her hair color and style so often you never knew what she might come up with.

Mary Lou had been so happy at Sylvia's wedding. She was like a princess in her white dress, holding her bouquet of white orchids. Mike looked so handsome and so in love. And he had a good future, studying to be an accountant.

The reception was held at a hotel and Mary Lou and Don hired a band and a caterer. There was champagne and an ice sculpture. Sylvia and Mike danced gracefully together and then smeared each other's faces with cake and were whisked away in a white limo. Mary Lou thought Sylvia could finish college now and be a teacher like Mary Lou had always wanted to be, or use her acting talents, if only for fun. Instead she had Billy right away, then came up with this stuff about finding herself and was still running around the country from pillar to post.

"She'll never get here," Helen assured Mary Lou. "She's too wrapped up in herself. And she can't stand anything unpleasant."

When the phone rang Mary Lou jumped to answer it.

"Mary Lou?"

"Penny."

Mary Lou tried to hide the drop in her voice.

"Long time no see. My neighbor said she saw you at the hospital."

As Penny spoke, an image of her friend as a young woman formed in Mary Lou's mind: a pretty redhead who, on the couples' boat rides wore a red and white polka-dot bathing suit like the one a model wore in a famous *Life* magazine photo.

"For Heaven's sake," Mary Lou said.

"So how is Don?"

Mary Lou described Don's situation and said he was doing fine. "How about Stan?"

Mary Lou pictured Stan as he was just after the men came back from Germany where he and Don had been together in the infantry—lean and tall, playing forties' hits on his guitar, piloting his cruiser on summer nights. He wore crisp white shirts and a captain's hat with an anchor stitched on it.

Penny said Stan had had heart surgery but was better than ever—walking miles every day and eating a low-fat diet. She had "lost a boob," but was happy with her five grandchildren (the offspring of Tammy, the daughter who lived with her boyfriend, now a middle-aged suburbanite).

After Penny hung up, Mary Lou went to the living room and got her old photograph album out of the bookcase. Evenings on the river on Penny and Stan's boat. There was Penny in her eye-catching bathing suit and Mary Lou in her white one-piece like the kind Betty Grable wore.

Stan would take the "Lucky Penny" out of the harbor, then ask Don to take over the controls while he shook up Pink Ladies and Singapore Slings for the women. As they sat sipping drinks out on the deck, loud friendly calls from other pleasure boats came across the water. The men whistled at Penny and Mary Lou in their bathing suits.

Mary Lou took the album up to Don and turned the pages for him.

"Remember those days?"

She reminded Don of Stan singing—everyone singing along—"Pistol Packin' Mama" and "Love, Love, Love." Don and Stan lifting Mary Lou and Penny on their shoulders and tossing them playfully into the water.

"You were always stronger than Stan," Mary Lou said.

"You were prettier than Penny."

"No one was prettier than Penny."

In those days, Mary Lou remembered, being "curvaceous" was the mark of sexiness. Now the popular movie stars had arms and legs like pipe cleaners. Exotic "glamorous" women (she could still see images of Hedy Lamar and Marlene Dietrich in her mind's eye) had vanished, and no more "come hither" looks, just lots of straight hair and raunchy talk.

"We almost got our own boat," Mary Lou said.

They had gone to boat shows and found just what they wanted: a cruiser about the same size as Stan's, with the same wooden trim and slick painted bow. Across the stern, instead of the name "Lucky Penny," they decided, would be the name "Merry Lou." They would have had to go into debt, though, to get the boat, and in the end didn't buy it.

Mary Lou looked up at Don to see if he was enjoying the photos. He smiled, but said, "Have you heard from Sylvia?"

Mary Lou had pretty well given up on her younger daughter. Helen was right about Sylvia; she could not be trusted.

She sometimes caught Billy with the same expression he'd had on his face after Sylvia first left him; during those days he still wet the bed and wouldn't talk.

"Guess what?" he said one evening at dinner. He seemed quite excited. Both Mary Lou and Don perked up. Did he have a girl friend, some A's on his report card?

"I decided I'm gonna go to college after all."

"That's wonderful, Billy," Mary Lou said. Don smiled for the first time that day.

"What changed your mind?"

"Well, Pop's been on my case, and my math teacher said I wasn't totally dumb."

"Of course you're not," Mary Lou said.

"And I think Mom'll be pleased."

"What?" "Who?" Alarms went off, of illness, death. Billy. Don. But Don was lying right there safely snoring. Mary Lou glanced at the clock: three-thirty A.M. She jumped out of bed to answer the phone before it woke Don.

"Momma?"

"Sylvia! You scared me out of a year's growth."

"Sorry, darling, but I'm here at the bus station. I didn't realize the thing would come in at such an odd hour. Can you come pick me up?"

Mary Lou thought of the car locked in the garage, the cold trip downtown, how she could leave Don. Yet she couldn't abandon poor Sylvia. She pictured her in the bus terminal full of suspicious looking men, people who would steal her luggage even as she talked on the phone. Dirty restrooms.

"I don't see how I can leave your Dad."

"Oh. Isn't he asleep?"

"Yes, but if he woke and needed me he'd be upset."

"Well, I guess I'll have to take a cab. If I can find one at this ungodly hour."

Why did Mary Lou feel this was her fault?

"Better do that."

"It might be awhile before I get there."

"I'll watch for you."

Mary Lou went downstairs, turned up the thermostat, and sat in the living room under her afghan, thinking about her daughter.

Sylvia was such a chameleon, changing colors with the times, whatever was going on around her. As a child in the fifties, she was forever singing and dancing the "Hokey-Pokey" along with Uncle Al on the television. She always had lots of kids at the house and Mary Lou kept pitchers of Kool-Aid, cookies and quarts of ice cream for them, enjoying serving the plentiful treats she could give out now that Don had his own business and was making good money.

Sylvia had a bright red bicycle (Helen and Frederick had gotten used bikes from the Good Will store); Don taught her to ride it, and took her skating. Mary Lou read to her—every time they went to the grocery they bought a pocket edition of Nancy Drew or the Hobbits. Together they pasted the 'green stamps' from the store into a book and then sent them away for items from a catalogue—a transistor radio and a record player for Sylvia.

Mary Lou loved taking Sylvia shopping: her perfect little size six figure made even the less expensive things they bought in the "Junior" department of the big department stores look good. And the "salesgirls" raved about her being slim and pretty enough to be a model.

Then when Sylvia was in her teens she suddenly changed. Her ingratiating smile faded and she looked at everything with mouth turned down and an expression of impatience and disgust. When her friends came to the house the group moped around, sang mournful folk songs and scoffed at anything Mary Lou suggested they do to have fun. They refused to wash anything but their hair, walking in the street barefoot, treading on too-long jeans that grew filthy at the hems. Even the boys' hair was long and Mary Lou had never before seen a male with long hair.

Mary Lou resented the uniform blue jeans, the dirtier the better, worn by the kids; those were for real workmen when she was a child, and the farmers' wives labored at their wash boards to keep them clean.

If Mary Lou came into a room, the kids who were once so glad to see her stopped talking and just stared at her with what looked like hate. They kept their marijuana and tequila bottles pretty well hidden. But it was clear they spent hours getting "stoned" and drinking. Mary Lou smelled the fumes on Sylvia's clothes and found a cache of empty bottles under the porch.

She lectured Sylvia, but did not dare tell Don.

At some point one of the girls was arrested at an anti-war sit-in, another left home and simply disappeared. One of the boys jumped off a railroad trestle while high on LSD and was killed. The country seemed to be splitting apart like a broken millstone.

Mary Lou watched the war images on tv of young people in the Viet Nam jungles (she always saw the big world second hand, through lenses, on film or tape or paper). Now it was kids being shot by snipers and blown up by landmines. Mud and swamps and killing pulling them in deeper and deeper, bogged down in futile, hopeless fighting. Our bombs dropping on the thatched roofs and destroying fields. She understood Sylvia and her friends' disgust. She had had a father in one world war and a husband in a second. Still, Don said they had to win the war, and Mary Lou left things like that to him.

"Don't trust anyone over thirty," the kids were saying. It was them against their parents and government. She and Don had been taught to respect authority, that there were teachers and doctors, presidents and judges, policemen and generals who knew what was best for them. No one she knew went on marches or protested.

She concentrated on trying to protect Sylvia. On tv and in the newspapers she saw kids tear-gassed in Chicago, the anti-war students going from sit-ins to blowing up college buildings, the four students shot and killed at Kent State in Ohio. No one would ever forget the photo of the girl holding her arms outstretched over a classmate's dead body.

Luckily for Sylvia, her own activities seemed aimed more at enraging her father than in action. Mary Lou was glad her rebellion was against someone who would never hurt her. She asked Sylvia how goading her father or addling her own brains with drugs could help change things.

"Oh Mom, Dad's part of the problem," Sylvia said, and pot made her see such incredible beauty in things like pine cones or magnolia blossoms. Mary Lou, with her love of nature, wondered how these things could possibly be more beautiful than they were.

In the garden one evening, she picked up a white petal from beneath her magnolia tree (the one she had planted when they moved into the house and that now spread across and shaded the whole side yard). She handed it to Sylvia.

"Feel it," she said.

Sylvia stroked the petal.

"It's like a lady's suede glove," Mary Lou said.

She watched every day a family of birds building a nest in a hole in the back porch rafter. Patiently, one of the birds flew back and forth from the garden to the hidden nesting place, adding twigs and grasses. Then it appeared regularly, each time with a worm in its beak. It would not enter the nest with Mary Lou on the porch, only if she went back into the kitchen. When the hole was repaired and the nest gone, the bird still came to the porch and hovered around the rafter, pecking on the wood.

Mary Lou thought *I am that bird.*

Then almost as swiftly as it came (it seemed)—was it before or after the images of more bombing and the soldiers clambering onto helicopters?—Sylvia's angry phase passed and she went out for theater.

Those years of the sixties and seventies, now reduced to memories of hippy styles and music festivals and quaint expressions, were hard ones for parents, Mary Lou thought, even the ones who had no children or relations who were in the war: the constant worry, the listening for a child's footsteps on the stairs when a son or daughter came home at night. While they were out, were they safe? When they came home, did their footsteps sound steady? Were they drunk, high on drugs? Of course parents had always worried when their children began their night time lives.

But the world had become darker, become more frightening than when Mary Lou was young. It began almost, it seemed, before Viet Nam—the day President Kennedy was killed. Mary Lou was in the dining room ironing Don's shirts when the news came on the radio. She watched the funeral on tv—shocked, deeply sad as though the bullet had gone right through the world and shattered it. And sad for poor Jackie and the children. The little boy was so brave saluting his father's coffin as it passed in the slow, somber parade.

Sylvia, who was nine then, said, "Will Mrs. Kennedy be President Johnson's wife now?"

She was always cute.

At five o'clock, Mary Lou heard the paper pitched onto the driveway. As the sun was beginning to faintly lighten the sky, she heard a car pull up. Looking out the window she saw Sylvia get out of a cab, long hair swirling around her shoulders, big floppy canvas bags in each hand, her feet bare in her earth shoes. She stood at the cab, talking through the window, then turned, lugging the bags up the steps, while the cab stayed put. Mary Lou opened the door.

"Momma!" Sylvia embraced Mary Lou fiercely. She was the only one of the children who hugged and kissed her and Don. Mary Lou had to admit the touch felt good: her daughter smelled of some sort of sweet herbs.

Honk! Came the sound of the cab's horn.

"Oh—you won't believe what this little jaunt cost: seventeen dollars. Have you got it? All I had was a check and the cabbie wouldn't cash it."

Mary Lou went to her purse and handed Sylvia a twenty dollar bill.

"I owe you twenty." Sylvia ran down the steps to pay the driver.

When she returned Mary Lou picked up one of the bags while Sylvia took the others and they started upstairs. Thank God for little tasks, Mary Lou thought. She was at a loss as to what to say to Sylvia.

Her daughter hadn't been home since Helen and Russell's wedding. Sylvia mostly left Billy to Mary Lou and Mike, and excused coming to see him so seldom on the grounds that her visits would only upset and confuse him. The result was that Billy saw his mother about two or three times a year, and he never knew when it would be.

Mary Lou concentrated on the back of Sylvia's bare heels. "No socks?" she said.

"You forgot to remind me to dress warm. No, actually I left in such a hurry and I couldn't find any stockings or even a leotard—I'd packed everything and I just ran for it."

In the bedroom that had been Helen's and then hers, Sylvia dropped her luggage and plopped down on the bed.

"Do you need help unpacking?"

"Oh no—I'll do it later. You can't imagine how awful this trip was.

The bus smelled so horrible I nearly threw up. I had to pee so bad I could taste it, but I couldn't go to the toilet because there were two guys back there making comments—I think they were drinking and the driver didn't stop them. They were so loud and repulsive I didn't know what they'd do. The seats were all cracked and loose and naturally I had to sit next to the fattest woman in the Western hemisphere."

Mary Lou was still standing by the door like a maid. She did this around Sylvia. By morning, she'd be doing her laundry for her.

"Sit, Momma."

"Oh." Mary Lou perched on the edge of the bed.

"I'm glad to be home. When I go back, I don't know if I'll have a place to live, and my relationship with Curt is up in the air. My job is driving me crazy. You can't imagine the things men say to you when you waitress."

Aren't you going to ask about your Dad, Mary Lou thought. Why was she listening to her daughter's problems when she had so many of her own?

Sylvia lay back on the bed.

"I'm so tired I could sleep for a month." She closed her eyes, and pulled the edge of the spread over her bare feet. In minutes she was sound asleep.

Mary Lou got a blanket from the closet and spread it over her daughter, tucking it in around her shoulders. She looked so tiny and young. Mary Lou touched Sylvia's hair fanned out on the pillow.

8

Nine o'clock came. Ten o'clock, eleven o'clock. Sylvia was still not up. Mary Lou wondered if she was sick or something.

Finally, just before noon, as Mary Lou was giving Don lunch, Sylvia appeared at the kitchen door. Her long hair floated in disheveled waves all around her face. She looked tired, but her cut off jeans and tight T-shirt revealed clearly that she had kept her figure. Her face fell when she saw Don. She hesitated, then rushed over to him and kissed him on the ear.

"Dad, how are you?"

Don blushed.

"OK. Well, as good—considering—"

"Do you want something to eat?" Mary Lou asked. "I'm fixing Dad a sandwich and some soup."

"No. Nothing. Just some coffee. You have some coffee?"

Mary Lou poured her a cup from the cold glass pot on the stove and put it in the microwave.

"Oh no," Sylvia said. "Let me make some fresh. I love the smell of brewing coffee, don't you? I'll do it. Where is it?"

She rummaged in the cupboards. Mary Lou pointed to the right one and Sylvia rinsed the pot and measured out fresh grounds.

She sneaked a look at her father, then returned to her coffee making, taking a long time to arrange a filter.

"You look pretty good, Dad. Your—color and all."

"Oh yeah, I'm a beauty."

Sylvia fiddled with the stove knob, got the flame way too high.

"Damn," she said, and turned it down.

"So, Dad, how are you managing this?"

"It's managing me."

"Now, Dad. I mean—are you doing any meditation or massage or anything?"

Don looked puzzled and Mary Lou tensed up. In a minute this whole thing would be her and Don's fault for not living right. Everything with Sylvia could be cured by some sort of self-improvement system. Over the years she had played with holistic medicine, yoga, tai chi, aerobics, and a vegan diet.

Don frowned and snapped, "I don't suppose I could meditate my leg right back, could I?"

"Of course not. I meant—"

For the first time Mary Lou could remember, Sylvia actually looked cowed. She busied herself with her coffee, offering some to both her parents. The rest of the meal passed with limp exchanges of weather news. After Don went off for his nap, the atmosphere relaxed a little.

"Gosh," Sylvia said. "I've never known Dad to snap like that. And he looks so thin." She sounded frightened.

"He's not himself. Remember he just lost his leg"—(*now she was doing it*). Sylvia winced. She picked at a piece of breakfast toast Mary Lou had left on the table to feed the birds.

"Well, Momma, I know you're taking good care of Dad—like his food and all. But is he getting enough—stimulation?"

"It's hard when you're sick."

"Yes, but he needs cheering up as much as medicine."

"We've all tried."

Sylvia's eyes brightened like stage lights. "I know what. I want to see Billy—and Helen and Russell of course. How about I invite them all here for dinner?"

"Oh, I don't think so, Sylvia. . . ."

"I'll do everything. You just relax. I'll make a big pot of chili and bake some of my famous muffins."

"I just don't know. . . ."

"It's settled. It'll be good for Pop."

It was impossible to say no to Sylvia; besides, Mary Lou thought it just might *be* good for Don. Seeing Billy was always a pleasure for him, and having people around could keep him from moping.

"You call them, Momma. I'm too nervous and I better run up to the store and get the stuff I need. Do you have fresh peppers?" Sylvia rattled off the names of two or three spices Mary Lou had never heard of, and was out the door before Mary Lou could protest further.

The afternoon kitchen was filled with the delicious smell of ground beef and onion cooking in olive oil. Sylvia chopped and stirred and shook up salad dressing, and ran back and forth from the table to the stove. She poured nuts and raisins and honey into batter and beat it to a smooth creamy yellow. Every dish and pan in the kitchen was piling up in the sink, and Mary Lou, when she had cleaned the bathroom and laid out guest towels and set out Don's afternoon medicine and snack and dusted the living room, came in and washed and dried them all. It was hard keeping up with Sylvia; it seemed the more things Mary Lou washed, the more Sylvia used. At last, Sylvia poured the chili into the crock pot, and had the muffins all ready to bake. The salad was covered with Saranwrap, and Mary Lou made room in the refrigerator for it.

"God," Sylvia declared, "all of a sudden I'm pooped. I've got jet lag. From a bus yet. Gotta go lie down a mo."

Mary Lou was almost relieved. She would like a little time off her feet herself.

"I can't wait to see Billy," Sylvia said. "Did you invite his father along?"

"No," Mary Lou said. "Of course I didn't."

"I don't see why not. I've got nothing against him. It's perfectly OK with me if he comes."

"It might be embarrassing for Billy."

But a chance for drama for Sylvia, Mary Lou thought. Her daughter could never resist a theatrical moment.

Mary Lou got no rest that afternoon. She noticed the dining room needed dusting. With Sylvia cooking, the floor in the kitchen would need to be scrubbed before anyone could safely work there again. Sylvia hadn't bothered to worry about dishes or setting the table. Mary Lou laid out plates and silver and ironed a tablecloth right on the table. By the time dinner came near, she barely had the energy to take a bath and get cleaned up. While she was in the tub, Sylvia knocked on the door.

"Gotta come in," she said. "I slept too long. Why didn't you wake me?"

"Just wait a minute," Mary Lou called. She really didn't want to share the bathroom with her daughter. She rushed through her bath and dressed in the bedroom.

Sylvia took forever getting herself cleaned up, and as the time for the guests arrived, Mary Lou gave Don his medicine and cracker, then went to the living room and, doubtful of their edibility, put the snacks Sylvia had bought into bowls—some sort of little green peas that looked as though they could break your teeth, funny-looking bread and a bowl of mushy stuff Mary Lou decided was the color of baby poop.

Sylvia came downstairs looking young and refreshed. Her eyes were bright and her makeup skillfully done to conceal any lingering fatigue. She wore a tight lycra and wool dress that showed her bottom in a way Mary Lou always tried to avoid: clothes plastered to your body were considered cheap and tacky when she was Sylvia's age.

"Do I look OK? Do you think Billy will be glad to see me? I want so much to get to know him again. I realize how important family is— that's one thing I found out in the last few years."

A little late, Mary Lou thought.

Sylvia studied herself in the mirror over the mantle.

"Do I look as haggard as I feel?"

Typical Sylvia, Mary Lou thought, everything was looks and sex. Well, maybe it was: even Helen had had her colors done when that was the thing and she died her hair and wouldn't be caught dead in glasses, even though she was a good thirty pounds too fat anyway. When Mary Lou was young she was taught not to be vain (or use "paint"), and still felt a little guilty every time she put on lipstick (at her age). The way Sylvia was carrying on, it was like she was meeting a lover rather than a son. She didn't even notice that the table was all set.

Mary Lou helped Don into the living room and into his chair. By this time, Sylvia was opening the wine she'd bought even though Don was not allowed to have alcohol and Helen was a teetotaler.

"Join me?" Sylvia said to Mary Lou.

"No thanks." Mary Lou would not drink in front of Don.

Sylvia gulped down a glass of wine and had started another when the doorbell rang.

"Helen!" She threw her arms around her sister and stood back, slightly emphasizing her slim figure at the expense of Helen's bulk.

"Russell!" Sylvia gave her brother-in-law a peck on the cheek. Russell looked pleased. Helen almost barged past her to get to Don and ask anxiously about his health.

Sylvia poured herself a third glass of wine and offered it to the newcomers.

"This OK? Or would you like something more serious?"

"I don't drink, remember?" Helen said.

"How about you, Russell?"

"I'll have whatever you've got there."

"So, everybody! Bottoms up, Russell! Isn't it good to have the family together?"

Helen shot Russell a disapproving glance and he put his glass down. "We expected you sooner," she said to Sylvia.

"I got here as soon as I could." Sylvia sat next to her father and took his hand. "Lighten up, Helen. We need some fun." She passed around paper napkins she'd obviously gotten from the bar where she worked: a man with a stemmed drink glass in his hand and spots in front of his eyes.

Mary Lou looked at her two daughters. They were some twenty years apart, with Frederick and Elaine in between. By the time Sylvia came along Helen was married and working as a secretary to a lawyer. She was embarrassed by her parents having a baby in their late forties (Mary Lou was embarrassed too). Helen had never welcomed her younger sister, and the two managed to conflict when they got together.

Mary Lou knew Helen resented her and Don paying Sylvia's college tuition and not hers.

"So are you still the pillar of the church?" Sylvia asked.

"We attend regularly and we're in lots of activities."

"Like what?"

"Lately we've been working with the CCV."

"What's that?"

"Citizens for Community Values. We monitor various materials—-"

"Dirty books," Russell said.

"Oh for God's sake. What do you consider a dirty book?"

Mary Lou left the room to get a sweater. She wasn't up to Helen and Sylvia's debates. When she returned Sylvia was saying, "A little smut never hurt anybody." She sang a few lyrics from the Tom Lehrer record she'd played over and over.

"We're beyond just books and movies now. We're concerned with the homosexual agenda," Helen said.

Luckily, in Mary Lou's opinion, the doorbell rang and the subject was dropped. She really didn't think the best thing for Don's health was listening to his daughters quarreling.

Billy stood shyly at the door. Sylvia went to him, her arms outstretched. As they touched, he put his arms around her. Sylvia kissed him on the lips.

"God, you're so grown up. You're a *man*."

Billy grinned happily. Mary Lou was amazed at how delighted he seemed to see his mother. It was as though she'd never left him.

"Want a glass of wine?"

Billy noticed Sylvia was the only one with a glass and nodded yes. It was probably his first, Mary Lou thought; he usually drank a little beer or ginger ale. When he had settled next to Sylvia on the couch, he took a fistful of the hard peas and popped them in his mouth; his eyes watered but he loyally crunched and swallowed. Mary Lou passed the dip and offered Helen and Russell juice. Don looked at his watch.

"What are you into now, Billy?" Sylvia asked. "Do you like rock? Rap? Metal? What?"

"Rap I guess."

"You should hear the awful stuff where I work—lounge music—old time musicals. We have a piano player." She sang out "Some en*chant*ed evening—"

"I like that music," Russell said. "*South Pacific* is my favorite."

"They're OK, just not exactly cutting edge." Sylvia spilled her wine on the arm of the couch and jumped up. "Club soda," she said. "Cleans anything. I know—I work in a bar."

While Sylvia was out of the room, Russell took advantage of her absence to spit the little peas he had tried to eat into a napkin. Helen said, "Are you sure you're up to all this, Daddy?"

Sylvia returned and scrubbed at the red stain.

"Don't worry," Mary Lou said.

Helen ignored the scrubbing and said to Don, "Our prayer group's been praying for you all week."

"That's good."

"You always said you'd sooner believe in the Easter Bunny, Pop." Sylvia didn't look up from her chore. "This goddam stuff is not coming up."

"Sylvia, I'd appreciate it if you'd not talk like that in my presence," Helen said.

"Oh, don't be stuffy, Helen."

"I'm not stuffy. I don't believe in taking the Lord's name, and I'd think in front of your own son whom you haven't seen for a year. . . ."

"Mom's just a little nervous," Billy said.

"Aren't you too young to drink?" Helen said.

The smell of burning muffins came from the kitchen.

"Oh Lord—is that better, Helen? My fucking muffins are burning."

Sylvia ran out of the room. In minutes she poked her head back into the room.

"Guess what? I forgot to plug in the crock pot and the chili's ice cold. It'll be a few more minutes till dinner."

The others tried to ignore the offstage noises, though the excitement was clearly in another room.

"Have you had any more visits from the roof squirrels, Mom?" asked Russell.

Mary Lou had complained of the scuffling sounds above the attic.

"I can hear them up there most nights."

"You need a gun."

"Russell, please," Helen said.

"Maybe some of those poison peanuts. I'll bring some over for you."

Helen looked at Don anxiously. "Are you OK, Dad?"

Don nodded.

The sound of breaking crockery came from the kitchen. Billy jumped up and ran to his mother. Mary Lou followed. They found a dismayed Sylvia standing at the stove with chili running down into the burners and onto the floor. Helen and Russell came to the door.

"What on earth?" Mary Lou grabbed a towel and started mopping while Sylvia wailed.

"I can't believe this happened! I put the crock pot on the stove cause it's so slow to heat and it broke."

"Of course," Helen said.

"I thought it was heat proof."

"Never mind," Mary Lou said.

"Oh, I could die. I worked all day on this and I wanted it to be so nice!"

"What's going on?" Don yelled.

"Chili exploded," Russell said.

"What?"

Sylvia looked so comical Mary Lou had to smile. Billy laughed.

"Never mind, Mom. Grandma's got frozen pizza I bet. And I for one ate so many snacks I'm about to bust."

"Pizza'll be swell," Russell said.

Sylvia picked up a wash cloth and mopped up some of the brown goo running down the stove. She laughed too.

"What in the hell is going on out there?" Don yelled.

Billy whispered to Mary Lou: "Mom's the only person in the world who could make somebody forget about having a leg cut off."

9

Sylvia and Billy looked like brother and sister going off to skate or run errands. Her face glowed when he came to the house to pick her up. And off they would go on Billy's motorcycle, Sylvia hanging on tight to Billy's chest, her hair streaming in the wind. It was like the days when she was dating: Sylvia rushing out of the house dressed for sports or an evening at a club, Mary Lou at the door saying drive carefully, now don't be late, her sitting up at night worrying about her daughter's whereabouts, mysterious fumes seeping from under her closed door.

Sylvia began wearing her hair in a ponytail. Her tight leggings, sweat shirt and big high-top gym shoes were mixes of bright pink and green, yellow and purple. She combined stripes and metallics, shiny latex and fuzzy wools. The result was always adorable. For evening she wore thrift-shop laces, old silk flowers, and a straw hat with a dusty pink rose. She might still wear the sneakers.

Billy looked so happy to be with his mother that Mary Lou wanted to approve, but she thought Sylvia was going too far in smoking pot with him—she was sure that's what the fumes were. Also, Sylvia talked about sex with him constantly, worried that he was inexperienced, gave him advice on how to attract girls.

Should she kiss him on the lips?

Sylvia could always get her mother tied in knots, and that's how Mary Lou felt now and she was not as patient as she should be with Don. Of course he wasn't easy to care for: his daily schedule of food, injections, and bathroom trips was more demanding than ever and Dr. Weiss repeatedly changed his medicines for blood pressure which meant Mary Lou had to memorize new directions and dosages. Sylvia was a cheerful presence, but not much help with details.

There was more than a little of the prodigal in Sylvia, Mary Lou thought, the way she was welcomed back by Billy so wholeheartedly. It must be fourteen years ago that Sylvia came over and told Mary Lou she was drowning, suffocating, had to leave. Mary Lou tried to talk her into staying with her husband and child, but she refused to listen.

"I'm going," she said, "I need space, I need time. I need to grow up myself. I haven't done anything, been any place. I have no life."

Mary Lou was still amazed at Sylvia's actually leaving: having needs was as foreign to her as the customs of some exotic people. She herself had wants, of course. But needs? She never heard of them when she was young. Not for women.

Did she have needs when she found out she was pregnant with Sylvia? She was working at a nearby lumberyard office, filing and answering the telephone. They had offered her a promotion and the chance to learn typing, and she wanted badly to accept. It had been a struggle for her to take a job to begin with, remembering her step-mother's disapproval of women working or going to college. Even her mother and grandmother had not encouraged her to be anything but a good wife and mother. And everyone she knew said a married woman with a job was taking the bread from the mouths of some man's family.

But her job was pretty much a woman's; the other two office workers were women and it was fun to work with them and eat lunch together at Mullane's Confectionary where they would have thin ham sandwiches and fountain cokes. Too, working and bringing home some money made her feel good, useful, a little independent.

When she found out she was about to be a mother again, she cried. I'm too old to be having a baby, she thought. She should be through bearing children. Elaine had been dead five years and Frederick and Helen were grown.

Would I have gotten an abortion? If there were such thing? Mary Lou asked herself. If it had been legal. . . . It was a good thing she had had no choice. She might not have had Sylvia. . . . And Sylvia had been a joy especially when she was little, and still was at times. But if abortion had been an option. . . . For nice people. Mary Lou tried to stop her musing: what disloyal, un-motherly thoughts. But you couldn't do anything to change your thoughts—they broke in, and sometimes robbed you of what you wanted to believe you were.

Mary Lou quit her job, and went back home and raised Sylvia. Sylvia was a beautiful child, as beautiful as Elaine, full of life, entertaining, demanding—Mary Lou wouldn't use the word spoiled. A girl was not a batch of burnt cookies. She and Don had probably indulged her too much, given in to her too often. But times were different from when Helen and Frederick were young; and Sylvia was hard to say no to. She was the star of the neighborhood, the star of her high school plays, the star of her own on-going drama, her quest for— whatever it was she was looking for.

Mary Lou postponed her own life (her needs?) once again when Sylvia brought Billy to her. Just when she and Don were planning to continue the traveling they had begun when Don's business suddenly took off after the war; they had been to Europe (nine countries in three weeks), Hawaii, and even Denmark and Sweden. With Don's retirement they were planning to take more trips. Then here was Sylvia presenting them with a child to care for. She claimed Mike could not take over. He was studying for his CPA exam and was "obsessed," always at his desk with no time to go out or have fun.

Mary Lou thought Mike was a good man; he seemed to truly love Sylvia and his son, but between his anxiety over the exam and Sylvia's desertion, he was preoccupied and depressed. Certainly in no position to care for a child.

Even once certified, he would still not have much time for Billy. He would be going to work and would have to leave him with baby-sitters all day. Still, Mary Lou thought, *we're old, we don't need this.*

Billy came up the front steps with a little suitcase in his hands. One look at his face looking up at her and Sylvia with such trust and doubt all mixed, and Mary Lou was glad she had said yes. She remembered how empty and frightening the world became when her own mother died and left her and how her grandmother took over and raised her with love.

Sylvia had a tearful goodbye scene with her son. She told him she would be back soon to get him and that he should stay with Grandma and be a good boy until Mommy would be able to come for him.

Billy stood at the screen door, watching her go to her car. He could just see over the bottom panel of the door. The strap of his overalls had slipped, showing his round white belly. He had been left with Mary Lou before for an afternoon or evening, but Mary Lou could tell he knew this was different. He was quiet as a mouse, hardly breathing; his shoulders drooped like a little old man's. Not cookies and milk, or tv, or a game, or Mary Lou's promise of a trip to the circus could tempt him away from his lookout. Finally he sighed, a deep resigned sigh full of an anguish Mary Lou thought no child should ever have to bear, and trudged up the stairs to the room she had prepared for him.

He would not let Mary Lou out of his sight for weeks. Sometimes he cried in his sleep, but never in the daytime when he thought anyone could see him.

He had the kind of sturdy strength, at least on the surface, of his grandfather. He even looked like Don. They were a picture as they shoveled snow in matching wool caps, hauled in the Christmas tree together, drank mugs of cocoa and ate Mary Lou's special sponge cake, wearing smiles with twin dimples. But Mary Lou could tell he never stopped hoping his mother would come back.

After Mike had passed his CPA exams and started working, he provided money for Billy, and was a sort of third parent, but his work involved long days and most weekends. He did not have much time for his son.

He seemed to hope Sylvia might return to the marriage, but after a few years, he received divorce papers which he silently showed to Mary Lou.

"How do I tell Billy?" he asked Mary Lou.

She did his explaining for him.

Billy lived with Mary Lou and Don for nine years. They bought him a fox terrier puppy and he and Mary Lou trained it. Buster slept with Billy every night.

When Billy was old enough, they took him on trips with them—the Grand Canyon, Williamsburg. Then Mike married again, and felt he was finally in a position to take care of his son. Mary Lou and Don were reluctant, in fact heart-broken, to let Billy go. He was keeping them young and engaged in life and they loved him as much or more (if the truth be admitted) than any of their living children. But maybe a teenager, especially one with so much of Sylvia in him, might be more than they could handle. They were in their seventies by then and Don was experiencing signs of illness. And they had to admit his father could offer Billy more than they could: a better neighborhood and younger parents. And Mike *was* the boy's father.

But Mary Lou would always feel that she and Don were Billy's real parents: they were there when he needed them most and had always been there. Maybe they weren't able to give the things Mike could. Nor were they flashy and fun like Sylvia. No one could compete with Sylvia. But they had been there.

When Billy left with Mike, Mary Lou once again stood at the front door; this time it was his back she saw as he walked the stairs—a larger boy with a larger suitcase in his hand.

And she was the one who was left behind.

10

Often, after Billy had dropped Sylvia off from skating or a jazz club, and Don was asleep for the night, Sylvia would come to Mary Lou's door in her nightgown, and invite Mary Lou to her room. They would each snuggle under a quilt, and over cups of herb tea, they talked more than they ever had before. Mary Lou finally got up the nerve to ask her daughter something she'd wondered about for a long time.

"Why couldn't you work things out with Mike?"

Sylvia did not hesitate.

"He was no good in bed."

Mary Lou thought, *Is that a reason to walk out on a husband and child?*

"Is that all that counts?" she asked.

"It's everything—don't you think?"

"You'd only been married three years."

"Three *years*—Mother, give me a break!"

Mary Lou thought back over her own first years of marriage.

Was Don good in bed? Was she?

That first night, no sooner had the justice of the peace in that Indiana "mill" pronounced them man and wife, than Mary Lou felt like running back home. What was she doing? What was the wedding night all about? She had never been in a hotel before. She was terrified going with Don into the one he picked out: they had to go up to the desk and ask for a room. The clerk looked at them suspiciously as if he thought they might not really be married. Mary Lou was mortified, but Don didn't notice the fishy look they got when they registered.

As they walked up to their room (the stairs smelled of Lysol and the halls were pea green and made of a pebbly plaster she would never forget), Mary Lou thought of her school friends and their whispered stories of broken hymens and bloody sheets and dreadful pain; how could that bring ecstasy? She cringed, trying to picture some big thing pushing into her body that as far as she knew had no opening big enough to push into. She had seen something on her father when he had come to the door of her room one night to close her window, and she peeked at the open fly of his under shorts—he seemed to have a whole cluster of organs.

Once in the hotel room, Mary Lou and Don looked at one another shyly. Don fussed with the blind, pulling it down to cut the light from the small Indiana street. Mary Lou unpacked her suitcase and laid out clean stockings for the next day. They undressed separately in the bathroom and came to bed fully clothed, Don in pajamas buttoned to his chin, Mary Lou in a long nightgown. They climbed into the bed like prisoners into a tumbrel and pulled the covers up to their chins. Don held Mary Lou in his arms stiffly. Having their bodies touch their whole length felt good, but Mary Lou was so nervous, she began to cry. Don patted her and said, "Don't worry, Mary Lou, don't worry." They fell asleep clinging to one another. When Mary Lou awoke she felt guilty. She was supposed to please her husband, to be a good wife, to have children, and she knew you had to do "it"—whatever it was— After the two-day honeymoon, she was still a virgin.

Late, late one night, when they had been back in their apartment a few days, Don slipped her nightgown up and began to push his "thing" between her legs. Mary Lou was startled, but submitted. And gradually he eased his way into her body. She didn't seem to have a hymen after all—there was no blood. She hoped he didn't think she was not a virgin. When he was through, he said, "There, that wasn't so bad, was it?"

After that night, Don frequently felt for her, and did the same thing. When he was finished she was pleased because he enjoyed it so, giving a groan he couldn't seem to hold in, but she was glad after to have it over with. She had felt only a mild discomfort and embarrassment. She liked the feeling she had afterward better than the act, being cuddled in strong arms.

Then when they had just moved into their house, she and Don started going out occasionally and they met Penny and Stan—Penny of the "curves" and the flaming red hair. They would have drinks and dance at a neighborhood bar. One night, while the men were at the jukebox picking out music and dropping in quarters, Penny announced, "I have to wee-wee. Let's go to the little girl's room." Mary Lou followed her into the women's restroom, and while Mary Lou washed her hands, she could hear Penny cursing softly, "this damned thing; it just pops out."

"What are you talking about?" Mary Lou said.

"Diaphragm," Penny said. "I think I'm gonna need it tonight. Stan's in the mood. So am I."

When she came out of the stall, she noted the puzzled look on Mary Lou's face.

"How's *your* sex life?" she said.

Again, Mary Lou didn't have to say anything.

"Get this book," Penny said, "*Married Love*."

Mary Lou burst into tears.

"Oh now, honey. It'll work out. Honest." Penny patted Mary Lou on the back and offered her a soggy hanky. "You deserve a little fun. Sex isn't just for men."

Mary Lou knew there was something missing in her marriage. She had read all those magazines, and she often had dreams in which while walking in a street or playing in a field on the farm, a strange sensation crept over her—dreams that woke her panting with pleasure, rubbing herself, feeling guilty because she enjoyed the feeling and Don was left out. She wanted to have what Penny had.

Mary Lou went to the library the next day, hoping as she approached the check-out desk with her book that the librarian wouldn't read the title.

Mary Lou wasn't used to the clinical language—Mother Nina made sex sound repulsive (her toothbrush description); her grandmother had said only, "Papa gives Mama a special kiss." This book used the words like intercourse and vagina.

Mary Lou didn't particularly like her vagina. When she was three or four, a neighbor girl called it her "piggy bank." With its tight little slit, it did look like a bank.

Money went in banks.

Money was dirty.

She didn't want a little slit.

But now she wanted what her book and Penny promised her. She learned all kinds of things she hadn't known before. The picture of a vagina looked like a peach opened to the seed; the text explained where the clitoris (something Mary Lou had never heard of before) was located and how to enjoy satisfaction from it. She was to tell her husband how to include her in their love-making.

She couldn't do it.

But she did begin to like her body a little. She was ready to have another baby.

After one of their evenings with Penny and Stan, Mary Lou whispered in Don's ear what she had learned in her book.

Soon she was pregnant with Elaine.

"Momma, you're blushing," Sylvia said.

11

Mary Lou bought a frozen turkey for Thanksgiving. Helen was fixing sweet potatoes with marshmallows and bringing pumpkin and pecan pies. Sylvia had promised to polish the silver and wash the good china and crystal which was dusty where it sat from one holiday to the next in the breakfront.

The day before the feast, Sylvia came to the kitchen for lunch dressed in what looked like skating clothes. Mary Lou noisily poured a package of cranberries into a pan and ran cold water on them. She rummaged in a drawer for the meat thermometer and pitched it on the counter, making a little extra clatter. Sylvia ate her lunch sandwich unconcernedly, seeming not to notice any special preparations going on.

Mary Lou went out on the front porch and smoked a cigarette. The snow had thawed, leaving the lawn mushy. Someone—she had no doubt who—had driven up on the grass and left deep tire marks all over it. This was a popular neighborhood sport, along with "papering" trees by slinging rolls and rolls of toilet paper on the branches.

Happily, Mary Lou saw Billy's motorcycle rounding the corner, and she shredded the butt of her cigarette into a flower pot. Her grandson would help her fill in the bad places in the lawn. But Billy jumped from the cycle and climbed the steps two at a time, barely stopping to say hello. Mary Lou took hold of his sleeve.

"Look at that front yard," she said. "Those no good kids have ruined the lawn."

"Geez."

Time was when he would have gone straight out back for a shovel to patch up the damage.

"Could you fix it up for me this afternoon? I'd like to have it looking decent for Thanksgiving."

"When we get back."

"Where are you off to now?"

"Skating."

Mary Lou followed Billy through the house and into the kitchen. Sylvia, just finishing lunch, hopped up from the table, kissed her son, then her father, and ran upstairs to get her jacket and backpack. Mary Lou went after her.

"Sylvia, you were supposed to wash the china and set the table."

Sylvia slapped her forehead.

"Tomorrow—right?"

"We're eating at noon. It takes a long time if you get the glasses clean."

Sylvia looked concerned but didn't stop arranging her scarf in the mirror.

"We'll only be gone a few hours. *Promise.*"

As Sylvia spoke she ran to the front hall, where Billy was waiting. Mary Lou was left on the stair landing.

"I'll stop and get the herbs for the dressing and the stuff for my muffins," Sylvia said. "And by noon the table will sparkle. C'mon Billy, we gotta skate fast."

Jumping onto Billy's bike, Sylvia and her son did look like brother and sister. Or lovers.

Mary Lou swallowed her annoyance like a too-big bite of an apple, and went into the kitchen. She found herself banging pots and pans as she worked, slicing vegetables as if her life depended on it, running the hot water so hard it splashed all over the counter.

First Sylvia foisted Billy off on me, now she's taking him away.

At four, Mary Lou began the job of cleaning the silver and washing the china. The ingredients for the stuffing and muffins arrived at five-thirty. And Sylvia brought something else with her: a tall, blond man with muscles bulging out of his sweat shirt.

"This is Thor," she said.

She opened two beers.

"Mom, you want one?"

"No thanks."

"Thor's a therapist and masseur as well as a terrific skater."

Mary Lou looked him over. He had a wide, knowing grin, big hands, a slim waist.

"I thought he might do Daddy some good, help him exercise, give massages."

"Thanks, but your Dad. . . ."

"Now don't speak for Daddy. Thor could help. He's fully licensed and has worked with lots of diabetics."

"Lots. I've done strokes and heart attacks too. I've done them all. The sick are depressed, every one, but with a little help, they're feeling better in no time."

His voice was deep, comforting, confident.

"I'm sure you're very good at what you do."

"Thor and I have had several conversations at the rink," Sylvia said. "He's explained his technique to me and it makes sense."

Thor nodded and smiled. "Your daughter is very concerned about her father."

Mary Lou shook her head, said nothing, ran cold water over the turkey.

"It took him a long time to come over and talk to us at all." Sylvia took a long swig of her beer, caressing the bottle with her lips, smiling at Thor.

He looked her over. "She looks so young. Like a high school girl, don't you think?"

"Thor thought Billy and I were lovers! Is that a hoot or what?"

12

Mary Lou got up early to put the turkey in the oven. She liked early morning in her kitchen, with the sun just lighting the yard. She liked being all alone, preparing for a big feast. She was so sick of fatless, medicinal food. She was looking forward to the pleased faces when the family bit into the browned drumsticks and wings. The cranberries and yellow squash, the green salad (she'd splurged and added avocados) would look pretty on the buffet. Good smells would fill the house again.

As she worked, Mary Lou kept a cup of coffee within reach; it would get cold during the preparations, but she'd sip it anyway from time to time. She whistled "Down by the Old Mill Stream," the tune her grandmother always whistled when she cooked. She felt good.

Frederick called to wish the family a happy Thanksgiving and ask how Don was doing.

"Fine," Mary Lou said. "Well, considering."

"Should I come out?"

"You don't need to."

Frederick sounded somewhat relieved.

He sounded so far away. Unbelievable, Mary Lou thought. Like Helen, her son was now what people called old, though he still skied and rode horseback.

He was a good son. He used to scrub the kitchen floor for her on Saturdays.

She visited California once in awhile, but had not been there since Don became ill, and Don had never like going—didn't feel comfortable in other people's homes. Frederick's wife was rather distant, too, very conscious of her family's higher income and bigger world. The daughter, Mary Lou and Don's other grandchild, was married now and *her* daughter seemed to be mostly interested in the brand names of clothing.

"Maybe at Christmas," Frederick said. "Tell everybody hello."

Mary Lou wanted to say more; to say how proud she was of Frederick's success. For some reason she remembered Frederick with his chest clogged by croup, sitting in her lap and posed over a humidifier. She remembered Frederick saying to her, "Don't cry Mommy."

"I'll put your Dad on," she said.

She passed the phone to Don.

By the time Mary Lou had the turkey underway and was whipping cream for the pies, Sylvia appeared. She poured herself a cup of coffee and went to work creating her muffins and dressing. The two women worked side by side silently. The smell of fresh celery and chopped onion wafted into the air along with the odor of sweet muffins and the sage Sylvia put into the dressing. They assisted one another without words. Mary Lou handed Sylvia the chopped parsley she knew Sylvia wouldn't know where to find. Sylvia rescued the water for Mary Lou's peas that was boiling over.

By noon they had everything ready, co-workers pledged to serve the meal nicely, players facing an audience that must be pleased.

Don looked at the table for what seemed to Mary Lou the first time in his life.

"Mom has a real knack for making things nice, doesn't she?" he said.

For Mary Lou it was a shining moment: the sunlight on her daughter's hair, the table gleaming and pretty, her husband noticing her work.

Helen and Russell arrived then, bringing the pies and sweet potatoes wrapped in foil. Mary Lou took the food to the kitchen, and Billy came in and joined her: his father and Sheri were off to a ski resort.

Mary Lou handed Billy the whipped cream beaters to lick (as she did every year).

At the table, the turkey was a perfect brown, just like the pictures in *Family Circle*. Russell carved, using an electric carving knife that Mary Lou and Don had never taken out of its gift box until today. Don usually carved with his favorite old knife. The white meat was moist, delicious with Sylvia's dressing. Everything tasted good, bringing grunts of approval all around the table.

"What are you studying in school these days?" Mary Lou asked Billy. She noticed the adults tended to ignore him, even Sylvia, who had Russell to charm, and her sister to annoy. Billy said he was supposed to do a report on America's wars. He asked Don if he hadn't been in one of the wars, and was it Korea or World War II?

"The big one," Russell said. "Your granddad was in World War II."

"What branch were you in, Grandpa? Army? Navy?"

"Infantry. Plain old infantry."

"He won a silver star," Helen said.

"What's that?"

"For bravery," she said.

"I didn't know that," Sylvia said.

"It was before you were born."

"Tell me what you did, I mean what it was like," Billy said.

"I was in Burma." Don's face came more alive than Mary Lou had seen it in days as he told Billy of the fighting he'd seen, how the men crawled in the monsoon mud to reach their trenches, how they had wiped out a nest of enemy snipers.

"Well, why were we in a place like that, Grandpa?"

"We were fighting the Japanese," Don said. "You know about Pearl Harbor, don't you?"

"Kind of."

"The Japanese bombed our base—a sneak attack. Destroyed most of a fleet, killed over two thousand men."

"How did you wipe out the snipers?"

"Flame thrower," Don said. "I killed more Japs than I could count."

Sylvia looked ill. "A flame thrower?"

Mary Lou saw a picture from the movies, of men spraying fire. She had never heard this story. When Don came home he never talked about his experiences.

"It was kill or be killed," Don said.

"Dad has a purple heart, too," Mary Lou said.

"I still have shrapnel in my shoulder." Don pulled aside his shirt collar and exposed a pair of lumps near his collarbone.

Mary Lou had not thought of the war for years. It was almost half a century ago that Don brought home the souvenir Japanese flag and his bayonet. They were buried under all kinds of old junk in the basement. Unpacking these trophies, he had looked them over, handling them thoughtfully, as if reminding himself that he had actually taken part in killing and had come so close to death himself. Then he forgot all about them. Or seemed to.

Billy looked at Don with what appeared to be new respect and awe. It was hard to grasp, Mary Lou thought, if you didn't know people when they were young, that they had once been full of life as yourself, and had been called upon to do things that you could barely imagine.

"I'll show you the bayonet Grandpa brought home," Mary Lou said.

She went hurriedly to the basement, digging through piles of old magazines, cardboard boxes and hunks of ancient carpet. She wanted Billy to see the proof that Don had been a soldier and even a hero. She found the bayonet and the Japanese flag, its red sun, once so menacing, now a meaningless symbol on darkening silk. (If people thought of the Japanese now, it was of well-dressed tourists with good cameras). She opened a splintery wooden box and rifled through old photos of forgotten great aunts and uncles, and found a crumbling newspaper article about Don.

Billy stood and helped her with mementos when she returned to the dining room. He handled the blackened bayonet and the raveling flag as if trying to project himself into his grandfather's past—to get acquainted with the young man he could never know.

"Was my Dad in any war?"

"Ask him some time," Mary Lou said.

Sylvia looked puzzled. If she knew, she'd forgotten.

"I doubt it," she said.

"Can I have these?" Billy asked Don.

"No," Helen said.

"Sure. What do I want with this old junk?"

Mary Lou handed Billy the newspaper to add to the other souvenirs. Billy laid them all on a chair in the living room. The others decided what kind of pie they wanted and passed the whipped cream.

"Whoa, the game's starting!"

Russell held up his wrist and pointed to his watch, then gulped down what was left of his pie.

"C'mon, Dad. Hey Billy, turn on the tv!" He helped Don to the living room where the men settled down comfortably for afternoon football.

Mary Lou and Helen began clearing the table, with Sylvia reluctantly joining in.

"Barbaric," she said. "Guys watching football, women doing the scut work. Just because we don't have penises."

Both Helen and Mary Lou reacted slightly to Sylvia's remark, but continued working without comment. Mary Lou thought maybe this was the first time she'd ever heard that word out loud.

Sylvia of course was a big women's libber. Mary Lou was a little skeptical; she'd never really thought things would be any different from her childhood when women just sighed and said, "It's a man's world." After all, when she was young, women weren't even allowed to vote.

When did women get the vote anyway? She couldn't remember. Had it made any difference? Maybe the new rights made things better for young women. It had come too late for her. Mary Lou's life was still centered in her household, organized around Christmas and Easter, Halloween, Fourth of July and Thanksgiving.

All sorts of "progress" had occurred since Mary Lou was young. Things that should have made her life easier. She had a dishwasher now

instead of the old dishpan and rubber dish drainer, a refrigerator instead
of an ice box and the ice man delivering his huge blocks of ice (which
she missed), a washer and dryer instead of the old wash tubs and the
electric washer with the hand wringer. She'd had an electric sweeper
since the family moved into their house (the women used brooms on
the farm and mill to sweep the carpets and beat them hung over an
outdoor wash line).

All the appliances and gadgets, fast cars, jet planes, atomic bombs,
television, men walking on the moon, computers—Mary Lou's life
went on the same: there were children to take care of, lunches to pack,
homework to check, windows to wash, garbage to take out, grass to cut.

And every year of her life a turkey to bake.

She laughed at the thought of all the turkeys she had cooked for
Thanksgiving—gathered together in a great crowd, trussed up and
frozen or running around gobbling.

Mary Lou said, "You girls bring the rest of the stuff off the table and
I'll rinse the dishes. I know just how I want the dish washer stacked."
She tossed turkey bones and paper napkins into a garbage bag, scraped
uneaten scraps into the disposal, arranged dishes in the dishwasher, and
laid her better glasses aside to be washed by hand. Helen and Sylvia
continued bringing out plates and utensils until the counters were
covered. Helen then helped Mary Lou at the sink while Sylvia sat at
the table "out of the way" and drank a third or fourth glass of wine.

"I think we have to have to do more to fight this damn disease,"
Sylvia said.

Oh God, Mary Lou thought, there she goes again. Everyone had
theories on how Don should be treated. Sylvia had been harping on
meditation and herbal concoctions. Helen was always suggesting
prayers. Even Frederick had an opinion; he didn't trust the local doctors
and wanted Don to go to the Mayo Clinic.

"I'm doing everything I know how."

"Maybe there're other ways besides conventional medicine."

"Sylvia, I barely have time to take care of his meals, his bathroom,
and tend to his leg."

"I know. That's why I want to bring Thor over for therapy."

"Who's Thor?" Helen asked.

"Thorsten Bourne."

Sylvia filled her in on the wonderful man she had met at the skating
rink.

"Things like that cost money," Mary Lou said.

"Besides," Helen said. Her face had registered distinct distaste at Sylvia's suggestion of therapy. "Who is this man? You can't just bring some person you picked up at a skating rink into Mom and Daddy's home."

"I didn't 'pick him up.' I've talked to him at length and was very impressed. I invited him here to meet Momma. He's a fully licensed massage therapist and has helped lots of people. I believe some of what ails Dad is depression, and Thor says I'm right."

"Your Dad has his ups and downs," Mary Lou said.

"You just want him not to upset *you*," Helen said.

"That's not true."

Sylvia's voice was growing louder with anger.

"I just think you have to fight back against illness."

"Hand me that pink sponge," Mary Lou said to Helen.

Helen silently squeezed a sponge that was floating in the left hand sink. Mary Lou was thinking Sylvia had a point, but she wasn't sure she liked the looks of this Thor. He was obviously attracted to Sylvia as more than a professional client.

"I've seen Dad so down and even crying. That's not him."

"That doesn't mean this man is the answer. Just because he's a boyfriend—you can't *use* Daddy that way."

"He's not a boy friend. How dare you! Mom, you tell her how Dad is some days."

Mary Lou shrugged.

"She knows."

"We can't just let him lie down and *die*."

"We're not the ones to decide that," Helen said.

Mary Lou felt an argument coming on. She did not believe in Helen's religion or in Sylvia's theories or whatever they were. Her daughters were equally doctrinaire as far as she could see, one preaching 'faith' and the other 'spirituality.' She had no answers of her own. It seemed to her she was doing the best she could for Don.

"Please don't start," she said.

"I'm just trying to say we can't be passive and refuse to try anything new."

The swinging door opened and Billy came into the kitchen with the Japanese flag draped over his shoulders. In one hand was Don's old bayonet and in the other the newspaper article about Don's silver star. He looked around, caught the flush on his mother's face, his aunt's rigid stance, and his grandmother's tired posture at the sink.

"You gotta hear this, Mom, Aunt Helen." He read them the

account of how, during a terrible battle, Sergeant Don Friedman carried a wounded corporal miles through the jungle to a hospital unit. Sergeant Friedman had been hit in the back and had to stumble and crawl over the dead to reach help.

Billy's eyes were proud as he finished reading.

"Grandpa was a hero. Is he a great guy or what?"

Later that night, when the dishes were put away and Mary Lou sat down for the first time in two days, she felt that it was a good Thanksgiving. Billy had cut off the argument brewing between the girls. Don had enjoyed watching football with Russell and Billy. By Christmas or New Year's Don should have his prosthesis.

She built a fire in the fireplace, put her feet up on the ottoman, and watched the pink light flicker on the blue and gray of the Rookwood tiles.

13

Within the week Thor was a regular visitor at the Friedmans' house. Sylvia had continued to press her point of view on Mary Lou. Mary Lou said she just couldn't afford to pay any further bills; they were stacking up as it was. Don was taking twenty different medications and the insurance paid for only a portion. But Sylvia would not let up; she came back at Mary Lou with the news that Thor wouldn't charge them a penny for his services.

"What does he expect in return?" Mary Lou said.

"We're friends."

"I don't think Dad will want—I mean—having another man—"

"Oh Mother, for God's sake, does Thor look like a fag?"

They finally agreed that Don should be the judge.

Thor arrived in hospital—white shirt and pants, looking very professional. He would, he told Don, help him learn to walk better with his walker so he could be more independent. He would also give him rub-downs to help his circulation. He made it all sound so manly, Don didn't object.

Thor came to the house three mornings a week, visits that Mary Lou began to look forward to. They took some of the pressure off her and gave her more freedom to get her household chores done.

Mary Lou could see why Sylvia liked him. He was helpful, cheerful, and nice looking with his broad shoulders, blond hair and blue eyes. Mary Lou liked him too; he didn't treat her like an old lady. So many people looked right past her as though her white hair made her invisible.

Every morning when Thor came to work with Don, he stopped in the kitchen with a friendly, "Hi, Mary Lou, what's happenin'?"

Still, she feared for Sylvia.

Sylvia always had some man who was the perfect answer to her life, then disappointed her. Mary Lou didn't want to see her hurt again. It was so easy to fall in love with someone who seemed whole, someone who seemed to have answers.

Like I did, Mary Lou thought.

Mary Lou had never noticed Dr. Robertson except as a competent family physician until late one night when she was sitting by Elaine's hospital bed. Her daughter was sleeping after a series of painful tests. The room was dark except for a small lamp by which Mary Lou was reading her tattered childhood copy of *One Hundred and One*

Great Poems. Dr. Robertson came into the room quietly. He had never abandoned the family to specialists but had stayed with them throughout Elaine's illness.

He was wearing a green hospital shirt that showed black and white curly hair at the V neck. He was solidly built, slightly heavy; his gray beard (unusual at the time) tended to curl like his chest hair.

"What are you reading, Mary Lou?" His voice was gentle, refined, deep in pitch. He tilted his head to see the page Mary Lou was turned to.

"Browning," he said. "One of my favorites."

No one before had ever noticed what Mary Lou read, not her parents, not Don, not her children. She wished she could share her books with Don, but he stuck to newspapers and magazines and his occasional engineering journal.

Mary Lou covered her sudden confusion by closing her book.

"That's my holy writ," the doctor said, "I read poetry when I need a voice to carry me through. . . ."

He put his hand along the side of her cheek, like a father comforting a child.

"How are you holding up?"

"OK."

He was so close, she could smell his mix of sweat and aftershave and ether from the work he had just witnessed. Then he moved away, over to Elaine. He felt her forehead and wrist, talking all the while.

"I happen to like Wordsworth, too," he said, "though I suppose he's hopelessly out of style."

Mary Lou didn't see how a poet like Wordsworth could ever be out of style, or in style for that matter. She wished, as she had so many times, that she had more education. That she could talk to people like Dr. Robertson as an equal.

His eyes were so kind. He seemed transformed in this moment, from someone she had barely noticed, to a man with power and strength. This was the first time they had ever talked about anything other than the Friedmans' symptoms, the first time she had thought of him, not as Dr. Robertson the family physician, but as a man.

She suddenly wanted him to know everything about her. The fatherly caress had almost made her weep.

"How's Elaine doing?" the doctor said.

Mary Lou fought for her everyday voice, her practical mother's tone.

"It took her awhile to settle down, but she's been sleeping pretty quietly." They both looked at the machines constantly monitoring the little girl's heart. Dr. Robertson studied them and nodded, seeming to carry on a dialogue with himself.

"She's so good," Mary Lou said.

"She's a lovely child."

This, too, was something Mary Lou badly needed, a respected person to tell her she was a good mother, to confirm the value of the little girl she loved so. She had had such confused feelings raising Helen. Helen was so fussy and difficult. It had taken her five or six years after Helen's birth to get pregnant again; she always laid the delay up to fear on her part, a bone-deep unwillingness to take on another child. And when she did have a second child, a boy, she was as perplexed as she had been with Helen. He was so good, so strict with himself and others, so unlike his father and the boys Mary Lou had known. She was very proud of him, but she wished now she had been able to be more relaxed, to be closer to her son.

Elaine was like a miracle when she came along. Mary Lou was over thirty and had learned more about raising children. Don was doing better at his work, making more money. They had the house they loved. Elaine was a dream child to look at and to raise. She was born with her bright brown eyes (like Don's) fully open; her skin was flawless and peachy pink. She had a head full of light brown ringlets and a sweet disposition.

Mary Lou had never been so happy as when she rocked Elaine to sleep at night. Everything else was forgotten: the two lived at those times in a nursery world where to look out the window you'd expect the stars to be the perfect five-pointed sparklers in children's books. The night enveloped them in a friendly dark blue while the rest of the family slept and just Mary Lou and Elaine existed, rocking and rocking, their bodies warming each other and no sound to be heard but the soft creak of the chair and an occasional satisfied coo from the baby.

Elaine learned to walk early, at six months. By a year she was forming sentences. She loved being read the books Mary Lou ordered from a children's book club. She bestowed sweet wet kisses on her mother and father.

Before Dr. Robertson there was no one to confirm the beauty of this new child, no grandparent, no sisters or brothers. Mary Lou's father and stepmother by the time of Elaine's birth were old and full of complaints. Their own arthritis was much more interesting to them than a child. Don's mother was dying. His sisters and brothers were scattered all over the country. One had visited once, Gertrude, a German woman with the toughness of a Cleveland ghetto, and Mary Lou had liked her, but that was before Elaine was born.

Sitting here in the shadowy room together, Mary Lou and Dr. Robertson were allies, witnesses to the struggle between her daughter's tiny heart and some dark thing that seemed to be lurking just outside the night window.

"She's a brave little girl," Dr. Robertson said.

Mary Lou took her daughter's hand; it was so slim and pretty. Her seven years had been full of pain, yet she was almost unfailingly cheerful. Not in a resigned, spiritless way. She fought back too. When she'd been stabbed by one needle after another as she was hooked up to an iv and given shots and had blood taken, she cried, and when the nurse said, "It's OK, Elaine, it's OK," she said, "It is *not* OK. It hurts." But she was laughing soon after.

"I'm constantly moved by the way the kids here endure illness," Dr. Robertson said.

Mary Lou too had been touched by the other children at the hospital, like the little bald fellow in the room next to Elaine's, who had liver cancer. When he felt good enough, he brought toys to Elaine and they played soldiers, using the bumps in the sheets as the forts on their battlefield.

Dr. Robertson looked at his watch.

"I must go now," he said. "I'll be back tomorrow."

He spoke with a kind of old-fashioned formality. With her new appreciation for him as a man and a real person, Mary Lou noticed in the dim light, how tired he looked. It had never occurred to her before what long hours he must work.

"Haven't you been home yet?"

"Not yet."

She felt selfish. He had given so much extra time to her and Elaine that she had never even thought about.

"Thanks for everything."

"My pleasure."

What a wonderful smile he had: kind, intelligent, and he looked as if he needed something from her. His eyes were touched by a sort of loneliness that seemed to match her own. Each time they met at the hospital, Mary Lou grew more dependent on him. She looked forward to their next moment together as she would warmth in the cold. No, no, no, she told herself: that's disloyal to Don to feel that way. But she was so desperate. And the world she shared with Dr. Robertson was not part of everyday life, but a separate place, a magic one.

Now Sylvia was in a similar place, reaching out to and depending on a man she barely knew. Maybe she should talk to Sylvia. It was hard, though, for Mary Lou to talk to her daughter. She didn't really know how. She had lost her own mother so young, then her grandmother, and had never been close to her stepmother or the second grandmother who was always off somewhere with her spirits.

And would Sylvia listen? She lived for thrills, the high of "passion." She had no idea, Mary Lou thought, of what love actually was. No one knew, who hadn't cleaned the shit from between the legs of another.

14

Thor ate two enormous ham sandwiches for lunch, and gulped down a quart of milk. Mary Lou watched his Adam's apple bob as he swallowed. There was something downright suggestive about the hard little knots moving up and down. Mary Lou caught Sylvia's eye. She was watching Thor too. So was Don. They had all become dependent on him. There was something about Thor that made people want his approval.

"I wish I had his strength," Don said one day.

Sylvia had more energy when he came around.

He was a caretaker, concerned about *your* health, *your* feelings, and he always seemed to be in a good mood. Once in awhile Sylvia went off with him for the afternoon or out for the evening. She saw less of Billy, but Mary Lou figured that was probably good; Billy had become too wrapped up in Sylvia. He needed his own friends, people his own age.

By and large, Mary Lou thought, things had worked out better than she had expected. The neighborhood was no less dangerous: Mrs. Wong had her purse stolen and a store was broken into. Billy had a shouting match with Harold, but the comings and goings of Thor and the others gave the house an air of busyness that was comforting, and with Sylvia there at night, Mary Lou felt more secure. Also, she was making progress with the pile of test results and documents and bills that came like a paper storm after Don's hospital stay. Mike was helping her with the tax and insurance forms that she figured you'd have to be a CPA or lawyer to understand.

He was at the house one evening when Thor called for Sylvia.

"Is that Sylvia's new man?" he asked Mary Lou.

Mary Lou explained about Thor.

"She picked him up at a *skating* rink?"

"Well, she met him there. Billy was with her."

Mike returned his attention to the papers in front of him.

"Your daughter. . . ."

Was he jealous? Mary Lou wondered. Surely not. He had hardly pined away for Sylvia after she left him. He had remarried and divorced and now had Sheri. He had a good life: a big job, plenty of money, a lovely house—skiing, boating—his son.

"I think Billy was hoping *we'd* get back together," Mike said. He chuckled. Mary Lou tried to gauge how farfetched he considered Billy's hopes.

She had sneaky hopes herself now that Mike was—well, not unattached—but not married. She wasn't fond of Sheri; she wore too much makeup; her lashes looked like a doll's—you thought her lids might go up and down if you shook her, and she was clearly jealous of the time Mike spent with Billy.

What could Sylvia have against Mike? He was good looking, with regular features, strong white teeth, springy black hair, an athletic build. His manners were good. He was successful. And nice. She still couldn't understand why Sylvia had rejected him (surely they could have worked out the sex part).

Of course, when Sylvia left he was struggling to start his career, and was not able to give her all the attention she craved. Perhaps he was just too quiet for Sylvia. She seemed to prefer Curt, the man she lived with in Akron, a sort of hippy garage mechanic, and now Thor who was all muscle and might.

It seemed you always wanted what you didn't have. Look at her feelings for Dr. Robertson. *Her* husband worked with his hands: he was intelligent, but had none of the assurance or well—command—that Mike or Dr. Robertson or men like them had. Don was steady and good and the salt of the earth, but Mary Lou couldn't help wondering if she'd done the right thing in marrying him. But to be disloyal to Don even in her thoughts was unfair. She still felt guilty about that earlier self, who, when she was with Dr. Robertson, was someone so different from the Mary Lou she was at home.

In the evening as Mary Lou hunkered down with Sylvia in the girls' old bedroom, her mind drifted back again to that other Mary Lou.

After their first chat about poetry, Dr. Robertson took her to the hospital coffee shop for a sandwich. It was well past dark. Everything was quiet.

"You've got to get out of this room once in awhile," Dr. Robertson had said. "Elaine will be OK for half an hour."

Mary Lou let herself be led away from her daughter for a brief break. In the coffee shop a lone workman was mopping the floor. There were no other customers in the room, just herself and Dr. Robertson. The plastic menu in the coffee shop swam before her eyes in the harsh light.

"Try the chicken sandwich," Dr. Robertson said. "It's not bad."

Mary Lou didn't argue, and when the waitress came to take their order, he said, "One chicken sandwich, two Pepsis."

It sounded funny to hear his formal, professional voice saying "two Pepsis." Mary Lou associated him only with moments and events outside time.

She would never forget the arrangement on her plate. There were a few broken potato chips next to the sandwich.

"Now eat," he ordered.

Mary Lou picked at the food: white chicken breast on white bread. Dr. Robertson took a potato chip and ate it.

"What do you think of Robert Frost?" he said.

Mary Lou couldn't answer. No one had ever asked her opinion on a subject like poetry. Don talked about whether he should buy new socks or get the car washed. She sometimes felt so lonely.

"I like 'Stopping by the Woods,'" she said.

"It's good you have something like poetry. . . ."

Is it? Mary Lou thought. Reading was something she didn't do for others, something unproductive, for herself alone. At the mill her father and Mother Nina complained that her nose was always in a book, and claimed she'd ruin her brain and her eyesight with all that reading.

Mary Lou had a sudden feeling of unconnectedness, as though she didn't know exactly where she was or what she was doing.

"What time is it?" she asked.

Dr. Robertson calmly looked at his watch.

"Midnight."

"I better get back."

"Miles to go before you sleep?"

Mary Lou smiled. And I have promises to keep, she thought.

And I have promises to keep.

"Don't you think Thor has the cutest ass you ever saw?" Sylvia said.

Mary Lou shrugged at Sylvia's question. You couldn't not notice the man was well-built, but while she liked Thor, she didn't see him as someone you'd want for a lifetime companion. There were other things besides good looks. When had this become so out of the question?

She would never understand Sylvia: not just her love life, but her whole outlook, her ways. Her lack of honesty about money. She had still not repaid the twenty dollars she'd borrowed for taxi fare the night she came home. She was deeply in debt in Akron and had run up enough bills in Cincinnati to receive frequent dunning phone calls from places she owed money to. Mary Lou and Don had never owed a penny to anyone in their lives since the Depression, and paid bills on arrival.

"Thor has buns of steel," Sylvia said.

She held up her own forearm and pushed at it.

"I'm flabby. I need to start working out. Thor says so."

She studied herself in the mirror.

"You look fine, Sylvia."

Sylvia turned to her mother.

"You know *you're* a really good-looking woman, Mom. You've always tried to hide it. But you have great bones."

Mary Lou shook her head. "Me? No. Not really."

Mary Lou looked in the mirror: with her pale skin and white hair, she seemed to be disappearing. When Sylvia was a baby she had her hair done regularly at a beauty shop. When it turned white, the operator talked her into a tint and a teased hair-do; the result was like strawberry cotton candy. Now she just washed it herself.

"You've got a sexy figure," Sylvia said.

"Did," Mary Lou said.

Once Billy pointed to her breasts and said, "My Mommy has those, but they don't hang down to her tummy."

Mary Lou told Sylvia the story.

When she stopped laughing, Sylvia said, "I'm going to give you a makeover." She got cleanser and a plastic tray of powders and rouge and lipsticks from the top of her dresser. "Now hold still and tilt your head up." Mary Lou obeyed and Sylvia soaked a cotton ball and wiped Mary Lou's face, then squinting professionally, she applied foundation and several shades of powder and rouge. The eye shadow and liner made Mary Lou's eyes water.

When Sylvia was finished she pulled back and observed her work like an artist. She held her mirror up for her mother. "See. You look great."

Mary Lou had to admit she looked younger and a bit more vibrant, if a touch overdone.

"You have perfect lips and great cheekbones," Sylvia said.

"You're the second person who ever said that."

"Who was the first, Pop?"

Wouldn't you like to know, Mary Lou thought.

It was during one of her talks with Dr. Robertson in the hospital coffee shop. He took her there often after that first night. Mary Lou talked to him about things she had never discussed with anyone: how she worried that Elaine's illness was some sort of punishment for being a bad mother, for not feeling what she believed she ought to for her other children. She took everything he said as truth; he seemed so wise, so experienced, such a man of the world. He assured her that she was not unnatural, just human, that the notion of punishment was primitive, magical thinking, something she could overcome.

They talked about philosophy and religion.

"I don't know what I believe, what to tell Elaine," Mary Lou said.

Her grandmother had taught her to pray and she had gone to Sunday school; she thought little about what she was taught except that they were good stories she vaguely assumed were true. But when her mother and then her grandmother died and the long-winded minister went on and on about how they would meet in heaven, she suddenly realized, though she was still a child, that she didn't believe a word of what he was saying.

"It's all right to say you don't know," Dr. Robertson said.

This came as a balm. No God she had ever heard of could take a child like her daughter. Not the judging and punishing God or the kind and merciful God. An innocent seven year old girl?

"You don't need to tell Elaine anything you don't believe. You are loving her and making her feel secure and when she passes she will always be with you in your memory and your heart."

Mary Lou noticed he said when and not if, and though she sensed this was true, a coldness came over her, the coldness of a winter mill stone.

Often in the dim room where Elaine's machines hummed the minutes away, she yearned for Dr. Robertson to touch her face as he had done that one time. She imagined what a kiss between them would be like. When he looked tired at night she longed to put her arms around him.

He was wonderful with Elaine. Unlike most adults, he took children completely seriously. He let her use his stethoscope on his chest and listen to his heart. He explained the workings of that "wonderful organ."

He praised Mary Lou as a mother and said Don was a "prince of a fellow."

Mary Lou tried not to compare the two men, but Don seemed clumsy now. He would bring Elaine useless gifts, once a giant aqua and pink teddy bear, too large to cuddle and too garish to love. He tried to make jokes that would lift Mary Lou and Elaine's spirits, but they fell flat. Mary Lou hoped he would notice her volume of Shakespeare, maybe bring her some new book of poetry. He brought her a box of chocolates, which she really didn't like and that Elaine wasn't allowed to eat.

One night, sitting in the coffee shop late at night, Dr. Robertson told Mary Lou about his failing marriage. He had married young, a nurse, a woman who had not grown in any way. He envied Mary Lou her children. Even though she had misgivings about them, he knew she really loved them. He and his wife had been unable to have children and that was another reason for their unhappiness. He was deeply involved in his work, while she stayed home with nothing important to do. She felt inferior to the other doctors' wives who filled their days with bridge, tennis, and children, who had college degrees and wealthy families and had never worked.

"Yet she does nothing to change all this," Dr. Robertson said.

Mary Lou felt flattered to be his confidante, but inadequate. She could offer no solutions. What had she ever done with her life? All that was expected of her as a young woman was to be a good wife and mother, and right now she felt like neither. Any activity she might take up for herself was in limbo. She could think only of Elaine, of keeping her alive. But the doctor had said when. . . .

During the endless months in Elaine's room, which had become Mary Lou's whole world, the newspapers were full of the war with Germany and Japan: stories and pictures of dying soldiers, bombed houses, the London blitz, tanks rolling into Paris, German cities leveled. In the South Pacific, Japanese kamikaze pilots who purposefully crashed their planes into troop carriers.

Don followed every battle in the newspaper and on the radio. For Mary Lou the war was there but far away, a dark worry that seemed to have no end.

Neighbor boys went off to the army and navy and gold stars appeared in the windows of houses on Mary Lou's street. Don, at forty-one, was too old to be drafted, so he and Mary Lou did not fear his going to the army. They had no close relatives fighting. The war's immediate effect on them was the shortage of butter and meat and gas ration stamps to get back and forth to the hospital. Mary Lou's battle was trying to save the life of one little girl.

Mary Lou brushed Elaine's hair and read to her, rubbed her thin spine, with its little ridge like a cabbage leaf. When Elaine began to fail badly, unable to get her breath, too weak to eat, colorless and listless, Mary Lou wanted to die herself. She would gladly have taken her daughter's place. But nothing, neither wishes nor prayers nor medicine could save such a sick little girl.

When Elaine died, Dr. Robertson was right there with Mary Lou, his kind eyes understanding exactly what she was going through, ready to listen to her anguished words. Once he held her in his arms as she cried, the father she had never been held by.

"So who said you had great cheekbones?" Sylvia demanded, "if it wasn't Pop?"

Mary Lou blushed again and Sylvia complained, "Mom, you never tell me anything about your feelings or anything."

Maybe not, Mary Lou thought. But she was ashamed of these memories and of what happened next with Dr. Robertson.

Although she wanted to warn Sylvia of getting too wrapped up in Thor, who was she to give advice to her daughter?

15

Christmas stuff was all over the stores. Mary Lou debated whether to put up a tree: she'd have to get Billy to haul it home and drag it into the living room and find the stand and the cloth and the boxes of ornaments. But it would be good for Don to have the regular things.

It was snowing hard the morning she decided to go ahead with the tree. She padded into the kitchen to start breakfast, feeling pretty content. She loved snow. Maybe it would be a white Christmas. As she made coffee and toast, she watched the blue jays and cardinals in the feeder outside her window, flashing red and blue—gypsy colors.

The familiar kitchen sounds were all she heard in the muffled world: the tick of the clock above the door to the dining room, the radio playing softly and Don rustling his newspaper. She laid out three cups, bowls and spoons, and put boxes of cereal on the table, corn flakes for her and granola for Sylvia. Mary Lou made hot oatmeal for Don.

She and Don went ahead and began eating, not waiting for Sylvia, who sometimes liked to sleep in. When they finished, Sylvia still hadn't appeared.

"I guess she's tired," Mary Lou said, "she was out late last night. I didn't hear her come in."

Don looked at his watch. "Thor'll be here in fifteen minutes."

Thor still hadn't arrived when Billy appeared with his skates over his shoulder, come to pick up Sylvia.

"Thor's late. That's a first," Don said.

"He'll be here soon."

"Where are you two going today?" Mary Lou asked Billy.

"Eden Park pond, it's frozen over."

"Your Mom's still in bed. Shall I go wake her?"

Billy looked unsure.

"Maybe I'll have a cup of cocoa first. If she's not up soon, you can go rouse her out."

Mary Lou fixed cocoa while Billy and Don made plans to start fishing again when the weather got better. Before Don got sick, they would go down to the river on Saturdays and make a miniature camp under the willows. Don had never had time to do things like this with Frederick; he was busy starting up and managing his business, often working weekends and late in the evening, and Frederick had been so self-sufficient and such a diligent student that he had not seemed to miss his father's attention all that much; he certainly never complained. When Billy came along Don had more time, and Billy loved their outings.

Part of the fun was fussing over their tackle boxes, selecting flies, and loading up their cooler and metal deck chairs. They enjoyed just sitting on the bank watching the big diesel towboats go by. Mary Lou would pick the two of them up at the end of the day and sit with them for awhile as the sun set on the coal barges hoving along the water. The steamboats were long gone. *When had they died out?* she wondered. Their wooden decks and black smoke existed somewhere, transformed (she'd read in one of Frederick's books that nothing disappeared completely, but became a gas or a liquid or something different): but the old boats had disappeared, something else gone and all but forgotten.

Mary Lou would fry the catfish Don and Billy caught and serve it slathered in Frisch's famous tartar sauce.

She served Billy's cocoa to him where he sat beside Don, and then went upstairs to call Sylvia. It wasn't fair of her to keep her son waiting; it always took her a good forty-five minutes to get ready to leave the house. Mary Lou pushed Sylvia's door open quietly, and called her name. No answer. She tiptoed into the room. Hard to tell if Sylvia's bed had been slept in; she never made it. Mary Lou checked the bathroom: it was empty. The hairs on Mary Lou's neck crackled with electricity as when she pulled off a blouse on a dry cold winter day. What now?

Mary Lou looked in Sylvia's closet; there was so much stuff it was impossible to decide if anything was missing. She checked the dresser drawers to see if they held any clue to Sylvia's whereabouts. They were almost empty. She must have gone off someplace. Why did Sylvia have to do these things?

Mary Lou dreaded going back downstairs and facing that boy who was always being disappointed. Where on earth could Sylvia be?

"Well, your mother seems to be out somewhere," Mary Lou told Billy.

Billy said, "No problem." As he put his coat back on, he added, "I suppose she's with that Thor."

"I couldn't say. Don't you like Thor?"

"He's so full of himself."

Billy left saying he'd check back later.

Mary Lou finished her morning cleaning and planned Don's lunch, then sat down at the dining room table. Trying to forget about what Sylvia was up to, she wrote a few Christmas cards: one to Penny and

Stan, one to a niece of Don's. She debated about Mrs. Wong; she was so nice, but did Orientals celebrate Christmas? She wrote a check to UNICEF for the child she was sponsoring, Jose. The agency sent her pictures of Jose, and he wrote thank-you letters. He was the third kid she'd "adopted." Over the years the first two had grown up.

Late afternoon—it was getting dark so early!—Billy reappeared. Mary Lou tried to coax Billy into another cup of cocoa and she laid out a plate of cookies, but he shook his head.

"Not hungry. Any news?" He looked worried.

"Not yet," Mary Lou said. "You go say hi to your grandpa."

Mary Lou finished writing a few more cards, then joined Don and Billy in the living room.

She had a bad feeling when the phone rang. She let it ring several times.

"Momma?"

Sylvia.

"Where *are* you?"

"Miami."

Mary Lou grappled with the name: there was a small town called Miamiville not too far from Cincinnati.

"Miamiville?" she said.

"No, of course not. Miami Florida. Thor's with me. We're getting married."

"Oh, Sylvia —"

"Be happy for me, Momma, please."

"But Sylvia, Billy's here. You were supposed to—"

"Oh God, I forgot. It was just one of those crazy nights."

"And Dad was expecting Thor."

"Oh. Well, we're not gone forever. We'll be back in four or five days."

"Why didn't you *say* anything?"

"It just happened."

"Why didn't you call earlier? We worried, not having the slightest idea—"

"I didn't want to call earlier—didn't want to wake you up."

How thoughtful, Mary Lou said to herself.

"I'm always up."

"Let me speak to Billy."

"Just a minute." When Mary Lou told Billy what Sylvia had done, he looked like the little kid his mother left the day she walked out on him and Mike.

"She wants to speak to you."

Billy hesitated, swallowed, shook his head no.

Don looked hurt and puzzled. What was happening?

Mary Lou went back to the phone.

"Billy doesn't want to talk now. I can't blame him. He came over to take you skating the way you planned."

"I guess he's mad at me. Tell him I love him very much."

In a pig's eye, Mary Lou thought. She hung up after a quick goodbye.

She explained to Don again what had happened. He and Billy both looked like someone had kicked them in the stomach

"Sylvia is always full of surprises," Mary Lou said.

Billy wouldn't make eye contact.

"It was kind of—thoughtless—not to tell us first," Don said.

"They'll be back in a few days." Mary Lou tried to think of something to say or do to ease the feeling they all had of being second best.

"I'd like to put up the Christmas tree tomorrow," she said. "Maybe you and I could go out to that little stand and pick one up, Billy."

Billy was still quiet and preoccupied.

"What?"

"The Christmas tree. Could we get it tonight?"

Billy still hadn't looked Mary Lou in the eye.

"I've got some stuff to do. Could we take care of it tomorrow?"

"Sure, whenever's good for you."

"Any time you say."

"How about first thing in the morning, say ten o'clock?"

"Fine."

Billy said he had to go now, and Mary Lou walked him to the door. She knew how painful this blow was, especially since it hit in the same place where he'd been hurt before. Billy was never first with Sylvia.

"She has a right to get married. It's just—she should have told you and not stood you up."

"No big deal," Billy said.

She watched him as he walked down the steps to where his cycle lay on the curb. His shoulders drooped like the child's of fifteen years ago.

But Billy was almost a man now.

Mary Lou went back to the kitchen and pitched the cookies she had laid out for him into the sink.

16

Mary Lou went to the basement to get the boxes of Christmas tree ornaments. Of course Sylvia had the right to get married, she thought, and Thor owed them nothing. But Don counted on his visits, and any little thing threw him off. And Billy: he had lost the smile he'd had since Sylvia came back. He mentioned her only once saying, "She actually married that guy?" Another time Mary Lou smelled liquor on his breath.

Helen was right about Sylvia: there was no one in the world but her. Helen was right about so many things. It didn't make her any more loveable.

The paper boy came to the door and Mary Lou hunted around for her purse. She must start putting it in one exact place so she wouldn't have to search for it every time she needed some cash. She located it on the covered radiator near the stairs, and pulled it open hurriedly to pay the boy who was waiting at the open door, cooling off the house: she had had four twenties, and they were all missing. All that was left was two one-dollar bills and some change. She knew she hadn't spent the twenties. She wasn't that forgetful. She asked the boy to come back later: she couldn't pay him right then.

Her face got hot as she sat down and tried again to think about the missing bills. She was positive she hadn't spent them. She hadn't been out of the house since Sylvia left. No one had been in the house but herself, Don and Sylvia. Billy had been with her or Don when he stopped over, and anyway Billy would never take money: he knew they would give him anything he needed or wanted if he asked.

Sylvia. Mary Lou could just see her: dashing off she'd need cash for taxis and hotel tips and so on. Mary Lou pulled the purse shut roughly.

Suppose she needed that money in a hurry? Sylvia would never consider that; it meant admitting someone else besides herself to her thoughts.

How embarrassing to have to stall the paper boy. He would be returning in the afternoon for his money. This was the first time since they'd been taking the paper, over fifty years, that she hadn't paid her bill right away. She was so angry she blurted out to Don what Sylvia had done.

"They're all like that anymore—young people," Don said. Mary Lou said he had a point.

"The ME generation."

Sylvia and her friends *had been* privileged, Mary Lou thought. Even soft. In their snug houses with electric heat and air-conditioning, they had never been hot, never been cold; they had never been hungry, never done without anything they wanted. They played in suburban yards, rode their bikes on safe quiet streets. They never had to do any work heavier than making their beds (which they didn't). There were vaccines for most every thing, including polio which Mary Lou had worried about all during the Depression and after (children in iron lungs and wheel chairs)—constantly making Helen and Frederick bend their necks to check for stiffness.

When Sylvia's teeth came in slightly less than perfect, she got braces; if the puppy was sick, it went to the vet. Sylvia never dealt with the pain and death that was always nearby in the country.

Still Sylvia and friends seemed to feel singled out by death. Mary Lou remembered Sylvia saying, "I could be annihilated any minute," when she was in grade school. She described how she and her classmates had to dive under their desks in a drill for an atomic attack. "Your generation brought this on us."

"And where will I be when you get annihilated?" Mary Lou asked. "Aren't I in the same boat?" She had to admit the world Sylvia would inherit was frightening, but the perils were far away, easy to forget in the daily scramble for the endless pain-free luxuries Sylvia and her generation seemed to feel entitled to: unlimited things, clothes that never got mended, sex that had no consequences, work that was exciting and easy, and so on. . . .

As though to underline her thoughts, Mary Lou got a call from a neighbor about Sylvia's age asking if she wanted to sell her Mercedes— his sixteen year old daughter needed a car and had her heart set on a Mercedes (and why, he implied, would an old woman need a fancy convertible?). Mary Lou assured him she was not selling her car, and rather snappishly suggested a less expensive brand.

He was one of those neighbors who never put his garbage cans away.

Mary Lou thought her own generation was too hard on itself, but Sylvia's was too soft.

Mary Lou dreaded calling Helen. She would have to listen to a lecture on how irresponsible Sylvia was and how stupid Mary Lou was to put up with her. She waited until Helen dropped in to see Don. She decided to tell her only about Sylvia and Thor eloping, not about Billy not being told or the missing money.

"I knew this performance wouldn't last. I don't think much of that Thor person, either," Helen said, pronouncing it eye-ther, Mary Lou noted with annoyance. "Daddy counted on him."

"They'll be back in a few days."

"So she says."

Helen had a way of making Mary Lou feel as though *she* were the guilty party. Or at least in cahoots with them.

"I don't know what we did to make our kids so—unthoughtful," Mary Lou said.

"You spoiled Sylvia to death."

"I suppose we did. But what about Frederick? I was hoping he would come to visit when Dad was in the hospital."

"You told him not too."

"I only hear from him at Christmas and Easter and then—"

"You never ask anything of him because he's a man. He's busy with his work. Like I didn't work—and pay board when I lived at home."

"Well, he could at least phone more often."

Helen looked frustrated.

"Mom you're avoiding Sylvia's problems by picking on Frederick."

"What?"

"You should face it. Sylvia will never be anything but a spoiled brat. And maybe Frederick feels you should have helped him with college. He was the smart one. But your little pet got to go and never had to do a day's work like me and Fred."

"We couldn't afford to send Fred. Or you."

"You gave Sylvia that big wedding too. I never got one."

Helen seemed to be waiting for this conversation. It seemed as though she'd waited a long time.

"What other crimes have we committed against you children?"

"You never loved me, Mother," Helen said.

Mary Lou gasped. "Of course I did," she said.

"No, you didn't."

Mary Lou didn't know what to say. She did love Helen. Maybe just not enough. She had done everything she could for Helen, always hoping her less motherly feelings were well hidden (*crying the day she found out from the doctor she was pregnant*).

"I changed your diapers, Helen. I fed you, I got you to school on time, I sat by your bed when you were sick. I mended your clothes. I made you a princess dress for Halloween and a formal for the prom. Remember? How can you say something like that?"

Helen, she could tell, was near tears.

"Oh, you were dutiful, Mother. I don't deny that. But you never loved me or Fred. And then when Elaine was sick you just disappeared."

Mary Lou knew she was right.

"We were completely shut out. Elaine's death belonged only to you. At least I was grown up, but Fred was still a kid. You did have another child, a son to turn to."

"He had his scouts. He was at camp. . . ."

Mary Lou was surprised at Helen's sharpness; she was more observant than Mary Lou had ever given her credit for.

"We had to tiptoe. There was nothing we could do to make you see that there were other people in the family. We were invisible. We felt *responsible*, like it was our fault Elaine died."

"Oh, that's not true."

"You were in like a trance, like Sleeping Beauty—until Sylvia came along."

Mary Lou was near tears now herself. Why did Helen pick a time like this to bring up all this old stuff? Didn't she have enough to contend with over Don's illness?

"I wanted to be a newspaper reporter, but you never once encouraged me to go to college. . . ."

Now she's being a cry baby, Mary Lou thought.

"We all have disappointments," she snapped. "I always wanted to be a teacher. . . ."

"Elaine and Sylvia were so pretty. You never once thought I was pretty," Helen said.

Mary Lou looked into her daughter's eyes and saw a child. Helen's well over sixty-five years old and still hurting from my words or lack of them, she thought. She studied Helen's dark pupils and the whites around them, shining with tears, her black cloud of hair. *You yourself still hurt from not being told you were pretty, why shouldn't your daughter?*

Now here they were, two old women, in tears over things that happened a lifetime ago.

"I was only sixteen when I had you," Mary Lou said.

She wasn't ready to be a mother.

Still, she was truly sorry Helen had caught on to her disappointment in her.

Now Helen was disappointed in herself: it seemed to signal forth from the roots of her black, black hair. Hiding behind the hair were Helen's slightly protruding ears. How could I have done such a thing? Taped those little ears back. *So cruel.*

She wished she could be a young mother again, one with more wisdom and experience so she could take back what she had done and comfort the humiliated little child peering out from her grown-old daughter's eyes.

"I *did* love you," Mary Lou said. "All of you. And so did Dad. We made mistakes."

Helen pulled a Kleenex from her purse and dabbed her eyes.

"You made me feel so ugly."

"No."

"Nothing I ever did was right."

"Well, I'm sorry you feel that way," Mary Lou said.

"You never approved of a single boy I brought home."

"Well, that one boy. . . ."

"It doesn't matter any more," Helen said. She blew her nose and closed her purse. "I'm sorry for picking on you, especially now." Helen reached for her coat.

"Wait, how about a cup of tea?" Mary Lou said.

"I have a lot of errands to do on the way home."

"Let me fix you some tea first."

"Thank you no," Helen replied.

Oh for God's sake, Mary Lou thought irritably. Why can't she sit down and drink a cup of tea with me? And why can't she just say no thank you like everybody else?

17

Mary Lou was up early again the next day, even though she hadn't slept much. Don's leg, the missing one, ached all night. Strange: when it was infected, there was no feeling in it, and now it could hurt as bad as a real limb.

The weather man had been right for once. Snow made the windows round as portholes, and the whole world like the skies outside a plane window. Mary Lou loved its softness, its mystery. The peeling paint on her wooden porch was covered, the garbage cans were white-capped, lurching gnomes.

As she went about her work she thought about her daughters. Sylvia had reached a new low (imagine her pilfering money!); things could not go on as they had, no one felt the same. As for the things Helen had said, thank God Don didn't hear them.

Helen was the most loyal of her children. But feeling the way she did, why did she stay so close, so protective of her and Don? Did she really love them, or was she a kind of prisoner, still trying to get the attention she had missed?

She couldn't blame Helen for her resentments. She too still felt things from long ago: big things like her mother's death, small things like never being told she was pretty; the change in her father after he came home from the first world war. He was hard as stone. Well, he was right about her being too young to get married.

Mary Lou threw on a jacket and went to the backyard to feed the birds. The steps were slick under the snow. She took little flat-footed steps. All she needed was a broken hip. She watched her own footsteps in the snow covering the grass: must be a good eight inches. She hated to be the first to spoil something so lovely. At the same time, she was tempted to run around and make a big circle for 'Fox and Geese'—the kind kids had made when she was young. You stamped out a circle and made lines across it, and there were bases or something: she couldn't remember how to play, but it was a lot of fun.

When the creek at the mill froze over, the kids walked and slid on it. Even her father once careened downhill on a garbage can lid. They chopped blocks of ice out of the creek and put it in the ice box to keep the meat and milk fresh.

Mary Lou lifted the bird feeder down and put a new piece of suet in it and scattered bread and cake crumbs on the snow. The sunlight on the white crystal surface reflected rainbow colors, so in spite of the low temperature, the day felt bright and pleasant.

She could hear car motors being urged into starting (she remembered when people used chains for traction and the sound of them clanking). The scrape of a shovel reminded her that she must get her own shovel out and start on the walk and driveway. Maybe Billy would do the big work when he came over.

They were supposed to go get the tree this morning: she could leave Don for that short a time. She would give him his shot when she returned and meantime he'd have cranberry juice and lifesavers by his chair.

"Wasn't Billy supposed to be here?" Don said.

Mary Lou took off the scarf she'd wrapped around her head, and peeled away her wet socks.

"What time is it?"

"Ten thirty."

"We said ten."

"Not like him to be late."

"No," Mary Lou said. "Boy, it's cold out and really slippery under the snow. I almost fell a couple of times."

"You shouldn't be shoveling snow."

"I enjoy it. I didn't do much."

That was true, she'd worked for an hour, but had made only a little headway. It was hard to lift the loaded shovel.

"I'm going to call Billy," Mary Lou said.

She got the phone machine, Billy singing: "You've reached the home of Mike and Billy/ You may think our message silly/ But leave your number when this song ends/And we'll call back cause we're your friends/ Wait for the beep."

"Call me," Mary Lou said.

"Probably on his way," she told Don. "Anything you want?"

"Nope. I keep thinking about Sylvia though. It wasn't right to run off without telling us she was going."

"We ran off."

"That was different."

Mary Lou looked in the refrigerator to see what she might fix for lunch. Billy still hadn't arrived by the time she laid out ham for him and herself and sliced turkey for Don. Maybe she should call Mike, she thought, but to call a man at his office was something she'd never done in her life. Even when the kids were sick she had never called Don at work.

By the time she had the sandwiches ready, she was getting really worried about Billy. He always called if he was going to be late. She looked out the kitchen window: the light had changed: no longer warm sunlight and bright reflections making the snow glisten. The light was cold, flat, the snow dead-white like a hospital sheet.

Mary Lou dialed Mike's office number. He had left it with her in case she ever needed him in an emergency. The receptionist said he was not in even though Mary Lou said it was urgent. Now Mary Lou was even more worried. She stared into space a minute, blank. She tried the home number again and got that stupid message again; she cut it off before it was over. Just after she hung up, the phone still in her hand, it rang.

"Mary Lou?"

"Yes."

"This is Mike."

She knew by his voice that something was very wrong.

"Where's Billy?"

"He was in an accident."

"Is he OK?"

Mike seemed to hold back as though he were choking on something. Finally he said, "Billy's dead."

"Mary Lou?"

"I'm here." Her hands on the phone were ice cold.

"He died instantly. He didn't feel anything."

"Billy dead. *No.*"

"It was about four o'clock this morning. He was coming home from a bar; the street was so slick, his cycle spun out of control, hit a stone wall. And well, Mary Lou, don't tell anyone else this: the police said he might have been trying to out-race another vehicle. I've been at the police station and the—the morgue."

Racing. It had to be with Byron and Harold. Why had she ever told Billy about those damned boys? Let him get into a fight with them? Oh my God, my God!

Mike was still talking and Mary Lou tried to listen while she was wanting to scream no.

"I'll let you know about funeral arrangements. Will you tell Sylvia?"

"Yes."

Billy evidently hadn't told Mike she was gone.

"Mary Lou, I'm so sorry to have to tell you this. You took care of him when Sylvia and I didn't."

A bar. Maybe run off the road. Why couldn't he let it be?

The click of the phone when Mike hung up was like a final blow punctuating his call. Done. Over.

Mary Lou looked out at the pointless, empty world outside the window. She noticed her geranium on the sill above the sink was drooping. She watered it, letting the water run slowly out of the plastic container.

She waited for the unbearable reality of Billy's death to hit her. But it didn't come. It would come later, she knew, an intruder chasing her with a club raised to strike her down. There would be no escape.

Now she had to tell Don. This would be the hardest task she had ever faced, harder even than telling him the day Elaine died. He had known that was coming, and he was young then with a life outside the four walls of the house and a future of his own.

Mary Lou's feet took her to the bedroom where Don was watching the news. He turned it down with the remote.

"Hear from Billy?"

"Mike called—"

"He coming over?"

"Billy was in an accident."

Don's ruddy face lost all color.

"A wreck?"

"He—was killed."

"No," Don said. "I don't think so."

He turned the tv back on. Turned up the volume.

Mary Lou went over to the set and turned it off. She took Don's face in her hands. She told him what Mike had said. Like a child being scolded Don kept looking away.

When she finished he looked beaten.

"Why couldn't it have been me?" he said.

Or me? Or me? Or me?

18

"Feral dogs," her father said when Tim came into the barnyard the night he died. They saw that Tim's right hoof was torn off and that he had a hole in his side. Her father got his gun from the kitchen and cocked it. "It's all we can do for him," he said. He held the gun out and made her hold it. She pushed it away and ran to Tim. She held on to him, begging for his life. His coat smelled of manure, his breath of fragrant oats. "Get away," her father said. Tim's legs buckled one joint at a time like a flimsy card table.

That was Mary Lou's first death. The death that had been around her all the time, that she had never looked in the face. And then had come the others, each one, her mother, her grandmother, her father, Elaine, tearing into the most fragile scar tissue. Why? Why? Why? she had screamed when Elaine died. Now she did not ask why. There was no answer.

And as always, there were jobs to be done.

There was Don to consider and Sylvia. Arrangements to be made.

Mary Lou called Thor's mother to see if she knew where Thor and Sylvia were in Florida. She called Helen. Helen offered to come over, but Mary Lou said no.

She called Frederick, feeling strange because of what Helen had told her about shutting him out. This time she would not shut him out. But how could she do that without breaking down and that she must not do.

"I'm so sorry, Mom," Frederick said. "I'll be out as soon as I can." He asked for details. He sounded far away, even farther than California.

"Call when you get your ticket settled. Helen will come and meet you at the airport."

"How is Sylvia taking all this?" Frederick asked.

"She doesn't know about it yet." Mary Lou told him about Sylvia's surprise marriage. Frederick made a sort of disapproving click.

"Oh Sylvia."

Mary Lou called Mike to see what she could help with. He asked Mary Lou to order flowers and food for the house; Sheri was out of town. He would make the arrangements with the funeral home. Mary Lou called Helen again and told her she had talked to Frederick, and asked her to pick him up at the airport. She made Don take his medicine, tried to convince him to eat. She cleaned the house, scouring the bathroom floors on her knees, scrubbing the grout between the tiles.

Don didn't say another word about Billy. Mary Lou told him about trying to contact Sylvia, and said Frederick would be coming home, but he paid little attention.

Before dinner she gave Don his injection. His poor stomach, she noticed, had been punctured so often, she had to search for new fresh places to jab. When she had helped him bathe and get ready for bed, he lay rigid with his eyes wide open. She knew he would not sleep and neither would she.

She turned off the light and went to Sylvia's room and sat on the edge of her bed: her duties were done, everyone had been called. Arrangements had been made. Had she forgotten anything?

She was cold but could not seem to muster the energy to reach for a blanket. She bowed her head as though to ward off a blow. She rubbed her swollen knee. She rolled back and forth across the bed: oh God, oh God, oh God.

"Mary Lou?"

Mary Lou ignored Don's call.

"Mary Lou?"

She got up from the bed wearily, joints aching, and went to Don. He felt weak and needed a glass of juice.

Mary Lou went to the kitchen and got out the carton of Tropicana with its bright orange and green label and the assurance of its added calcium and vitamin D. She sat at the table and stared at it.

The funeral was held two days later in Schmidlapp's funeral home. Billy's casket was closed, a decision made by Mike. Mary Lou wanted to see her grandson one last time, but that was not to be. Mary Lou had to agree that Billy's father had the right to make the decision. She barely heard the words of the minister as she tried to grasp the fact that her grandson, a young man alive and full of energy two days before, was actually lying in the long, flower-covered box in the aisle of the chapel.

The cemetery ground had thawed enough for Billy to be buried, and the mourners followed him to the cemetery and saw him lowered into the earth. Mary Lou stood at the gravesite between Helen and Russell. Don sat in a wheelchair with Frederick standing beside him. Mike and his parents were nearby along with Sheri, who had come back from **her** vacation (Mary Lou noticed her stiletto heels were sinking into the wet earth).

Billy was laid next to Elaine, whose shiny granite stone reflected the sudden cruel sunshine. As the minister spoke, melting snow ran down the tree trunks and headstones and trickled into the gutters as though even nature could not bear this death.

That night, after she had taken care of Don, Mary Lou crept back down the stairs and sat on the bottom step. She rubbed her cold arms. Moonlight through the windows lay on the living room floor like sheets of ice.

She stared through the stair rails at the snow outside the window, now blue in the moonlight. She smoothed down the hem of her robe. The phone on the hall table was just beyond her hand. She stared at its black form for a long time, then quietly, almost guiltily, she reached out, picked up the receiver and pushed a button. A voice came on:

"You've reached the home of Mike and Billy. . . ."

She listened to the beloved voice, all that was left of her boy, until the cheery "Wait for the beep." Then she slammed down the receiver and her icy heart split like a frozen pond.

19

Mary Lou knew Don was bad off because of how fast the hospital got him to a room and hooked up to an IV.

Dr. Weiss was there in fifteen minutes. He observed Don closely, took his pulse, studied the various monitors.

"Severe insulin reaction. Blood glucose has fallen dangerously low."

"But I gave him his shot and he had—"

"It's nothing you did wrong." The doctor's voice was kind and reassuring. "These things happen. Stress or severe shock could exacerbate—"

She told him about Billy.

"I'm so sorry, Mary Lou. This is beginning to make sense." Dr. Weiss tested Don's reflexes, and got little reaction. "Don has suffered a big blow here: his body is trying to close down."

"He's in a coma, Mom," Helen said.

They sat there all morning, waiting, and watching as Dr. Weiss and various nurses and assistants bustled in and out. Every once in awhile Mary Lou crept over to the bed and peered at her husband's face. He was just not there, further away than when he was in the army. When he was in the army she got letters—news from where he was. He was nowhere now.

Toward noon Dr. Weiss came into the room for another look at Don.

"What's going on?" she asked Dr. Weiss. "Is he ever coming out of this?"

The doctor took a deep breath, looked upward, seemed to search for the right answer.

"You have to be prepared that he might not—survive this."

"Oh."

Would she bury another this week?

She sat down and tried to grasp what was happening: the funeral two days ago, Don falling down in a faint early this morning; herself frantically calling the hospital to try and get an ambulance.

"You'll have to call it yourself," the woman on the line said.

"But it's an emergency."

"Sorry, honey. We don't run ambulances. It's a service." She gave Mary Lou a number to call.

"Two hundred dollars," the man on the phone said.

Mary Lou was shocked. Why did she think ambulances were free?

Helen excused herself to go and "feed Russell." Mary Lou tried to get comfortable in the hospital chair.

Why were they being punished like this? Hadn't they had enough? It seemed as though they were being punished for getting old. People were living too long now.

She muttered the little German prayer her grandmother taught her, "Ich bin klein. . . . Mein herz ist rein. . . ."

She began to doze.

When Mary Lou awoke, she was stiff. Don was still quiet and unresponsive. The room was too quiet. Mary Lou tiptoed to Don's bed and whispered his name. No response.

Helen's voice in the hall was welcome. She came bustling into the room, carrying bags of food from the hospital coffee shop. Mary Lou had missed Helen, but the odor of the food was not tempting.

"You have to be prepared that he might not survive this." She kept hearing Dr. Weiss's words.

How could he deal so familiarly with life and death, she thought, he's so young. What can he have ever lost? Mary Lou realized Dr. Weiss was about the age now that Dr. Robertson had been when Elaine died. And she had thought Dr. Robertson was so mature and wise. Dr. Weiss could be her son. Maybe her grandson.

Mid-afternoon, he appeared again. He looked Don over, checked the bags of urine attached to the bed. He left the room and returned half an hour later with an orderly pushing a stainless steel machine. "Maybe you should step out," he said. "We need to hook Don up here."

Mary Lou stayed and Helen with her.

The orderly began inserting a catheter in Don's side, attaching it to the machine.

"What are you doing?" Mary Lou said.

"He's suffered renal failure. . . ."

"What's that?"

"Kidney," Helen said. She looked frightened.

"Mary Lou, I must tell you," Dr. Weiss said, "If Don does survive, he'll be dependent on this."

Mary Lou thought how Don would hate this thing.

"Glomerulopathy is a blockage of tiny filters in the kidney and—"

The doctor seemed to be talking from far away. She could barely hear him. "He may also have significant brain damage."

Don would not want a half life, Mary Lou thought.

When the doctor and his assistant left, Mary Lou resettled herself in the chair by the window, with a sweater draped around her shoulders. Don was still as death, his mouth open in a kind of silent howl.

He looked like Mary Lou's father right before he died. The nursing home had tied him to his chair with a strip of soft fabric, to keep him from wandering off. His mind was like a walnut dried up inside its shell. He wore diapers.

Sometimes he would sit through Mary Lou's visit and not say a word; other times he would cry with anger. The home celebrated his birthday with balloons and bright-colored streamers: King Lear in a party hat.

Mary Lou became aware of Helen gathering up the containers of food that she hadn't touched and pitching them in the waste can.

"I'm going to run on home. Is there anything I can bring over later? Maybe some of that roasted chicken from the Dinner Bell. You like that."

"Don't bother, please."

"Mother, would you pray with me?

"Sure. Why not?"

As Helen muttered a prayer, Mary Lou listened to the sounds of the hospital: a nurse's shoes passing the door, a blower going on, a man down the hall crying, "nurse, nurse."

After Helen left, Mary Lou moved from her chair to the window, and back to her chair. She noticed the floor was dirty. She looked in the closet and found a mop and broom. That was one change since Elaine was in this hospital: the rooms weren't kept clean. She swept in the corners and scrubbed the sink.

She stopped by Don's bed and tried to see through his skull: where was he? Would she ever talk to him again? If he did wake up, what would he have to look forward to? He would have to face Billy's death, his own damaged brain, dependence on a machine. She tried to relate the body on the bed to the Don she knew. Even in the last year of sickness he had had his wits about him. He read the paper, and after all these years had begun to enjoy having her read poetry to him. He was especially fond of Kipling and Robert Burns.

New growth out of old wood: some plants were like that, and Don had been like that too. Dead wood was different: the heart of the bush or tree turned to soft brown dust. Nothing could grow from it.

Everything was taking place outside Don's body by machine: instead of a heart beat she heard the faint clink of electronics, the sucking noise of liquid moving from glass to vein and back to glass.

Mary Lou was so tired. Could she fight death again? The hospital sounds, bleeps and whispering shoes, a far-off cry, the squeaking wheels of a cart brought back her days in this same hospital with Elaine. So many days trudging through the long underground passageways to the children's wing, always producing, as her grandmother had taught her, a smile for her daughter in spite of her own discouraged heart. Late afternoon shopping for her and Don's meals, cooking and washing up and then back to the hospital.

She cleaned the house late at night.

Mary Lou begged and cajoled the doctors for information about Elaine's condition, trying to follow their professional talk. She read every article or book they mentioned about heart disease. She took Elaine to Texas for an operation that could only be done there—living out of a run-down hotel for weeks. Back to the hospital for more long days and late nights. Nothing did any good.

When Elaine died, Mary Lou wished only for her own death. She was barely aware that Helen was around. Frederick came and went, going off to classes or with his friends. She turned on Don. Why was he not ready to die the way she was?

He was like stone like her father. He bought their daughter's coffin and arranged her funeral. He stood by the open grave silently. The next day he was back at work.

Mary Lou was left alone in the empty house frozen in grief like a fish in a winter pond. Alive but dead. Not yet middle-aged and her life was over. She could not stop crying, but Don never cried. He left her alone in the house to grieve alone.

And soon he seemed to be the same as before, going to work, doing his chores at home. Had he forgotten their child? Mary Lou tried to bring her back to life in her mind: seeing her before she got so sick, splashing in a big pan of water in the yard, wearing her yellow bathing suit with the ruffle around her rear, arranging her dolls at the child-sized table in her room. She saw her in the hospital, playing soldiers with the boy in the next bed.

Mary Lou tried to read, to find some comfort in the words of others who had seen death take children. Nothing meant anything. She thought of calling a friend but couldn't lift the phone. What good would it do? She could not bear any occasion Elaine had enjoyed. Valentine's Day was one of Elaine's favorites; she loved to cut pink and red paper into hearts and trim them with lace. Now red and pink meant blood and Mary Lou hated the sight of the valentines and candy.

She dreamed of Dr. Robertson, his knowing touch on her cheek with his hand, the solid feel of his body the day he held her in his arms as she cried. He was the only person who would know how to say what she felt. He was her comrade in death.

The day Elaine died, he had taken both her hands in his and told her it was over and how sorry he was. Don had never said a word. He pretended in a way it hadn't happened, that Elaine had never been. He hadn't mentioned her name since they buried her.

Mary Lou could not touch him. She spoke only when she had to, to get through the day. She wanted the other man. He said Elaine was wonderful, that she, Mary Lou, was beautiful.

She longed to hear that voice once again. She could almost hear it: "What do you think of Robert Frost?" "She's a wonderful child."

Weeks passed and still Mary Lou yearned to feel the instinctive understanding, to see the knowledge in his eyes of what she felt.

She hoped he might call to see how she was, or just to talk to her. Hadn't he hinted he'd needed her as much as she needed him?

One gray winter afternoon she could stand her isolation no longer.

Against everything she was ever taught, she called him.

Her hands felt weak as she held the phone.

"Dr. Robertson?"

"Yes."

It was his voice, warm, and intelligent.

"It's Mary Lou Friedman."

"Mary Lou. How are you?"

"Fine."

"What can I do for you?"

He sounded so brisk now, so impersonal. She had been sure he wanted more than friendship: the confidences about his wife, the sharing of poetry and feelings.

"Have you got the bug that's going around?" he said.

"No."

"Don got it?"

"He's fine."

"What is it then?"

Now he sounded impatient. He probably had a crowd of people in the waiting room.

"I—thought you might like to come over—one afternoon. For coffee? Just to talk?"

There was a silence on the line.

"Oh—well, I'm awfully busy. This season's been hectic."

She could not speak, vaguely debated whether to hang up or try to say goodbye or I'm sorry or what. . . . The indecision spread and the silence grew.

"Mary Lou," Dr. Robertson said. He seemed to try to make his voice as kindly as possible. "It's awfully nice of you to invite me. I understand, I think, why you called *me*." He paused again. " We've had several little superficial chats and it's natural that you might think I could be of some help now."

"I—"

"But you must return to your everyday life now, and me to my professional role in it."

Mary Lou said nothing.

"Are you OK? You understand, don't you?"

"Yes." It was like she understood she mustn't break down at her mother's funeral, or cry over Tim when his legs buckled and he crashed to the ground (such a big body). And she shouldn't be hurt when her father refused to help her and Don, and she mustn't complain when her husband left her with a new baby, and she shouldn't mind giving up her dreams. . . .

She put the phone back on the stand and stared a moment into its black face, humiliated.

She thought their "chats" had been more than superficial.

She felt so foolish.

She stayed in her suspended state: maybe others could see her, frozen in time. She couldn't see them, nor the sunlight, nor the birds. They seemed to be singing far away in some other world.

She saw Don sometimes looking at her, not saying anything. If only he would speak. Cry.

The weather stayed gray and cold. The pain was physical. She sat in a chair and stared at the walls, let the house get dirty; she cooked, but ate little.

Don lit the furnace every morning, carried out the ashes, shoveled the driveway when it snowed, went to work. In the evenings he went down in the basement to his workshop.

When spring came, time to plant her flower garden, Mary Lou stayed in the house. The new green stubble poking through the earth was a mockery, ugly as hair poking through a woman's stocking.

She wanted to stomp on it, push it back down into the soil. Mary Lou usually planted petunias, impatiens, marigolds, and geraniums by the first of May, while Don put in tomatoes and did the spring repairs. This year she turned away from the trays of annuals at the grocery store.

When the sun grew warm, on the kind of day that normally would have had her outdoors and working in the garden, Mary Lou lay on her bed with the blinds pulled shut. Her head ached. She groaned to herself "go away" when Don rapped on the window.

There was already too much of her in the ground. She tried to keep Elaine inside her as though she were not yet born. Months had gone by, and still Elaine was waiting to be let go, bringing Mary Lou's grief with her on a tide of blood and tears that could wash her into the world and bring back its color.

The summer made Mary Lou feel even less alive; the air was smoggy and damp, the heat overbearing. She stayed in the house as much as possible, not even turning on the air-conditioners she now had in her bedroom and kitchen. She should water the lawn, but the thought of dragging the clumsy hoses around the yard seemed impossible.

She was stripped naked as a branch peeled of its bark.

September was hot and dry; the grass under the trees was listless and brown along with the withering butterfly bush. The leaves of the walnut and hedge-maple, that always dried up before the season could take on its colors, were already skittering around with a papery death-rattle.

Don bought the candies for the trick or treaters and handed them out. Mary Lou wanted no part of it. Elaine's birthday, November 1, a date she would carry around her neck forever like a convict's number, sent her into a special hell.

How should we celebrate? she asked herself with ironic fury.

The day came and passed. Nothing changed in Mary Lou. The air grew cooler. She heard the fluttering and cawing of the hundreds of crows that filled the trees every year like black leaves.

She had carried her grief nine months, let it take her bones and teeth, let it have all her nourishment, kept it warm. Just the time she had carried Elaine. And when it came to term it was blighted and black like blasted corn. A monster, a waste. Seed scattered and wasteful.

She began to feel ashamed. What would her grandmother think of her? She who had lost two sisters and a mother in a flu epidemic, and several children too, and her daughter who died before her.

Mary Lou would never stop mourning. Elaine would be her last thought on earth. But she must not let her grief destroy her. Because it wouldn't. That was the cruelest thing about losing so much.

Some time in mid November, she roused herself from her lethargy and went into the garden. She walked hesitantly as though learning to walk for the first time. There were a few shreds of fall color clinging to the trees. She saw that Don had planted the usual impatiens and geraniums and marigolds. He must have been keeping them watered and fed all summer. It was nice of him, Mary Lou thought. He had done this planting to lure her back into life. Now the oak tree had covered them with dry leaves and their stems were breaking down but they were still putting out small blooms. Mary Lou brushed the leaves from the geraniums and nipped off the shattered heads.

She wandered to the side yard where her huge magnolia tree spread its limbs over the lawn. She picked up a pod. It was brown and soft as a mouse. She petted it aimlessly.

Later that week, she bought an azalea plant for the dining room table. It was Elaine's favorite color, pink, and would be blooming when the summer things and chrysanthemums were gone.

She lived another whole life after Elaine.

Don went in the Army as older men were drafted toward the end of the war. She fell back in love with him when she saw him in his uniform and realized how much she had always needed him. She began to follow the war news carefully. She knit sweaters for the soldiers and wrote letters to Don every day, and when he came home they went on their boat rides with Penny and Stan and were happier than they had ever been in bed at night, and then she took in her parents and cared for them, and then she got her job, and then along came Sylvia, and then Billy, and now Billy was dead—and Don needed her help.

How many endings she'd had, only to begin again.

20

It was dusk. The gray cement decks of the hospital garage were a labyrinth of sloping lanes and confusing signs: NO PARKING, EXIT, ONE WAY, NO EXIT. Mary Lou got off the elevator on the floor where she thought the car was, but it wasn't there. She had left it near an opening through which she could see the other hospital buildings. She was sure she had. But where? Was she on the strawberry or the cherry level?

She took the elevator to another floor, walked around the inner circles. The ramps were dark. She trudged up another level: no car. She turned back. She had been here before. Maybe it was another time she had parked by an opening. Oh, there it was, a cream-colored coupe hidden by a van. What was her license number? It wasn't her car. What should she do?

All the rows of cars looked alike. All the floors were the same. Her knees were aching. She wanted to sit down and give up. She rested for a moment, then continued her search. The sky beyond the gray cement was getting dark. This was like a dream. But it couldn't be, could it?

There seemed to be no way out.

She tried once again, starting back at the elevator, trying to remember which way she had turned earlier.

The toll booth was a long walk down.

She would have to find help somehow.

Cars were whipping around the curves. Finally a slow-moving car came by, and Mary Lou waved at the woman driving, and when she rolled down the window, asked if she would take her around a floor or two until she could find her car. The woman nodded for her to get in, and they drove around a few floors until Mary Lou spotted it.

"Dumb me. I should have written down the name of the level," Mary Lou said.

"Happens all the time. I did the same thing last week," the woman said.

The next day in Don's room Mary Lou tried to read a magazine, a month old issue of *Redbook* with a model in a Santa Claus hat on the cover (for the first time in her life, Christmas had slipped by with no tree or celebration). She started when a young man came in, felt Don's pulse, and checked his monitors.

"Vital signs are not bad," he said. He detached a plastic bag from the dialysis machine. Mary Lou looked away. Helen arrived, bringing coffee and rolls. Very shortly, Dr. Weiss appeared. He looked Don over carefully.

"Mr. Friedman? Don?"

Don groaned slightly. The first sound he had made since they found him staring at the ceiling of his bedroom. Dr. Weiss listened to his heart, took his pulse. He conferred with a nurse who had entered, bringing a tray with several little paper cups of medicine on it.

"I was afraid we were going to lose him," he said. "But he's coming around. I think he'll make it." He smiled at Mary Lou and Helen, and looked at his watch. "Now I have some other patients to see. I'll be back in a little while and we'll talk about what comes next. OK?"

He sounded so pleased. I guess it's a triumph for him, Mary Lou thought, but what about Don? He was still in another world, with only a half life ahead.

"You see," Helen said. "Prayer does help. You prayed and Daddy came through."

"Yes," Mary Lou said, "but I was praying he wouldn't."

Mary Lou walked down the hall to the visitors' waiting room, found the smoking area, and lit a cigarette. *That was a horrible thing to say to Helen.* Did she mean it? Maybe. This had to be the very lowest moment of her life. She had nothing to look forward to but the care of a terribly sick man, and no Billy.

She felt her grandmother's hand at her sleeve. It was selfish to be thinking of herself: she should be thinking of Don and how he would feel when he opened his eyes to the light and saw that he was dependent on a machine and left with a damaged brain.

Another woman sat nearby nervously going through the contents of her purse.

"Lost my car keys," she said. "I've been losing things ever since my husband got so sick."

"Me too," Mary Lou said. "What's your husband here for?"

"Triple by-pass. Sixty thousand dollars! We're going to have to sell our home."

Mary Lou pictured her tall Victorian house. At least she still had a home to go to. And anyway, what was she going to do? No one had given her a choice about the things that had happened. Her grandmother always said, "Grin and bear it," and that's what she would have to do or go crazy. Her determination was false as a wig, something she put on to better the image she saw in the mirror—but it was all she had.

She squared her shoulders and went back to Don's room. Don's eyes opened and made contact with hers, but he was different from the man who emerged from surgery in the fall. The fight was gone.

The house was still standing when Mary Lou went home. She was always surprised at its being there after some painful event that took her away. The earth in the yard was swollen from melting snow, a bloated invalid.

The house was silent and empty.

She wished the old custom of neighbors dropping in during bad times were still alive. But it was long gone. The new people who had moved into the neighborhood worked all day and watched television all evening. Mrs. Wong was busy at the family's restaurant.

The doorbell interrupted her thoughts. She looked through the front window before opening the door: Sylvia and Thor stood on the porch with a few pieces of light luggage. She had almost forgotten about them. They were laughing happily, tan and rumpled from the plane flight, wearing blazers thrown over island-bright shirts. Mary Lou opened the door, rattling the Venetian blind over the glass fiercely.

"Momma!" Sylvia cried.

"Hi, Mary Lou," Thor said. "What's happenin'?"

21

"I killed him."

"No you didn't, Sylvia."

Mary Lou said this to calm her daughter, though she did feel Sylvia must bear some blame for Billy's death. The roads were bad the night Billy died. But Billy would not be out drinking at four o'clock in the morning, not unless he was very upset. Of course, he had plenty of things working on him—everyone did at sixteen. But Sylvia had never seemed to realize how much her leaving him still hurt and how her second rejection touched the sore spot. Because Billy tried to hide it, didn't mean the hurt wasn't there. People were so willing to believe a cheerful front: it made them feel better, took away their guilt.

Well, now Sylvia was facing things, but it was too late, and Mary Lou couldn't allow her to hurt herself as well as her son. What good would it do?

"I can't go on living," Sylvia cried. "I cannot."

She poured over Billy's childhood photos and the pictures of him with the high school swimming team and the bikers' club in his year book (which was inscribed to Mary Lou).

When she went to the hospital, Mary Lou was half afraid to leave Sylvia for fear she might be serious about taking her life. Mostly, she figured it was talk, from guilt on top of sorrow, but she couldn't take chances.

All she could say was, "I know how you feel, Sylvia. I lost a child too, remember? We have to go on—"

"But why? Why did it happen?"

"I don't know. Why did your father get sick?"

Mary Lou tried to appeal to reason, to Sylvia's obligation to Don, but Sylvia spun herself tighter into her grief. She spent hours lying on her bed crying or just staring into space.

Her whole body had crumpled and seemed to shrink the day she and Thor returned from Miami, and Mary Lou told her about Billy. She would not go home with Thor—he lived with his brother and the brother's family in a small house, and Sylvia could not face these strangers. She treated Thor as though he were taboo—the cause of Billy's death. She clung to Mary Lou like a child, as Billy had done when she left him.

"You have to snap out of this," Mary Lou told her.

Sylvia had been back for almost two weeks and Mary Lou had tried everything else: now she figured a cold-hearted approach might be the only one left. She was losing patience, getting angry at Sylvia, who never once acknowledged Mary Lou's loss or that Mary Lou had raised her son.

And Mary Lou had her own grief to deal with. She sometimes felt Billy was in the room with her and forgot for just a second that he was gone. She would think, *I'll tell that one to Billy.*

Then the emptiness, the loss would be so unbearable she wanted to take a broom and smash out the windows. Or, slicing vegetables, cut off her own hand.

There should have been an open casket. And that Sheri with her stupid shoes and Barbie Doll eyes came traipsing into town at the last minute and criticized the caterer Mary Lou had picked out, and refused to serve the ham Mary Lou brought over. And then she kept the ham.

God, how petty can I get? Mary Lou asked herself. But she could have served that ham for several meals and saved herself some work when she was already exhausted.

And Sylvia never let up.

"I don't know what I'm going to do with her," Mary Lou told Helen. "I can't handle two sick people."

"Tell her so."

"It's hard," Mary Lou said. "I feel sorry for her."

"I feel sorrier for Daddy. And you. After all, you raised Billy. Sylvia didn't."

"She's his mother."

Mary Lou finally got Sylvia out of the house to visit Don in the hospital. He was in and out of consciousness, taking a light diet, talking a bit, though very depressed, and angry at the machine he had to rely on. He had trouble with words, and slept a great deal of the time.

He was asleep when Mary Lou and Sylvia came into his room. Sylvia looked revolted at the sight of her father hooked up to all his machines, at his pallor, his drooping jaw.

"Did I do this too?"

"Oh, Sylvia, of course not. How could you?"

"He went into this state the day Billy was buried. Helen said so."

"That's just a coincidence."

"I wish I could believe that."

Sylvia sat by Don's bed and took his hand, and put her head down on the sheet. She stayed that way for a long time until Mary Lou began to worry about her.

"Sylvia?"

Sylvia raised her head.

"He won't want to live like this! He won't."

Mary Lou figured Sylvia was beginning to recover somewhat when she said she wanted to go and see Billy's grave. Thankful, Mary Lou called Helen and asked her to drive them to Spring Grove cemetery.

Billy's grave was a short walk from a lake, guarded by a statue of a Civil War soldier pointing his rifle at an invisible enemy. Nearby was a grove of redbud trees and a miniature Gothic cathedral.

Mary Lou tried to imagine coming here as many people did just to enjoy the scenery and elaborate monuments. Each tree along the way bore a label: Mary Lou read the names, "Purple Juniper," "Japanese Mimosa," "Golden Rain Tree," concentrating on them to keep from breaking down.

Though she loved Billy more than anyone in the world except Don, Mary Lou had yet to come here and would never have come on her own. She had visited Elaine's grave only a few times. Her grandmother and mother said life is for the living, and they did not follow the customs of cemetery visits or taking flowers to the dead. Nor did Mother Nina and her father. Leave that to the gypsies, they said, who put masses of orchids on their family plots every Memorial Day.

Sylvia carried an azalea that she meant to plant. Helen had brought a bouquet of plastic flowers, of which Sylvia said, "That's not for Billy, is it?"

"It's for Elaine."

Sylvia looked to Mary Lou as if to say, you wouldn't let her put that ugly plastic thing on Elaine's grave would you? But Mary Lou ignored her. Any sign of Helen acknowledging Elaine was good. Helen didn't miss Sylvia's snide tone.

Sylvia knelt down by Billy's grave and ran a hand over the still raw earth. There was a small, temporary white stone. Mary Lou had to turn away.

Frederick had insisted on paying for a more elaborate marker which was on order. Mary Lou was very glad he had come home and was attentive and kind to Don. Always the perfect one. He had not stayed long: business and the family pulled him back to California, but Mary Lou felt that when he saw the weakness and pain of his father, he had forgiven her and Don for whatever they had neglected to give him. She only wished her daughters could forgive each other for whatever kept them enemies.

"I can't believe Billy is under this ground," Sylvia said.

Mary Lou could not bear thinking about this. She put her hands in her pockets and walked to Elaine's nearby grave, where Helen was arranging her bouquet in the metal holder chained to the headstone.

"You never get over losing a child," Mary Lou said.

"I never had any children at all."

Mary Lou was surprised at Helen's bitterness. She had never realized her childlessness meant that much to Helen. Maybe she should have.

"Don't you remember I had that miscarriage?"

Mary Lou didn't. Another omission.

She gave Sylvia a few more minutes, then said, "Maybe we better go. It's awfully cold."

"I was going to plant this," Sylvia wailed. She held up the azalea in its clay pot. She had not brought a digger.

"Maybe you can just set it by the headstone."

"It'll die," Helen said.

Small loss, Mary Lou thought. With two children buried here, worrying about a plant didn't seem worthwhile.

"Is there anything in the car I can dig with?"

Helen turned resignedly and headed for the car, with Sylvia following. Mary Lou heard the trunk raised and then slammed. In minutes they were back, empty-handed.

Sylvia picked up her plant.

"I wanted something that would grow, and be here next year, and the next."

"We can come back another time, in spring, and plant a different azalea or maybe a rhododendron," Mary Lou said. "Let's go now. My feet are freezing."

Sylvia reluctantly arranged the azalea by Billy's stone, and looked back at it sadly as they left the graves with their few notes of hopeful color. Mary Lou didn't say anything, but the azalea Sylvia had brought was a florist plant, not a hardy variety, and would not live outdoors anyway.

At the house Mary Lou made coffee. Poor Sylvia looked so cold and pinched and she herself needed the good smell and something warm in her body. Helen must be tired too. She had been driving Mary Lou back and forth to the hospital often, and spending long hours by Don's bed.

Sylvia sat at the kitchen table, her head propped in her hands. Mary Lou struck a match and lit the gas burner on the stove, bringing the blue and red flame to life, and a familiar gassy smell. It was these small things that linked her to everyday existence. She took some English muffins out of the freezer and put them in the toaster: the tiny red coil of heat told her life was going on. She put cups on the table for her daughters and herself, poured the coffee, buttered the muffins.

Helen spread jelly on hers and ate. Mary Lou did the same.

"It's supposed to snow again," she said. "I can't remember a winter this bad."

Sylvia was still glassy eyed, abstracted. "Why?" she said. "Why, why, why?" She rolled about on her chair.

"Here, Sylvia, drink a little coffee," Mary Lou said.

"I don't understand," Sylvia said. "I don't understand."

"We don't know why the Lord takes someone," Helen said. "But He must have a reason."

"No!" Sylvia said. "There can be no reason for taking my son."

"Maybe if you pray," Helen said. "You'll be able to accept this."

"Oh God!" Sylvia shouted, "couldn't you once just have a human reaction? Couldn't you just once see how I feel and treat me as a human being instead of a heathen to convert?"

"I know you don't believe," Helen said. "But I'll pray for you."

"Why can't she just feel with me, Mama?" Sylvia demanded. She began to cry.

"This is no time for preaching, Helen," Mary Lou said.

"I was only trying to help."

"Yeah, right. You're always trying to get at me. I don't think you even believe all this stuff. You just go on and on about it to feel superior."

Mary Lou sometimes had the same feeling about Helen; it was like her tirades on smoking. *Though of course she was right about cigarettes.*

"You're just jealous of me. You always have been."

"Sylvia!"

Helen said nothing.

"You were jealous the minute I was born. Jealous of my popularity. Jealous because Mom and Daddy sent me to college. My looks. The fact that I had a baby and he was a wonderful beautiful boy and—"

Helen looked at her sister as though she'd been struck, picked up Sylvia's coffee cup and hurled the contents into Sylvia's face.

"Helen!" Mary Lou said.

Sylvia sputtered as Mary Lou leaped to her feet, grabbed a cloth and began mopping at her daughter's face and white sweater now covered with brown spots. Sylvia didn't appear to be burned, but she was shocked into breathlessness, and gasped for air.

Helen sat back down in her chair and burst into tears. She looked as though she couldn't believe what she'd done.

"Maybe you should change your sweater," Mary Lou said to Sylvia. She sat down too, still holding the coffee-soaked cloth. No one moved.

"We're all upset over Billy and Dad," Mary Lou said.

22

"Can you believe Helen being so insensitive? She's like the 'get on with your life' people. The 'closure' people." Sylvia was driving Mary Lou to the hospital.

"She meant well."

"No she didn't. Mother, what would it take for you to have feelings?"

"I have plenty of feelings."

"I mean to express them. Your two daughters act like savages and you pretend nothing happened."

"Watch out for this driveway. They come out of here fast."

That day Dr. Weiss announced that Don could go home. He was more alert, reading the paper—with difficulty, but able to understand most of what he read. He was taking an interest in the news on tv.

"You'll bring him in soon for a stress test," Dr. Weiss said. "The heart can be affected with this blood pressure of his."

Mary Lou wasn't sure she was glad the hospital stay was over. How would she do all the things this big staff of people did for Don?

On the way back to the house, she asked Sylvia to stop at the Best Western store to look at new tires for the car.

"Billy—well—I—noticed they're awfully smooth. I better be ready to go in case of an emergency."

Mary Lou was preparing for a long lonely battle. Sylvia would be leaving soon. She had started going to a support group for mothers who had lost children. They assured her she had no part in Billy's death, and she was beginning to believe it.

"You'll be wanting to go back to Thor," Mary Lou said.

"Do you think I should?"

"That's up to you."

The set of tires cost five hundred dollars. Sylvia suggested letting Thor put them on, and Mary Lou said OK. It would save her some money, and perhaps be helpful to Sylvia. Mary Lou had hoped she and Thor wouldn't get back together, but now she was all for anything that would lift Sylvia's spirits.

The day Thor came over to put the tires on, Sylvia went out in the backyard for the first time since she'd been home. She hung around while Thor worked. At one point Mary Lou heard her laugh: what a welcome sound, like the few birds beginning to chirp even though it was still winter.

At first Don seemed glad to see his own things: sheets with a little color instead of the hospital white, his favorite pillow and clock radio, his old chair. Having Sylvia around helped too. She was not much practical use: she could not bear to look at the plastic bags of urine beside his dialysis machine—it was Mary Lou's job to unhook them and carry them to the trash. But Sylvia was pleasant to look at and kept Don company when Mary Lou had to catch up with cooking or cleaning.

Don complained of being too hot, too cold. He was irritable when he couldn't think of a word. He would start a sentence and then get stalled and grapple with his memory and faltering brain and finally just curse and say forget it. After Mary Lou had been talking with the paper boy in the living room one day, he said, "What did Billy want?"

He sometimes soiled the bed or yelled at Mary Lou. Once he lit a whole book of matches Mary Lou had absentmindedly left on his night table, and dropped them into the waste can by his bed. When Mary Lou had put them out and cleaned the can and gotten him settled down with the newspaper, he said, "That Dr. Kevorkian has the right idea—why don't we call him?"

"Shut up," Mary Lou said. "Just shut up."

It was the first time she had ever spoken harshly to him, but she couldn't help it. She was immediately sorry. She went out on the porch and smoked.

Sylvia, who had not heard the exchange, came out and lifted the cigarette from Mary Lou's hand.

"You should not smoke, Mother."

Mary Lou snatched her hand and grabbed her cigarette back.

"I quit last year and got a horrible cough," she said. "Besides, I need something."

She told Sylvia what Don had said, and about his thinking Billy had come over.

"He thought I was Elaine the other day," Sylvia said.

They stared out at the backyard. The snow and ice had crippled the trees; the driveway cement was crumbling from the weather and old age.

"This place is falling apart," Mary Lou said.

Sylvia put her arm around her mother. She pointed to Mary Lou's cigarette.

"Give me one of those damned things."

They smoked for a moment.

"He threw a lunch plate at me day before yesterday, while you were washing your hair," Mary Lou said.

"This is not Daddy."

Sylvia dropped ash onto the earth below the porch, studied the smoke from her cigarette. "Have you thought about nursing homes?"

"I promised him I never would. We promised each other."

"I don't see how you can go on like you are."

Mary Lou held out her hands. The fingers were crooked as ginger root.

"Look like witch's hands, don't they?"

"Do they hurt?"

"They're weak. My knee hurts."

"There's too much work around this place. You need some help."

"I know. We should have listened to Helen. I don't see how we can pick up and move right now though. Dad's confused enough as it is."

"He's never going to get any better."

"Probably not."

"How long can you hold out?"

"As long as I have to, I guess."

"You're not made of iron—even if you do pretend to be."

Mary Lou couldn't endure all this sympathy and understanding.

She stubbed out her cigarette in a flower pot.

"I'm going in."

"Mother, Thor belongs to the Hemlock Society. He gave me some of their literature. I think you should read it."

"What's that? Where people kill themselves?"

"It's taking things into your own hands while you're still rational enough to do it."

Mary Lou went into the house, slamming the door on Sylvia. In the kitchen, she studied the teddy bears on the pot holders. She watered the red geranium over the sink, her hands shaking. Sylvia followed Mary Lou into the room.

"I'm not talking about right now," she said. "But later."

Mary Lou reached for an iron skillet. Her weak wrist couldn't hold on to it and it clattered into the sink.

"Damn!"

"Dad is losing it, Mom. He is. But he's got the heart and lungs of a horse. What kind of life will it be for him as a vegetable? A piss and shit machine?"

Mary Lou put her hands over her ears.

"How can you *talk* this way?"

"Because somebody has to. I showed Dad the stuff Thor gave me the other day. He's all for checking out on his own when the time comes."

"He's not clear-headed."

"He was when we talked about this. In fact, he brought it up."

"Sylvia, get that stuff out of my house, do you hear? I won't have it."

Mary Lou went to her room and sat on her bed. She felt as though she might fall off, as though the bed were moving. She would manage. Do what she had to do. You don't "check out" because things are tough, or get rid of someone because they are an inconvenience. And who's going to take care of me when I start going downhill? Not Sylvia. Not Frederick. Maybe Helen, but she could never live with Helen. . . .

Somehow she'd felt if she did her duty by Don—as she had for her father and stepmother—someone would care for her. Magical thinking again? No one would. They'd just put her and Don to sleep like a pair of old dogs. Well it was wrong wrong wrong. And if Sylvia didn't move out soon, she would throw her out. She would manage as she always had, by herself.

Sylvia didn't mention the Hemlock Society or what they'd discussed again. She was on the phone with Thor frequently, talking about getting back together.

Mary Lou found the pamphlets Sylvia had brought over, on Don's bed table. She took one into the living room and opened it, handling it gingerly, as if it were poison. About two paragraphs were all she could stand: ways to kill yourself and discussions of which was quicker or more painless. There was carbon monoxide in the garage, a plastic bag over the head, a mix of tranquilizers. Mary Lou couldn't even like killing the squirrels in the attic. She was supposed to help her husband into a dry cleaner bag or mix him a tumbler of forty Librium and thirty-five barbiturates? Where was she supposed to get all those drugs and who could drink such a concoction? She closed the booklet.

Don called from the bedroom. He was feeling better and apologized for his latest outburst. Mary Lou gave him a glass of milk and a back rub.

Another thing Sylvia hadn't figured on: Mary Lou didn't want Don to die, even so impaired and unhappy—even if he wanted to. She loved him. She had never forgiven him for not loving Elaine as much as she did. Her anger burned on, low and dangerous as a persistent infection. There was no reaching it.

But she could not imagine life without him.

"We should have bought that boat," Don said.
Mary Lou nodded and said, "And gone to Mt. Rushmore."

23

Mary Lou and Sylvia were laughing and eating popcorn.

"Ulp, I better be careful," Sylvia said, "I'll need the Heimlich maneuver."

On the tv, Laurel and Hardy were selling Christmas trees. It was the funniest thing Mary Lou had ever seen. She had to admit it felt good to laugh, to be sitting, feet propped next to Sylvia's on the coffee table, drinking beer and eating popcorn.

Sylvia had read that comedy tapes could help sick people: she had Thor bring over a V.C.R. and she rented tapes from the video store. Don wouldn't watch them; he would have nothing to do with Thor. He blamed him for Billy's death.

"I love to see you laugh, Mom," Sylvia said.

Mary Lou wiped her eyes.

"It was nice of Thor to bring this thing over."

"He's a nice man," Sylvia said. She rewound the tape. "He wants me to come back with him."

"Do you want to?"

"I think so."

"Why don't you?"

"You should see that brother's house where he's living. Dogs and kids all over the place. The brother is a cop and he's always flashing his gun around. He's scary. Even Thor takes orders from him. And the place is—dirty."

In Sylvia's hippy period she wore T-shirts she never washed, and her room was a mess of bottles and pizza containers and God knows what. Now she was always showering and her clothes were spotless, her room clean beneath the clutter.

"Nobody ever picks up after themselves. The kids are totally on their own. Nobody can count on anyone. I remember how I used to make fun of you and Pop: I could set my watch by you two, you were so always on time. But you were always there. These kids have no discipline at all, except when Jack gets fed up and starts knocking everybody around."

Mary Lou wanted to tell Sylvia not to go with Thor. The brother's house sounded awful, and she would miss her company. She would not have any more evenings with the two of them so close. She had heard from Mrs. Wong that Byron had gotten into another fight at school and injured the other kid. She would feel less safe with Sylvia gone. She had to force herself not to comment. It had to be Sylvia's choice.

"I'm getting more like you and Daddy as I get older," Sylvia said. "You would clean things before they were dirty. Now I find myself picking lint off things and re-washing the dishes. Jack's wife never gets anything all the way clean."

The day-to-day realities could never be exciting as eloping to Florida with Thor, Mary Lou thought—and maybe Sylvia was exaggerating about the place where they lived.

"Thor's better away from Jack," Sylvia said. "Jack thinks women have to be kept in their place."

"Could you get an apartment of your own, you and Thor?"

"Maybe if I get a job here, and we can save a little money. . . . "

Mary Lou would have liked to ask them to stay here at home, but Don's mind was made up.

"So what should I do?"

"I can't say," Mary Lou answered. "It's up to you."

Sylvia stood up and took the tape out of the V.C.R.

"I have to take this back to the store." She hesitated. "When I went to get this, there was a gang of real creepy-looking kids hanging around there."

"Take it back tomorrow."

"And pay twice? Naw. I'll be all right."

"My paper boy was mugged in that parking lot."

"Animals."

This was the Sylvia who had always been on the side of the delinquent, the drugged out, the disaffected. "I'll be careful," she said.

"I'll go put the porch light on for you."

Sylvia zoomed off in Mary Lou's car with the radio Billy had gotten at Value City at top volume.

Thor *was* basically a nice man, Mary Lou thought. Wasn't he? Sylvia and he had made a mistake in just taking off without thinking how anyone else would feel, but everyone had good and bad points.

Mary Lou waited by the front door until Sylvia returned. She worried when she took a few minutes longer than seemed necessary and was relieved when the car pulled into the drive. Upstairs, Mary Lou heard Sylvia take a shower. Soon after, she appeared in Mary Lou's room, dressed in a white cotton nightgown. She looked like a little girl.

"Mom, how did you get through menopause?"

"Oh boy."

Sylvia could certainly keep a person off guard.

"I thought we were talking about you and Thor," Mary Lou said.

"We are."

Sylvia sat on the bed next to Mary Lou. "I haven't had a period since Billy died. Maybe it's stress—maybe it's the big M."

"You're young yet."

"Yeah, but how bad is it?"

Mary Lou remembered sudden feelings of panic and nausea while she went from burning up to freezing. She dreamed of empty houses and crying babies.

"It isn't so bad."

For cramps Mary Lou had taken a drugstore tonic, "Lydia Pinkham's." All she had been told about "the change of life" was a story Mother Nina whispered of a neighbor woman running into the street in her nightgown. In those days you weren't supposed to mention your symptoms. Any kind of "woman's problem"—depression, bloating, pain—was just hysteria.

She couldn't tell Sylvia all this.

"I had you to take care of and that got me through," she said.

"But how did you feel? You had to have some problems."

"I gained some weight."

"And?"

"Well—"

Mary Lou blurted out a story she had never told anyone.

"When I mentioned it to the doctor, he just said, oh what's the difference? You're fifty-six years old."

He had scoffed at the idea that she should care about her looks and still be attractive and sexual—while that part of her life had actually changed to an urgency she hadn't felt even at her happiest. She was suddenly unusually eager for sex. At the most inappropriate times. Once in a movie theater she couldn't wait to get home. And in fact, she felt like plunging the doctor's hand up her skirt right then and there.

Mary Lou felt miserable at this recollection—embarrassed and angry both. She tore a tissue out of the box by Sylvia's bed and dabbed at her eyes.

"The bastard," Sylvia said.

She put her arms around Mary Lou and held her tight.

It felt so good. Mary Lou had never been close like this or talked this way with other women, not even with Penny. In fact, she was lonely for any feminine companionship. Her small circle of friends had narrowed: her sewing club had dried up, her card club members were mostly dead.

Mary Lou laughed at herself.

"How silly can you get? That was at least thirty-five years ago."

"Doesn't matter."

Which was the mother and which the daughter? Mary Lou had learned a lot from Sylvia in spite of everything. She would miss her terribly if she went back to Thor.

Sylvia kissed Mary Lou on the cheek, and got up and walked to the door.

"Goodnight," Mary Lou said.

Sylvia paused and looked back, a little sheepishly. "I guess I'd better go back to my husband," she said. "I want to have a baby before I get all dried up."

"You won't," Mary Lou said.

"I can't cling to my Mom forever."

"No."

Nor I to my daughter, Mary Lou thought.

24

Don's stress test, done on a trip to the hospital, showed his heart to be in fairly good condition, though his blood pressure was high. Mary Lou was instructed to continue his diet and dialysis and injections. She told Dr. Weiss of Don's mental lapses and depression. "There will be ups and downs," the young doctor advised, "just take it one day at a time."

This, Mary Lou thought, from a man in his forties, to one who had lived through World War I and the Great Depression, who had built his own business from nothing and fought in World War II, who had lived through the death of his daughter and grandson. She decided not to advise Don to take it one day at a time.

Don was crabby on the way home. He didn't seem to care whether his heart was functioning or not. He harped on Mary Lou's driving.

"For God's sake, look out. Did you see that car pulling out there?"

"I saw it. I saw it," Mary Lou said. "*You're* going to cause a wreck yelling like that."

At least he knew where he was and what was going on. He even asked about Sylvia, and got her name right.

"I wish she'd stayed married to Mike," he said. "Then none of this would have happened."

Mary Lou couldn't wait to get home, take off her stockings and lie down.

There was something off about the house. Mary Lou realized it the minute she opened the door. She was so accustomed to her house, so much a part of it, she could tell right away something was wrong. As she walked through the door she saw it: the living room television set was gone.

"Stay here a minute," she said. She settled Don in his big living room chair.

"What's going on?"

"Just sit down."

She made herself go through the house. The kitchen door had been pried open. The room was empty. She grabbed a broom for a weapon and went upstairs. She was pretty sure the persons who'd broken into the house were gone: she would be able to sense their presence. She carefully peeked into each room, then went in and opened the closets. She went to the basement, gave it the same examination, with Don yelling, "Where *are* you, Mary Lou? What in hell are you doing?"

Mary Lou returned to the living room.

"We've had a break-in," she said. "Just stay there a minute till I call the police."

Two officers arrived in about half an hour: a tall Puerto Rican man and a tiny blond woman named Debbie.

"Did you have your name and I.D. number on each of the stolen items?" Debbie asked.

She made it sound as if Mary Lou were to blame for not initialing her property.

"I didn't expect thieves in my house," Mary Lou said.

"No, of course not, but to retrieve your stolen property—"

"Now you think this young man down the street is the perpetrator. . . ." the man said.

Mary Lou told them of the Halloween night garage break-in and about the boys coming up on the porch and threatening her.

"He and his buddy."

They took names and addresses and examined the kitchen door once again.

"How long before we get our tv back?"

"Depends. Better get a dead bolt on that door there."

"Sure."

But what about the front door, the basement windows, all the other ways to get in? There was no way to make this house safe.

Now Mary Lou really wished she'd moved when Helen first suggested it, before Halloween and those kids started getting dangerous.

She called Helen, who, she was relieved to note, didn't say I told you so, but did bring up the subject of a burglar alarm, for the fourth or fifth time.

"I'm having Russell check them out. You are not safe in that neighborhood."

Mary Lou called Sylvia: she was upset, but had no suggestions as to what to do. She sounded far away.

"How are things going?" Mary Lou said.

"OK."

"Are you sure?"

"Sure. . . . Yeah."

Mary Lou thought this wasn't like Sylvia, to have so little to say. But she had more pressing worries.

"I'll put a new lock on the door tomorrow," Don said, just before Mary Lou got him into bed.

"You know you can't. . . ."

Don wore a goofy, hopeful look.

"That'll be good," she said.

What on earth would Don do without his tv, Mary Lou thought. He could read less and less. The tv was his one link with the world outside the house.

"Billy can help me."

Oh God, she wished he'd stop doing that, talking crazy. It was going to drive *her* crazy.

Those hoodlums! If they came into her house again, she would kill them.

25

Twenty tv sets: the same program on every one. Some woman sobbing to a talk show host that her husband was sleeping with her sister. Mary Lou couldn't think. She hated this place. There was a Ferris wheel in the giant atrium, rock music pounding, fifty places to eat, the smell of hotdogs and frying grease everywhere.

Helen kept pushing her to make up her mind.

"Do you want a big screen?" — "How about this one, it's on sale."

Mary Lou drifted around, barely listening. She could not keep her mind on tv sets.

"Tell you what, Mother," Helen finally said. "I have a few things to pick up. I'll leave you here to decide what to buy. Meet you back here in half an hour, OK?"

"Seven hundred dollars they want, and no clerks," Mary Lou grumbled.

"OK?"

"Fine," Mary Lou said.

Why did she let Helen bring her out here instead of driving herself? She had to admit the parking lot was a mess, and she would still be meandering around looking for a spot, but Helen was like a watch dog. Thank God she'd gone.

As soon as Helen was out of sight, Mary Lou left the tv section of the store. Big stores used to have a directory near the elevator, but this one was all different. She went round and round looking for an elevator, but couldn't find one. Pretty soon she was lost. She kept confusing the mannequins with real people. Every two seconds a loud explosion came from the toy department.

Finally she circled back near the television sets, where she found a clerk at a computer who looked like he might be able to steer her in the right direction.

"SPORTS," the sign said. Under it were laid out about two hundred guns: all lengths and sizes, bright metal barrels and burnished wood handles gleaming under the fluorescent lights. Mary Lou never dreamed there could be so many kinds. She wandered down the aisle, intimidated by the variety of magnums and calibers and the number of rounds they could shoot and the boxes of bullets that looked like giant deadly suppositories.

"May I help you?"

A male clerk appeared at Mary Lou's elbow. He seemed to be struggling to keep a straight face. Was that a smirk? Would he take her seriously? Could you just up and buy one of these things? The rifle her father kept to shoot foxes that got into the chickens, and that he used when he shot Tim looked like everybody else's in the country: dull, well-worn, nothing like these sparkling deadly things.

"Well, yes, I want a gun."

"Hunting? Target practice?"

Again the man seemed to be struggling to control his amusement. He was about Mike's age, early forties; he wore a neckerchief held by a turquoise pin. Imagine him selling these guns to kids like Harold and Byron. Did he smirk at them?

"It's for my grandson. He's in a gun club."

"Oh yes. They're very popular now. May I suggest this Remington? This sports model is good, very nicely priced."

He picked up a rifle and held it to his shoulder.

"Do you think he'd like this? *You* lift it—see if you think it's too heavy."

He thrust the gun into Mary Lou's hands, then lifted it with her arms and propped it on her shoulder.

"What do you think?"

The weight was too much.

"He—Billy's not a big boy," Mary Lou said.

The clerk took the gun back and laid it down.

"Let me see."

He thought a minute, then selected another rifle.

"Try this. A Henry Golden Boy."

Mary Lou lifted the rifle. She was getting a little less jittery about handling these things. This one was lighter. She never thought this would be so easy.

"A lady about your size, maybe your age or slightly older, bought one of these last week. Saved her life. She was alone at night and a prowler came into the house. She blew him away like dirt."

"How do you load it?" Mary Lou said.

The man got a box of bullets from a display and opened the chamber of the gun.

"I won't really put these in; just watch, though, I'll show you where they go."

"Mother!"

Helen's voice cut through the store like a fire alarm.

"I've been looking all over for you!"

Mary Lou wished she could turn this rifle on herself. Her eyes met the clerk's. Now he really thought she was a crazy old woman.

"What are you *doing* here?"

"Looking at guns," Mary Lou said levelly. "I'm going to buy one."

"For her grandson," the clerk said.

Helen gave him a look that clearly said there was no grandson.

"Mother you can't do this."

"I can. How did you find me?"

"I was running all over. Finally this man near the tv section asked if I was looking for a little . . . lady and he said you asked where the guns were. I couldn't believe it was you!"

"Helen, calm down."

"Is this about that break-in?" Helen said.

"People have the right to defend themselves," the clerk said. "It's the second amendment of the Constitution."

"I am buying this rifle to get rid of those damned roof squirrels," Mary Lou said.

"Get an exterminator."

"They're not allowed to poison squirrels."

"Are you actually thinking of climbing up into that crawl space and shooting them?"

"Russell will do it."

"No he won't! Now come on. We're going to buy a tv set like you said and we're going home."

"I'll take the rifle," Mary Lou said.

The clerk picked it up and laid it by the cash register.

"That'll be three hundred and fifty dollars."

"Three hundred and fifty *dollars*?"

"And twenty dollars tax."

Mary Lou was now totally humiliated. She looked pointlessly in her purse. She had brought two hundred dollars cash with her, thinking she'd have change to spare.

"I don't have that much."

"We take all the major credit cards."

Mary Lou and Don had never had a credit card in their lives. Mary Lou looked to Helen.

"Don't look at me," Helen said. "No way am I going to finance this crazy idea."

"Just give the man your credit card. I'll write you a check when we get home." Mary Lou spoke through clenched teeth, but of course the man could hear every word.

She was burning up. Her hands were slick with sweat as she searched her purse again. She felt like a bad child.

"Helen, I will pay you back."

"Guns mostly kill family members. What if I come over and you think I'm a burglar?"

She would shoot Helen now if she had the damned gun.

"I'm leaving," Helen said. She turned away and marched toward the down escalator.

"Helen!"

The clerk looked puzzled.

"Coming?" Helen called. Then disappeared into the escalator.

Mary Lou stood her ground by the gun display, determined to wait Helen out. She'd come back. She always did.

But she didn't. She had never been so independent that Mary Lou could remember.

"You could open a charge account," the clerk said.

Mary Lou ignored him, anxiously scanning the direction in which Helen had disappeared. The clerk left her for another customer. She waited another ten minutes. Finally, Mary Lou had to give in—that or be stuck wandering around this mall all day, or find a phone and get a cab, but from way out here it would cost a fortune.

Mary Lou's clerk returned.

"So did you decide?"

Mary Lou could not look him in the eye. Utterly humiliated, she slunk off in the direction Helen had gone. Going down the escalator she almost got her foot caught in the works. That would be the end of a perfect day, she thought: Helen having to come back and pry her out of an escalator.

She went as fast as she could through the atrium, bumping into groups of giggling teenagers, people in running suits getting their exercise indoors, racks of marked-down shoes, a garden of plastic flowers with a whirring mechanical bird singing "tweet, tweet, tweet, tweet."

Would Helen actually go off and leave her?

She walked to the front door that opened so fast it scared her. The fresh cold air outside felt good, reviving. There were hundreds of cars in the parking lot, and one after another rolled past the doorway. None familiar. Where was Helen?

26

Mary Lou wasn't speaking to Helen.

Of course Helen had come back to the mall entrance and picked her up, but the damage was done. Neither woman said a word as they drove home. Mary Lou felt like a delinquent being punished. Did Helen actually think she couldn't tell the difference between her daughter and a burglar or a squirrel? She had humiliated her in front of that clerk. She didn't care if she never saw Helen again.

When Helen called to ask if she and Don needed anything, Mary Lou curtly said no they would manage. When Helen suggested a visit, Mary Lou said Don didn't feel up to company.

Sylvia thought the whole episode at the mall was hilarious.

"The clerk must have been scared to death of getting caught in crossfire. You and Helen should have grabbed Saturday Night Specials and shot it out."

Sylvia mimicked pulling six-guns from a halter.

"Shoot-out at the Okay Mall!"

Pretty soon she had Mary Lou laughing as well.

"I guess it was sort of funny," Mary Lou said. "But she shouldn't have treated me like I'm senile."

"That's true, Mom. But then Helen treats everyone that way."

Like Billy, Sylvia could make everything seem better, even fun— when she wasn't worrying you to death. After her light-hearted visit, she didn't call or drop in for several days.

When Mary Lou called to ask when she'd be visiting Don, she said, "I'll be over soon."

It bothered Mary Lou that she said "I" instead of "we."

Threatening signs began turning up everywhere. At the Walgreen's way out on the expressway, an old man ahead of Mary Lou at the prescription counter was trying to pay a dollar or two on a sixty dollars' worth of medicine. She felt so sorry for him. Near the bank she saw an old woman about her own age tottering along the street, urine running down her legs onto the pavement. Mary Lou pictured herself pushing a shopping cart bulging with rags and plastic bags.

When Helen called for the fourth time, Mary Lou decided it was time she stopped feuding with her daughter. Sylvia wasn't about to take over all the things Helen did for her and Don.

She was surprised at how eagerly Helen responded when she said OK to a visit. Russell would bring the pellets he'd mentioned to get rid of the roof squirrels.

Helen seemed very ill at ease when she and Russell arrived. Don was asleep, so she just peeked in at him. She seemed to be poking around the house more than usual.

Mary Lou left her downstairs and followed Russell to the third floor where she steadied the ladder for him to climb up into the crawl space.

"Those durn critters are between the floor boards," Russell said. "I'll poke this stuff down into these little gaps in the furring strips." He worked while Mary Lou waited.

"Hear you wanted to get a rifle," he called.

"I still do."

"I don't blame you." Russell reappeared at the opening to the crawl space and sat on the top step of the ladder "Getting ripped off in your own home stinks."

"You better believe it."

"Helen is just afraid you'd get into trouble. Like it seems wrong but some guy the other day shot a couple of delinquents that kept trespassing after he told them not to, and they sued *him*."

"In the country, trespassers got a backside full of buck shot. Or worse."

"Right on."

"Well what if they come in the house?" Mary Lou said. "Didn't you say that was self defense?"

"If they come in your house, yes. A person has the right to defend themself."

"That's what I thought."

Russell climbed down the ladder and folded it.

"Thanks, Russell."

"Any time."

Russell carried the ladder down the stairway, with Mary Lou guiding him to make sure he didn't bang into the walls; then he took the ladder and the extra pellets to the basement while Mary Lou joined Helen in the kitchen. She had run a sink full of soapy water and was wiping the stove with a sponge.

"What are you doing?"

"Thought you might need a little help."

Mary Lou looked at the stove. There were food and grease stains around the burners. When had it gotten like that?

"I usually keep it wiped off, but I've had a lot to do with Dad and all."

Mary Lou grabbed the sponge from Helen. Her kitchen had always been spotless.

"I think maybe you should get your eyes tested, Mother."

"There's nothing wrong with my eyes," Mary Lou snapped.

But maybe there was—or maybe she was just forgetful. How rundown was this place?

There were streaks of dirt on the back door. Well she couldn't do everything.

"It's really time for you and Daddy to get out of here," Helen said. "This place is too much for you."

Helen opened the oven, winced, and began scrubbing the inside.

"I can try to find you an apartment. Or—I've been meaning to ask: have you thought about some sort of assisted living?"

Mary Lou pictured old people stuck in a sort of death house.

"You talking about a nursing home? No thanks Helen. Why don't you just put a bullet through our heads?"

Mary Lou saw Helen stiffen; she supposed their struggle over buying that gun had come back to her daughter as it had to her. How *did* she appear to Helen and others? Like some helpless dotty old fool, too out of it to clean her own stove and take care of herself? Assisted living? She'd sooner join Sylvia's Hemlock Society: it sounded less phony.

Mary Lou took a few swipes at the oven, and slammed the door.

"I'm only trying to help," Helen said. "There are some nice facilities in town. They aren't nursing homes."

"I don't need your help."

Russell came into the kitchen.

"Are you girls fighting again?"

"Your wife thinks Dad and I belong in a home."

"I didn't say that—"

Russell sat down at the table.

"Could I have a Diet Pepsi?"

Mary Lou pointed to the refrigerator.

"Help yourself."

"Mom," Helen said. "You know you don't feel safe here in the house any more. I'm trying to find a solution."

"How 'bout a burglar alarm?" Russell asked.

"Hate the things," Mary Lou said. "I'll look into it."

"Let me see what I can come up with. Hey, incidentally, Mom, if you hear any more activity from your roof rats, let me know and I'll give 'em another dose, OK?"

"Fine."

After Helen and Russell went home, Mary Lou looked around at her house. The dining room needed paint; the carpet on the steps was a little loose and could trip someone. She had to admit she was not keeping up the way she should.

She went back to the kitchen. Her string mop was leaning against the wall like an old woman with dirty hair. She plunged its head into the bucket of water that was cold by now and mopped the floor and then she washed down the cabinets.

At dinner she could hardly move. Her knee was more swollen than ever, and her back hurt so she could not straighten up.

Night was falling. She checked every door, preparing for another onslaught of fear. She never slept anymore, it seemed. The house was full of odd sounds that could be someone breaking in: the ice cubes falling into the refrigerator tray, the steam heaters making those funny clunks.

Mary Lou prowled the house while Don slept. She heard a noise in the back yard and ran to the kitchen window. She saw a shape moving by the garage. It looked human.

She watched for ten minutes. There was no further movement.

She went upstairs and dozed in the chair beside Don's bed. She awakened remembering the night Tim came home covered with blood. She could hear the long-ago scream of the rabbits attacked by the owls in the woods.

27

Sylvia had returned to skating: besides needing exercise, she felt she should not avoid everything associated with Billy. She came over to Mary Lou's one afternoon with her right arm in a sling.

"It's not broken, just sprained," she said. Mary Lou had never seen such terrible bruises. She hoped this wasn't some sort of self-punishment: it could happen—she remembered a neighbor who had wrecked his car, killing his wife, and soon afterward he "accidentally" burned himself, cut himself with a saw, and fell and broke his hand.

"Sylvia, take care," Mary Lou said.

Her daughter had interrupted her trying to fill out her income tax form and going through the many bills for doctors, hospitals and medicine that Don had run up. The tax forms made her dizzy: reams of small print she could never hope to understand and couldn't see too well (she should call the eye doctor and would as soon as she had time). The medical bills were an equal maze: what did they actually owe? The bill would say so much and then the balance would be a percentage of the total and the government paid some. She couldn't believe the amounts.

Don had always taken care of these financial matters. She wished Frederick were closer—in every way. He could help her with these figures: he had a head for numbers ('anal retentive,' Sylvia called him).

"How do other old folks do this?" Mary Lou asked Sylvia.

"Don't know." Sylvia looked over Mary Lou's shoulder, tried to read one of the forms and gave up.

"How 'bout a service?"

"Hmm."

"How about Mike? I bet he'd help you. This is what he does."

"He helped me before. But I'd hate to ask again. And we aren't—"

"Give him a try. He likes you. Tell me when he comes over. I've got something to ask him myself."

Mary Lou prepared all the papers she needed help with, so they'd be ready when Mike arrived; she didn't want to waste his valuable time.

He came to the house on an unseasonably warm and sunny afternoon. He looked good as usual, slim and fit. His hair was still dark brown with no gray streaks, and even Sylvia had little streaks of gray starting up—which of course she tinted.

He sat at Mary Lou's desk in the dining room, put on his glasses, and got down to business. Mary Lou hovered about in case he needed her; every once in a while he did look up and ask her a question.

They had worked about an hour when Sylvia came breezing in: she looked divine in tight jeans and a matching jacket. While Mike and Mary Lou looked up, she pulled the jacket off, showing her cute figure in a white cotton T-shirt with short sleeves and a low neck. Mary Lou instinctively glanced at Mike to see how he reacted. His glasses slid almost imperceptibly down his nose. She worried that he might notice the tiny bits of black bruise peeking out at the neck and sleeve of Sylvia's shirt.

"You're looking good," Mike said.

"You too."

"Me? The old hair line's starting to recede. But you could be about eighteen."

Sylvia gave him one of her dazzling smiles.

"Well," Mike said. He returned his attention to Mary Lou's papers. "What about this one?" He pushed a paper toward Mary Lou.

"Isn't there like Medicare or Medicaid or something to take care of all those bills?" Sylvia asked.

Mike smiled, and started to explain the difference in the two plans, but Sylvia stopped him.

"Never mind," she said. "You two wizards figure it all out. I'll get out of your way and go see Pop."

She walked toward the stairs, and Mike watched her.

"I can't get over how well Sylvia looks," he said.

Mary Lou's hopes began to grow, but then she remembered Sylvia was married to Thor. Still. . . .

Mike and Mary Lou worked together another hour.

"You and Don never invested in stocks?" Mike said.

"Didn't believe in it. The crash. . . ."

"Hmm. Your savings haven't grown much. Have you and Don thought of transferring your assets to yourself, out of Don's name?" Mike asked. "I wish I'd thought of this before: what worries me is if Don would need extra care or a nursing home—and it looks like he might, Mary Lou. I mean, you can't go on forever trying to do everything by yourself. The thing is your savings and house don't represent large amounts, and they could be eaten up in a hurry. . . ."

"We promised each other no homes."

"That's good, but what about home care? That's not covered. But for Medicaid you have to be below a certain level."

"Isn't that the same as welfare?"

"Otherwise you could lose your house, Mary Lou. As I said, I wish I'd thought of this before, but I—none of us—knew Don would go downhill so fast. But you can only do what I said for two—or maybe three—years before letting Medicaid take over, and even if we do this now, you'd have to pay for several years of whatever care Don needs."

"He would never go on welfare."

"He's paid for it with his taxes."

"It's for poor people. Don made good money. We're not poor."

"I hate to say this, but you will be if you don't do something about the current situation."

Mary Lou remembered when she and Don had to borrow from a finance company in the Depression—the shame of having to put off the collector another month—or hide from him, pretending she wasn't at home.

"You have to think about yourself, too, Mary Lou."

Before Mary Lou could get her thoughts unmuddled, Sylvia came back into the room. She pulled a dining room chair at an angle and joined Mary Lou and Mike.

"Pop called me Elaine again."

This was just what Mary Lou needed at this moment. Mike nodded his head; this confirmed everything he had been saying.

"I get names mixed up too," Mary Lou said. "Most of the time Dad's perfectly OK."

"Mom, Daddy is definitely worse than he was the last time I was over here. You need to give up this idea that you can take care of him forever."

"He won't be here forever."

"Helen told me Dr. Weiss said he has the heart and lungs of a horse."

"I would never put him in a home."

"I've been trying to convince her to place their assets in Mary Lou's name to protect them, just in case he does have to have more care." Mike explained his plan to Sylvia.

"That's genius. Mom, listen to Mike. He knows what he's talking about."

Was Sylvia trying to help her, or flirt with Mike?

"I'll think about it. But Dad will not be put in any home, not while he's still in his right mind and I can take care of him."

"OK, but promise me you'll shift your assets to yourself," Mike said.

"I'll talk to Don about it. I hate it that everybody treats him like he's just a burden or a side of beef. He's still a human being, a man!"

Sylvia reared back in shock at her mother's anger. She had never seen Mary Lou let loose. She smiled.

"Way to go, girl."

Mary Lou was totally surprised at her own outburst. Anger was for beasts—so said her grandmother and Mother Nina.

"I'm sorry," she said. "You came to help and I yell at you."

"You're right, Mary Lou. Of course you need to talk to Don about all this. I didn't mean to imply. . ."

Mike shuffled some papers.

"How about you kids take a break?" Sylvia said. She looked at her watch. "The sun is over the yardarm. I'll fix some drinks."

Mike looked at his watch.

"We better finish up. I just have one more item I wanted to check out with Mary Lou."

"I make a mean martini."

"I'd love to stay," Mike said. "But Sheri and I are leaving for Sun Valley today. She's grading term papers this afternoon, and we'll just make it to the airport."

"She teaches?"

"Psychology. At the university."

"Oh."

Mike and Mary Lou returned their attention to business matters. Sylvia straightened the supermarket lilies on the dining table and brushed up the pile of tiny match-sticks they had dropped.

It took only a few minutes for Mike to finish, and he soon stood and said, "If you have any more things I can help with, Mary Lou, just call me. I'll be back in town in a week." He looked at his watch again. "Better run."

"Thanks for helping," Mary Lou said.

"Thanks," Sylvia added.

Mary Lou saw Mike to the door. After he left the house, Sylvia joined her at the window.

"I want to see what kind of car he's driving."

The two watched Mike go down the front steps and get into a silver BMW.

A moment passed, and Mike's car pulled away. Into the dead silence, Mary Lou sighed and said, "I have to fix Dad some juice and crackers."

Sylvia followed her to the kitchen She opened a pack of crackers while Mary Lou poured cranberry juice.

"Psychology, eh?"

Sylvia had lost the bounce she had when she came in. Mary Lou was dejected too, not only about Don and their financial situation but about Sylvia and what she had lost when she left Mike: her child, a good man, security, perhaps an education.

Sylvia was obviously thinking about the same things. Their mutual doubts silently filled the air.

Mary Lou headed for the bedroom with Don's snack; Sylvia put on her jacket.

"I'm going to get control of my life," Sylvia said. "I am."

28

"Why don't you call Dr. Robertson?"

That was Don talking, some years after he had come back from the army. Mary Lou was suffering chest pains. She didn't want to call because of the embarrassing phone call she'd made after Elaine's death. She didn't want to see the man again. But Don kept worrying and pressuring her to call.

"He was so helpful to you—before."

How could she explain her reluctance?

Finally she did make an appointment. Surely the doctor had forgotten her earlier call.

Dr. Robertson greeted her as though nothing had ever taken place. It had been a long time.

"So how is the Friedman health?" he said. "Seems you have been fine."

"Yes," Mary Lou said.

"And Don?"

"We've been lucky."

Dr. Robertson asked her several questions about the pain she was experiencing and what medicines she was taking, and then asked her to sit on the examining table.

"Would you slip off your blouse and put on this little blue business?"

He handed her a gown open in the back. Mary Lou sat on the white paper, slipped off her blouse, and slid her bra to her waist.

Dr. Robertson tapped her on the back and put his cold stethoscope on her chest. Her felt her neck muscles.

"Let me look at that chest with the fluoroscope," he said. He led her into an adjacent room, she clutching her bra. The room was dark and dominated by a large white machine.

"Stand right over there," Dr. Robertson said. He placed Mary Lou against the wall where a plate was located.

"Let's take a look."

Mary Lou was horribly embarrassed. Her gynecologist always had a woman nurse in the room when he examined her.

Dr. Robertson turned on the fluoroscope and peered at the images on his screen.

He flicked it off and came over to Mary Lou.

"Could you drop just one side of your gown?" he said. Mary Lou did as she was told.

Very tactfully Dr. Robertson took hold of her bared breast and felt it. His hands were cold. He held the breast in his hand like a lump of clay. He lifted it up.

"Other side," he instructed. Mary Lou pulled her smock to one side and pulled it over the other breast.

He did the same thing with the bared breast. Mary Lou felt nothing but embarrassment. But her face grew hot.

Dr. Robertson carefully lowered the gown from her breasts and asked her to place her hands at her sides. This time he held both breasts for a moment as though weighing them.

He lifted her brassiere and put it in her hands. "You can have this back now," he said. His voice was reassuring. Mary Lou quickly slipped back into her gown.

"I see nothing wrong," Dr. Robertson said.

Mary Lou followed him into the office.

"Your heart is OK. The discomfort may be muscular. Would you like a relaxant?"

Mary Lou shook her head.

"Take this pain killer then," Dr. Robertson said. He handed her a sample medication wrapped in plastic.

"Call me in a week or two if this doesn't let up."

Mary Lou felt foolish. She hoped he didn't think she had come to see him out of loneliness. She enjoyed her happiness with Don now (her resentment had been stored away like all the useless stuff jammed in their closets).

She was eager to leave the office. On the way home, she felt uneasy. Until several days later, she did not know why she felt this way, and then the way Dr. Robertson had touched her breasts came back to her. Was the fluoroscope necessary? And the way he handled her breasts? Her pain was inside her chest, not in the breasts. He had seemed to be, not caressing, but manipulating, evaluating her breasts, and he had seemed taut and there was no attendant. She flushed again as she had in the room. It had not occurred to her that he could be anything but right and honorable. It was strange. Later she read of doctors taking advantage of women patients and felt convinced that that is what had happened.

Why had he done this? Had he changed? He had had some ill health himself. A heart attack she heard. Perhaps he wasn't himself.

Why was she remembering this now?

Dr. Robertson was dead. Another person who had entered her life and left it, like a person in a dream.

29

A day or two after her conversation with Mike, Mary Lou heard a car door slam in front of the house. She went to the front window, and saw that a taxi had pulled up to the curb. Sylvia got out and walked toward the porch. She was walking slow, and the cab did not pull away. What now?

Sylvia stepped into the house, but did not call out to Don or throw her arms around Mary Lou as she usually did.

"I'm leaving Thor."

"Since when?"

"It hasn't been working out. Ever since I moved into that pigsty."

"Well, I know it hasn't been pleasant, but. . . ."

"I have to, Mother. I've already left. I have a room at a motel for tonight and then I'm going back to Akron. Tomorrow."

"But what about Dad? What will he think?"

"I feel bad, Mom."

"Do you have to go all the way to Akron to leave Thor?"

"Believe me, I have to put major space between myself and him. If I'm around here, he'll come and try to get me to come back. I don't have a choice."

Mary Lou focused on the bruises on Sylvia's neck and arm. Were they really from skating? Sylvia actually seemed afraid of Thor when she spoke of him. She would like to ask Sylvia, but she didn't want to humiliate her any further. Maybe she was just imagining things: Thor had never shown any signs of a violent streak. But the brother. . . . The bruises were turning a bit green and yellow.

"Don't you want to stay here tonight?" Mary Lou said. "You don't have to stay in a motel."

"This is the first place Thor will look. He'll definitely come after me if I'm anywhere around. I won't even tell you where I'm going."

Mary Lou must have looked frightened, because Sylvia said, "He won't hurt you. He's not the type to pick on you and he'll believe what you tell him."

"I'm just so surprised. I thought things were working out."

"No you didn't. You just hoped. You saw me flirting with Mike the other day."

Sylvia looked so different from the way she had pranced in that afternoon. Her shoulders drooped, and there were two little lines beginning to show between her eyes.

"I feel terrible about leaving you and Pop. But with Mike around, you're in good hands. And you have Helen. She may be annoying, she'll never desert you like I always seem to do."

"But Sylvia—"

"And Frederick," Sylvia said, "He can help if you need anything."

"He's so far away."

"Just bypass the wife. God, does she ever take her finger out of her ass?"

"But if anything happens, how will I know where to reach you?" Mary Lou said.

"Soon as I think it's OK, I'll call you."

"Aren't you going to tell Dad goodbye? He'll be awake soon."

"You tell him for me. I can't bear to face him."

Sylvia looked so little and fragile and unhappy, Mary Lou wanted to gather her in her arms and comfort her.

"I deserve to be happy," Sylvia said. "I do. Why can't I ever get what I want?"

Mary Lou reached out for Sylvia, but she had turned away, and Mary Lou dropped her arms.

"I hope you find what you're looking for," Mary Lou said.

She watched Sylvia go down the steps to her cab. If only she could protect her. If only she could have her back, a child again in her pink Dr. Denton pajamas, bathed and all ready for bed.

Mary Lou postponed talking to Don about Mike's suggestions. She knew Mike was right, but she couldn't bring herself to mention his plan. Don would take it as a criticism or her taking over from him.

Then she thought of the old woman on the street, pee running down her legs, and the man in the drug store.

Don was watching the tv set she had ordered for him, switching channels like mad. That meant there was nothing on he really cared about like baseball or football or the news. She sometimes wondered why he kept the tv on at these times—maybe it was because the little metal remote was about the only thing left in his life he could control.

She tried to be tactful in bringing up money, not knowing quite how to broach the possibility of a nursing home or long-term care.

"What good were all those savings?" Don asked.

"They're fine, but our money won't last forever."

"I hope I don't live forever."

"Oh now. You've got plenty more years."

Don sulked awhile, but then said, "Just do whatever you want."

"It's not what *I* want."
"I wish you didn't have me to bother with."
"I didn't say that."
"You shouldn't have to do all this."
"I'm not complaining."
Don switched channels.
"Here's the five o'clock news."
Mary Lou gave up.
"Do you want cranberry juice or orange?"
"Makes no difference."

Mary Lou waited a few days, and then brought up the topic again.
"Don, my own health is not too good anymore. I showed you my knee. It's not any better. It might be me that needs care."
"You're healthy as a horse," he said. "I wish I had your constitution."
He turned the tv down and looked at her anxiously.
"Are you really in bad shape?"
He looked so much like a child needing his mother to be strong and well that Mary Lou did not have the heart to tell him about how bad she sometimes ached.
"I'm fine. It's just that I do have arthritis."
"Is it really bad?"
"I guess not."
He turned the television back up.
"So what shall I do?" Mary Lou asked.
"Get somebody to draw up the papers."
"Are you sure it's all right?"
"This makes it final. I haven't been a man for a long time. Now I'm not even a person."

Mary Lou decided she would wait until Mike got back from his vacation, and ask him how to go about doing what he said. But the week went by and she was still postponing action. It would be a long time before Don needed more care. They were getting along. They had time.

30

"There's that crazy old bitch."

The voice seemed to come from inside her mind. But turning slightly she saw Byron and Harold. They were on bicycles and had crept up behind her without her hearing them.

"Maybe we should pee on her porch some time."

Mary Lou stared straight ahead and walked as fast as she could. It was only one more block to the bank where there would be other people around.

"Got you a new tv set, ain't you?"

"I'd like to come over and watch some night."

How did they know about the new television? Must be the box she put out in the garbage. She wished she'd stowed it in the basement. She could hear their bicycles crunch on the gravel in the soft gutter. They were close enough to knock her down.

"That old tv wasn't worth much," Harold said.

"How do you know?" Mary Lou cried. "You did steal it!"

Mary Lou jumped to the bait, and was immediately mad at herself. They could easily push her down and she was terrified of a broken hip—that was always the end for old people.

"Watch who you accusin' of stealin'," Harold said. "The Basher here just meant ole televisions ain't never worth watchin'."

"But a new one now, that's different."

Mary Lou clenched her teeth. Where were the cops when you needed them?

The boys turned their bikes around and waved.

"Don't think it ain't been fun," Harold said. "'Cause it ain't!"

"You take care now, old woman!"

"'Bye," Harold added. They sped off and disappeared around a corner. Mary Lou walked on to the bank stiffly, praying they wouldn't come back her way.

When Mary Lou got home she almost fell into a chair in the kitchen; her legs wouldn't hold her. She smoked a cigarette.

Those boys had practically confessed to breaking in and threatened to break in again. And now, with Sylvia gone, she was totally alone. She had to have some protection. She had not given up on the gun idea. Billy wanted her to have it. She would drive back to the mall where she and Helen had their fight, and pick out a rifle. This time she would take plenty of money.

She was getting dressed to go when Helen called. Her daughter seemed to have read her mind.

"Did you remember to renew your driver's license on your last birthday?"

Mary Lou said of course, but she was lying. In all the turmoil of the year, she had let her birthday slip by and forgotten all about it. Now it was only a few months until her next.

"Good," Helen said. "Because you know if you go past six months after your birthday, you have to take the driving test over."

Oh God, Mary Lou thought, with my eyesight I'll never pass. They'll take one look at me and decide I'm too old. I'll get so nervous I'll flunk the parking test.

Helen seemed to see right through Mary Lou's little fib.

"You're sure you renewed, Mom? Remember, if you're driving around without a license and get into an accident they can arrest you."

"Oh they wouldn't do that to a nice old lady, would they?"

"Yes. Mom, you shouldn't be driving anyway."

Mary Lou hated it when Helen noticed her weaknesses. Reluctantly, she informed her about Sylvia's move.

"Typical Sylvia. Did she ever pay back the money she stole when she ran off with that Thor?"

"How did you know about that?"

"Daddy told me."

"Of course she paid me back." Mary Lou was lying again. Sylvia had never even mentioned the money. "And she didn't steal it, she borrowed it. I feel sorry for her, Helen. She doesn't have much, and to lose Billy . . . ."

"She's always worked on your sympathy. She's a master at it."

"Helen, where's your Christianity?"

Mary Lou knew that would get her where she lived.

They hung up enemies as usual.

Mary Lou decided that she would stop at the newsstand next to the bank, and get some information on guns. Since she had better not drive to the mall, maybe there was a place to order one through the mail— from a magazine or something.

The newsstand had been on the square for years, a hole in the wall that carried a few magazines, four or five newspapers, cigarettes and candy. She entered to the tune of a wind chime and several adolescents guffawing over *Hustler*. The place still carried *Time* and *Newsweek*, but the rest of the merchandise was a slick-paper orgy of nude women,

men, and even dogs in ugly positions and covered with leather and
chains. Mary Lou turned away. She gave the boys and the proprietor a
disapproving look, but they just stared at her like creatures from outer
space. What had stolen their minds? Television, pollution, war?

Mary Lou was embarrassed to be seen here. When she and Don
were young these magazines were sold in brown paper wrappers, and the
newsstand owner would be ashamed to display them.

She backed out of the store. The boys chortled.

What now?

Maybe the library.

She had always loved the library: it was in one of those neat, nice
old buildings. The quiet atmosphere, the smell of books, the half-
drawn blinds and the intelligent-looking women librarians had always
made her feel peaceful. Today's library was not the same as the old: the
books were squeezed into a small room instead of the generous paneled
room of earlier years. Fluorescent lights made it less soft and inviting
as a place to browse. And racks of video tapes and talking books were
the first thing you saw when you came in. But Mary Lou was glad to
see that there were displays of children's books, and cutouts of spring
flowers in the windows as always.

Billy and Elaine had made cutouts just like these. They had loved
the library, and so had Sylvia. Only Helen had resisted. She seemed to
mistrust books the way she did insects and water and grass and animals.

"Can I help you with anything?"

"Just browsing." Mary Lou edged away from the librarian and
over to the magazine section. *Seventeen, You, Cosmopolitan* (whatever
happened to *Atlantic Monthly* and *Harper's*?). What was she looking for?
The mall considered guns part of sports. She glanced at *Sports Illustrated*
and *Field and Stream*. She was too embarrassed to tell the librarian what
she wanted. What on earth would she think?

Mary Lou picked something with a rifle on the cover and took it to
a table, glancing around, and trying to fold the cover back so no one
could see what she was reading. There were lots of ads for the NRA and
story after story of people who had saved their own lives and those of
their 'loved ones' by having a gun at the ready.

One little old lady—they were big on stories about little old ladies
and invalids—helpless people—had rigged up a wire-pulled trigger
and totally decapitated a burglar. Each tale was more gory than the
next. They seemed not only to be about saving life and property, but
about revenge—revenge against everyone you didn't like: black ghetto

youth, teenagers, drug addicts, foreigners. Even though Mary Lou felt threatened herself, these stories were too much—she couldn't imagine herself pulling a trigger.

More tales: police that didn't arrive on time, 911 operators asleep on the job. Well, those were true enough, she thought: the paper had just run a scary item about a shooting at an all-night Laundromat where 911 did not respond quickly enough. The tv news played the last anguished cries for help of the clerk who was shot dead, and the paper showed a picture of his body with blood running onto the floor among the dryers. A kid whose little brother ate lye, a woman stabbed by her husband—all had been questioned at length by 911 until it was too late to be helped.

The magazine had just about convinced Mary Lou to send away for a gun from one of the companies that advertised. Could she do that? They were out of state. Further, she had no pencil and paper. If she got a library slip and a pencil at the desk wouldn't they expect her to ask for a book? She could tear out the little ad, but she would never tear a library item.

Was she actually giving in to Helen? That would be the day. But this magazine didn't mention the people who shot their own relatives mistaking them for intruders, or the husbands and wives who killed each other during arguments, who if there were no gun handy, would have lived to make up. They didn't mention the kids playing with Daddy's gun who accidentally killed a playmate. Maybe she was crazy to be thinking about this at all.

Mary Lou closed her magazine and returned it to the rack, glancing around to make sure no one was looking. When she got home, she took in the mail and sat at the kitchen table, sorting the bills from the junk mail and laying aside the catalogues she'd look at, the ones with pretty clothes and things for the home. She had never received a *World Merchandise* before: wonder where that came from? She thumbed through it: lots of flashy diamond jewelry. She'd always wanted a really nice diamond ring, but she and Don couldn't bring themselves to spend the money. She turned a page: the last section of the catalogue hit her right in the eye: guns, page after page of guns: pistols, rifles, automatic weapons. It was as if she'd sent for this thing. Mary Lou stared at the pictures for a long time. What was it now the mall clerk had suggested? A Something Golden Boy. She tore out an order form. The decision had been made for her. She didn't believe in a lot of mystic stuff, but it did seem like sometimes things just fell in your lap, and something said "do it."

31

"I haven't seen Elaine for awhile," Don said one evening.

"You mean *Sylvia.*" Mary Lou sounded cross and angry. She missed Sylvia. There would be no more Laurel and Hardy and popcorn, or girl-to-girl chats in nighties.

She softened her voice. "You know which is which, you just get your tongue twisted."

"Maybe I'm getting that Alzheimer's business."

"Some lady at the hospital called it 'Oldtimers'."

They actually had a good laugh, something Mary Lou and Don hadn't shared for a long time.

This was the last time Mary Lou and Don ever laughed together. In fact, looking back later, Mary Lou thought it might have been the last time she laughed at all.

She explained once again to Don that Sylvia had to go back to her job in Akron; Thor, she lied, was out of town.

"But why didn't Sylvia tell me goodbye?"

"She wanted to, but you were asleep and she couldn't miss her bus." It sounded weak and Don looked puzzled and sad. So many blows he had had. . . . He reminded Mary Lou of the alligator at the zoo when she was a kid. Children and uncaring people tossed coins and even things like apples at him to rouse him, and the stuff just stuck on his back and his hide grew over them, the lumps of more and more wounds.

Much of the time now Don couldn't put two and two together, couldn't remember people, misplaced his glasses—forgot he wore glasses. Talked about Elaine when he meant Sylvia, said Sylvia when he meant Helen.

He spent more of his time in bed, pleading fatigue and age and the slowness of his healing wound. He talked constantly of death as if death were a boarder sitting in the living room.

"Why am I still alive?" he said. "I can't think. I can't work. I can't eat. I can't walk. What good am I?"

"Now hush, hush that talk," Mary Lou would say.

He slept a lot during the day, and when he did, he looked dead, lying on his back so white and still, his mouth gaping. It scared Mary Lou, though she was glad he could get some time off from his pain.

Since Helen had noticed how rundown the house was, Mary Lou had been working harder than ever to keep it up. A tear in a slipcover reminded her of the hopelessness of Don's situation, a cracked lamp shade symbolized their shrunken future. The place was so dim. With Billy gone and Don sick, there was no one to climb ladders and replace the burned-out ceiling bulbs.

Mary Lou was vacuuming the hall steps one day when she turned awkwardly and caught her foot on the loose carpet. Pain shot through her ankle and up her leg. The sweeper fell over and was still running as she sat down and rubbed her ankle, feeling for broken bones. Wasn't there going to be any end to all this? It seemed not. And there would be no one great catastrophe—a heart attack, a flood, a tornado—that would take the two of them off, but burned out bulbs and dimming brains.

Mary Lou stood tentatively, holding onto the banister, and yanked the sweeper cord out of the wall. You weren't supposed to do that and she never had before in all her life, but this time she did. She tried to take a step but the ankle wouldn't let her. Oh God, she thought, she needed help: where was Sylvia, where was Billy, where was Don?

Helen took Mary Lou to the doctor, where the ankle was ex-rayed and taped. It was only a sprain, but she would be limping for awhile.

Don's face turned white when he saw the bandage.

"What *happened?*"

"Nothing much. Tripped. It'll be OK in a week or so."

Meanwhile she could barely keep Don going. Helping him from their bed to his chair hurt, and he could see her wincing.

"You can't handle all this. You've got your own self to take care of."

Once Don mentioned the papers Mike had suggested they sign.

"We better go through with that. Don't you think?"

"Soon as I can get to it."

The ankle was on Mary Lou's mind now: it was minor but it showed what would happen if she got really incapacitated and couldn't care for Don any more. She would have to check out nursing homes.

Victory Manor sounded good. But how to get there? She could not face that driver's test. She couldn't ask Helen to take her. Anyway, if Don ever did go into a home, she would have to get there on her own. She decided to drive in spite of not having a valid license: maybe if she was stopped she could explain her situation. *Sure,* she could hear Billy saying. Right. Like the police are going to miss a chance to make a collar (actually the newspaper recently ran a story about a grandmother being arrested for not putting the correct coins in a parking meter).

Mary Lou had never gone through a red light, no matter how remote, or what time of day; she never drove over the speed limit. She'd never gotten a ticket. She never ever littered. She had been known to drink a whole cup of something she didn't want rather than pitch a container with liquid in it into a public waste can. The plastic liner might leak. On plane trips she mopped the stainless steel sink in the lavatory as the sign said.

But today she was planning to break the law. She had no choice. Bus service was all but non-existent. To get from her suburb to Victory Manor would mean making two or three transfers and would take all day.

"Don, will you be all right for an hour or so?" she said. She put the phone with its long extension cord on Don's pillow.

"Now stay put." She worried he might try to stand, try to put his weight on the missing limb, and take a fall.

"Sure. I'll sleep. Where are you going?"

"Oh I need a few things. Helen has the front-door key. If you need anything in a hurry, call her."

Mary Lou vowed to drive super-carefully, and she started the car. She hadn't driven much lately and when she put her foot on the gas, the car kind of jumped backward and hit the side of the garage door. Good beginning.

By fits and starts she backed the car out of the garage and down the sloping driveway. She checked the gas gauge. Better stop at a station and fill her up. Mary Lou was proud of herself for thinking of this: she didn't want to get caught out on the expressway and run out of gas.

Approaching the entrance to the expressway she almost panicked: so many cars streaming on, and the ones in the lanes didn't yield an inch. Once in the flow of traffic, Mary Lou felt more secure, but she worried about making it off at the right exit. She wasn't familiar with this part of town. If only those trucks wouldn't get you surrounded (they loved to pick on her Mercedes). Suppose she had to stop in a hurry? Her convertible would be crushed.

Victory Manor was a pleasant looking building, not distinguished, lacking the neat proportions of the library and the firehouse, buildings she liked, but there were cheerful pansies in two planters out front. Mary Lou plucked off a couple of strings of dried blooms. She could not bear to see a dead flower.

Just inside the door was a plastic fountain with a little boy pouring water out of a bright red sprinkling can. The smell of urine and aromatic candles was sweet and sickening.

The woman at the reception desk was very polite. When Mary Lou told her what she wanted, she said, "I'll get Mr. Conners." She went into an office and returned with the manager, a man of about seventy. Thank God he was not some kid, Mary Lou thought. She was tired of dealing with kids.

The halls were decorated with colorful posters and schedules of activities: bridge, arts and crafts, volleyball. Just the thing for Don, Mary Lou thought. Who were they trying to kid? The people she saw were in no condition for games and sports. One man was making a quacking sound and another was groaning as steadily as a motorboat. Most were in wheelchairs, parked along the hall haphazardly as if the vehicles and their owners had run out of gas and crashed into the walls.

"How are you today, Mr. Solomon?"

It seemed as though the manager thought he could get Mr. Solomon back to his senses if he pretended he was going to answer his pointless question. He adjusted Mr. Solomon's bib.

"Raspberry sherbet for lunch today. Your favorite."

He led Mary Lou to a small room.

"This is our double—our most popular accommodation. Hi, Mrs. Scott. Mind if we come in?"

Without an answer, he ushered Mary Lou into the small space. Twin beds and two dressers took up most of the room. Mrs. Scott was a shrunken woman in a blue housedress, with her head nodding toward her lap. On the bed table next to her wheelchair were a pot of ivy and a group of colored photos. The pillow on her bed said "World's Greatest Grandmother." The other bed and dresser in the room were bare.

"Her roommate has flown," Mr. Conners said. "So this space is available."

Flown? Mary Lou thought. Then caught his meaning. Nursing home talk for dead.

"How are you, Mrs. Scott?" Mr. Conners asked. His voice was again pointlessly loud and cheery.

Mrs. Scott waved him away with a hand that looked like a small bag of blue worms.

He was doing his best, Mary Lou thought, seemed to mean well. But everything was shrunk to the narrow world of the lives within— lives shrunk to a bed, a food tray and a toilet. The bright colors and hopefully planned activities, the cloying scented candles aside: this was the end of the line.

"What does this cost?" Mary Lou asked.

"Twenty-five hundred."

"A month?"

"Right."

"That's how much a year?"

"Thirty thousand."

"Thirty thousand dollars?"

"Our rates are very competitive," he said. "Check around."

A year or so would eat up much of their savings for sure. They would definitely have to put everything in her name. But what if Don had to come here next week?

Mary Lou felt sick at her stomach. They had postponed too long taking care of their few assets.

Anyway she could never bring Don here. What on earth was she going to do?

"Thanks so much," she said to Mr. Conners.

The expressway was even busier on the way home; it was close to rush hour and people were speeding toward the bridges to Kentucky or to downtown events. Mary Lou got the usual honks as she hesitated getting on. The man behind her rode her bumper aggressively, trying to push her to drive faster. She tried to keep herself steady, and ignore him, but he was so close. She was overly warm, and suddenly a black, blank, horrible feeling came over her; it was as though her brain were going dead. She was just an instant from passing out. Panicked, she headed for the next exit, trying to cross several lanes.

She saw a truck in her rear view mirror, a van on her right. She was afraid to change lanes, but finally just pulled into the line of traffic. People were honking from every direction. She looked in her mirror again, and in the side mirrors, confused by all the directions where she could see things moving. The truck was still close, like time itself bearing down.

She took another wild chance, hopping another lane, and pulling in front of a pick-up truck and into an exit where cars were streaming off the expressway at full speed.

When she got onto a quieter road, she pulled over to the side, and stopped. She took a deep breath. She felt even more light-headed for a moment. She was unable to go any farther but she couldn't stay here forever. Should she head for a police station, a fire house? Who would

help? She thought for a moment, remembered she couldn't ask the
police for help because of her lapsed driver's license. She took another
deep breath and began to drive home, very slowly, staying in the
extreme right lane, taking the long, long way.

It seemed to take forever to navigate the streets that led back to her
house and she concentrated hard on not getting lost. When she finally
saw her street, she felt her body relax a little. Almost there. Finally
in the safety of the garage she pushed the brake down with relief. She
would never drive a car again.

"Where were you so long?" Don asked when Mary Lou came
upstairs. He sounded upset.

"Oh, the mall," she said. "Are you all right?"

He pointed to the sheets that were sopping wet.

By pulling and tugging Mary Lou got him to his feet, and stripped
the bed the way they did at the hospital—half at a time. When Don
was comfortable again she said, "Now what would you like for dinner?"

Without waiting for an answer, she rushed to the kitchen and
worked extra hard on Don's meal. She had always felt people could
tell what she had been doing, whether it was a stolen moment with
Dr. Robertson or a childhood mistake—she had once actually buried a
ticket she forgot to give the ticket taker at a school play.

Don glanced at the tray of food Mary Lou brought him and turned
away. Mary Lou placed a fork in his hand, but he just dropped it.

"You have to eat," Mary Lou said.

She took a bite of sweet potato and said "Umm, good," like she had
with the children. But Don was too agitated to concentrate on food. He
was often like this in the evening.

"Sun-downing," the nurses at the hospital called this. Mary Lou
tried to feed Don another bite of potato, but he closed his lips firmly.
He seemed far away. She tried to picture him in Victory Manor. She
couldn't imagine him letting the nurses give him his sponge bath at
bedtime. He was too modest. If he were as out of it as the old man
quacking in the hall. . . . Anyway she enjoyed making him comfortable
and clean

When Don was in his pajamas, Mary Lou brought him a cup of milk
and some crackers. No way, Mary Lou thought, was he leaving this
house.

She got out her photograph album. Don was more relaxed now, and
looked on as she turned the pages. The older pictures, black and whites,
were curling and slipping out of their plastic holders: Don among the

men at her father's mill, so handsome and big and strong. Helen and Frederick wearing their Easter outfits, posed on a photographer's pony. Penny and Stan on the "Lucky Penny," life in color now. Sylvia's wedding. Billy at Yellowstone. Folded in the page was his school report on "Old Faithful" with the teacher's penciled "A" at the top. Elaine holding her beloved stuffed kangaroo.

"When Elaine died, I felt like dying too," Don said.

Mary Lou dropped the album in her lap.

"I did. I felt like dying."

What was he saying?

The anger hoarded in her deepest self was still there, for all those days she spent alone, in despair, and so desperate she turned to another man.

"I thought you—well, you said nothing."

"I know. I didn't want to make you feel any worse. But I felt like I failed to protect Elaine, or that I gave her a bad heart."

"We didn't know where her illness came from. . . ."

"I couldn't let down. We had to hang on. If we hadn't, we wouldn't have had Sylvia, and we wouldn't have been able to take Billy and raise him."

He had felt like dying.

Mary Lou stood and placed the album on the dresser. She looked out the window at the trees moving in the wind. They seemed blurred.

A terrible pain in her head blocked out everything around her.

Then it opened, like a big fist unclenching.

It moved to her heart, her chest. She stood by the window another moment or two, letting it pass through her, forgiving tearing her apart.

When relief came, she went over to the bed and sat down beside her husband.

"Drink your milk," she said.

What a waste of time and emotion. What unnecessary loneliness and unhappiness their grief had spun. If only Don had said how he felt when Elaine died. Or she had been less tightly wrapped in her anguish.

Don took a few sips of milk.

"Shall I read a little?" Mary Lou asked.

Don nodded his head.

She opened her *One Hundred and One Great Poems* to Robert Burns.

"Elaine would be forty-seven years old this month," Mary Lou said.

Where was she? What would she be like if she had lived? Was there a grown-up Elaine destined to be?

Mary Lou held Don's hand. Of course he had shared her sorrow.

His hand was dry and veined as a fall leaf. She held it to her cheek, the same hand, once so young and steady, that held the reins of his sleigh the day he asked her to marry him.

Mary Lou began reading:

". . . John Anderson my jo, John,
We climbed the hill together. . . ."

32

The mail man stood on the porch, holding a long, thin cardboard box.

"What'd you order here, Mrs. Friedman? A shotgun?"

He chortled at the idea and held out a form for Mary Lou to sign. She'd almost forgotten about the gun.

"Doing a little target practice?" he joked.

"Curtain rods," Mary Lou said.

"Kind of heavy ones. . ."

"Quite a few of 'em."

She was glad to be rid of him when the pink paper had been signed and she was alone with her purchase. She felt awe at herself—as she had at her first period, her first kiss, her first pregnancy. She could barely lift the heavy awkward box. She dragged it into the kitchen and laid it on the table, thinking about the contents. With the solemnity of a priest she got a knife from the cutlery drawer and sliced off the cords wrapped around it. She pulled and pulled at the heavily-stuck plastic tape. Finally, there it was: gleaming, deadly. She was as afraid to lift it as though it were a newborn. She found the box of bullets and laid them on the table. Could she remember how the clerk at the mall had shown her how to load them?

Almost in a dream, Mary Lou took the rifle from the box and held it to her shoulder. She walked over to the window, got the back garden and garage area in its sites. That's where they would come from when they came again. And they would: they as much as said so that day they followed her on their bikes.

Mary Lou took bullets from the box and dropped them into the chamber. The click was a sound like a door opening. Or no, she actually heard a door. Who? She swung the gun in the direction of the noise.

"Mother!"

Helen stood in the doorway.

"For God's sake, Mother. Are you crazy?"

Mary Lou lowered the gun.

"I was just loading this up."

"Where on earth did you get that thing?"

"Mail order. Helen, what are you doing here? Why did you sneak in that way?"

"Don't you remember? You asked me to bring over some new pajamas for Daddy? The ones on sale?"

"Oh yeah."

"I rang several times. You didn't answer. I thought maybe you'd gone up the street, so I came on in."

Mary Lou felt like a guilty kid again. She laid the rifle on the table. Helen looked at it with distaste.

"Let me take that away. I told you you'd do something awful. You came close to killing me."

"I did not. I wasn't going to shoot—you just startled me."

"That's how it happens. Mother, I'm going to put that thing in its box and take it home and get rid of it. Is it loaded?"

"Yes."

"Oh God."

Mary Lou put her hand on the rifle.

"Helen, those hoodlums threatened me the other day. I need protection, and I am an adult and perfectly OK in the head and I will decide what I will do about this gun."

Helen moved toward the rifle.

"No. You're going to kill somebody."

"I know how to shoot. My father taught me. He wouldn't let anybody come in his house. Even Russell said if they come in the house, you have the right—"

"Mother, you are upset. You are making no sense. This is not the farm or the Old West. I'll get you an alarm tomorrow."

"I don't want an alarm."

"We'll move you out of here."

"I won't be scared out of my own home."

"Mother, please listen to reason. . . . You're blaming everything that's wrong on those two neighborhood kids. You can't . . ."

"I'll decide what I can and can't do."

"If you insist on keeping this thing, I will not have any part of it. Russell and I are not coming into this house again until you get rid of this gun."

There she went again, Mary Lou thought, taking that tone, taking control, whether it was cigarettes or god or apartments.

"Suit yourself," Mary Lou said.

"I mean it."

"I believe you."

Helen looked her in the eye.

"This stupid gun and being obstinate is more important to you than your daughter and son in law?"

Mary Lou didn't answer. This was like the times Helen threatened to run away from home as a child. Following her grandmother and mother's example, Mary Lou had said, "I'll pack your bag."

Helen slapped down the package she had brought in and turned toward the door.

"I wish you luck, Mother. But don't call me when you want a ride some place or you want to use Russell for your handyman."

"I'll remember that."

"Goodbye."

Mary Lou wouldn't say goodbye. Helen left, slamming the front door. Mary Lou sat down, weak and angry.

"Good Riddance," she said.

33

Regrets gnawed at her like rats chewing away at spring bulbs. She had not been a good mother. Maybe not a good wife. She was so strict with Helen and Frederick: withholding love from Helen, afraid to just love her. Made her ashamed of her poor little ears, and she used Mother Nina's method on Frederick when he played with himself—painted a circle of mercurochrome on his belly while he slept, making it bigger each time he was caught. Today she supposed this would be called "abuse," as would the spankings Helen and Frederick got, but she and Don were raised on "spare the rod and spoil the child," and all the old notions Dr. Robertson had said were outmoded.

Her love for Dr. Robertson—her favoritism toward Elaine and Sylvia—not letting Helen and Frederick share her grief over Elaine, turning cold toward Don.

Don either slept or acted confused all afternoon. She was in for another rough night. When she took him his snack she noticed his bed sores were awful, red and raw. There were black spots on his foot.

He saw Mary Lou looking at them.

"I won't go back to the hospital," he said.

"Maybe you won't have to."

"So they can chop off my other leg."

"We'll get it early."

"I can't fool myself. There's nothing left for me, Mary Lou. Except you, and I've taken enough from you. More than I deserve. If I could get to it, I'd take that rat poison Russell left in the basement."

"Don, stop that."

"You could leave it out where I could get it—by mistake."

"Don!"

"You'd do it for an animal."

"I won't listen to this." Mary Lou went out on the porch and smoked. A dog was barking somewhere down the street.

Mary Lou shuddered with the memory of Don's words and went back into the house. In the kitchen the Mr. Coffee machine held the dregs of breakfast coffee. She fixed Don a snack and took it upstairs.

Don obediently drank his juice and nibbled a cracker.

"Let me talk, Mary Lou. There's nothing left for me but becoming a burden—a vegetable."

He wouldn't quit!

"Half the time already I don't know where I am."

"Well I do. You're here in your home. . . ."

"Where I'd like to die."

"You mustn't let despair take over."

"It hasn't. I just see things very clear: I've been down before and thought of—well, taking my own life, but there was something better coming. When I lost my job with Mr. Neiderhelman, loading at the mill—that was the first really bad thing that ever happened to me. The family had problems, my mother sick and so on, but I never met any personal upsets. I was so ashamed."

"It wasn't your fault."

"It just killed my pride. But I was young and strong. And I finally got a new job, a better one eventually. Something good came of it. I didn't want to be drafted. I was too old. I'd never held a gun. I was afraid, and I thought I'd rather die than go. But if I hadn't, I wouldn't have been there to help that young soldier. And do my part in the war. It was like some good came out of all these bad things. No good can come out of this."

"We don't know that. . . ."

"Yes, we do. We know it."

"Now, now. Please don't talk of it anymore."

"But I might lose it so bad I won't be able to tell you what I want."

"You won't, Don. You rest now. Things will look better tomorrow."

"I'm trying to tell you, Mary Lou, they won't. . . . If they chop me up any more there won't be anything left. . . ."

Mary Lou rushed from the room. She held her ears. What *did* he have to look forward to? But what he wanted her to do was a crime. Could she watch him gasp for breath, watch his veins collapse?

She kept thinking she heard the phone ring, but it didn't ring until late afternoon. Helen, she thought. She rehearsed what she'd say. She would forgive her daughter for being so nasty and walking out, but she wouldn't promise anything.

"Helen?" she said, lifting the receiver.

Nothing for a moment, then a click. It wasn't the first time this had happened. Those goddamned kids, she thought; they were checking to see if she was home so they could come and rob her—maybe worse.

No matter what, she would *not* call Helen.

Don stayed in a kind of stupor. It was as if with his recent suicidal talk he'd said all he had to say. He must have been building up to it for a long time, reasoning out what he wanted to tell her. He hadn't mentioned Helen.

She should call Dr. Weiss. But she put it off. She would let Don rest, let him be, at least for another day. The doctors would keep Don alive forever, no matter whether he wanted to live or not, they and his yeoman's lungs and his heart that kept its relentless beat though he wanted it to stop so he could be at peace. Tomorrow she could have to call. Maybe he would pass away in the night.

Mary Lou looked at the row of pill bottles lined up on Don's dresser, each with different instructions to be given at different times of the day. She could barely remember what to give him when; the writing on the bottles was small and hard to read. She pictured Don gone: no more trying to remember all the details of his medicines, no more cleaning messy sheets and soiled pajamas, the house clean and neatly run, the bed made, slick and flat and white, her lying peacefully on it—

But no way could she live without Don.

Helen would be back. She always came back. Sylvia would call, maybe come back home. Frederick would come out if she asked him. She decided she would. Or maybe she should call Mike and tell him to go ahead and try to salvage their finances. But Sheri might answer and all Mary Lou could think of was the ham she wouldn't serve and then kept.

She was so *tired.*

Late that afternoon the phone rang again. Mary Lou jumped toward it and grabbed the receiver after the first ring.

"Mrs. Friedman?"

"Yes."

"It's Tammy Brown. Penny's daughter?"

"Oh yes." The girl who moved in with her boyfriend.

"Mom passed away this morning." (Penny with the flaming red hair, the red and white polka-dot bathing suit that excited the men). "You were on the list of people she said to call when—she passed—"

"I'm sorry," Mary Lou said. She asked the usual questions and said the usual things, then hung up the phone.

Penny dead. The past was disintegrating, dry as old newspapers.

She and Don had lived through so much—the Depression (Don loyally trudging off to look for work in his scratchy wool suit). They had lived through five wars, (her father returning from the first World War changed, herself tormented by the neighborhood kids, the end of the German language in her school—she had almost forgotten that). They had lived through World War II, her mind on Elaine, and then when Don was drafted, herself frantic when Don's letters slowed down. The atomic bomb. They had lived through the Korean war so far away and strange, terrible images on tv of men being marched to death camps, the "38th Parallel" (what was it? she had forgotten, but still remembered the names of the Dionne Quintuplets—and the Beatles, though she had assured Sylvia no one would remember them a year or two after they hit America); Frederick in the army, she and Don proud he'd been picked for officer's training—a neighbor boy killed in Korea and a ribbon hung on the mother's door. They lived through the civil rights battles; the city riots. They lived through the Viet Nam war, napalm and bombs, years she worried about Sylvia—Sylvia getting hooked on drugs, being hurt. The Iraq war in January, with Mary Lou so absorbed in caring for Don she paid little attention to the tv images, this time of bombs and blazing buildings.

So many great battles in the world while all her battles were small. So many changes, while her small life moved on. Some of them affecting her like a local rain and most just drifting over, far away clouds in ever new patterns.

The Depression was still with her in the way she hated waste— never wasted a bite of food or made a risky investment, saved and saved for the future as if anything she had could be taken away. The second world war had brought her and Don security, when his business took off. The takeover of cars and the race riots changed their community, made them dependent on driving, their neighborhood dangerous. The war in Viet Nam nearly tore Sylvia from them, and drugs and "the pill" colored her life. But clones and computers, AIDS and transplants, Grenada and Panama, African hunger remained far off. So much had come and gone. Or was it all still drifting about and taking new shapes, fading like jet streaks or the tails of comets, or changing from solid to gas like vaporizing elements?

They had lived through sixteen presidents.

And all through the years, Mary Lou just hung on, trying to keep the family safe, her nest intact.

Oh, how she missed Billy—it was physical, a gnawing away of her heart. The house was so quiet: only the ticking of the clock above the kitchen door to the dining room, the one Billy had fixed. In place of his laughter and silly jokes the relentless ongoing tick.

To get away from the emptiness of the house Mary Lou went outdoors. The early March weather was its usual unpredictable mix of wind, sun, and sudden rain. Clouds gray as dirty wash scuttled across the bright sky. Would it make up its mind?

Mary Lou walked among the flower beds. She noticed for the first time how much death there was in spring: the withered leaves clinging to the oak tree finally being pushed from the branches by aggressive buds, the rose bushes with gangrenous black spots. She spaded one out whose roots had rotted away. She pulled up arthritic chrysanthemums, their woody stems split apart. Nothing stank like rotting garden stuff.

Everything died: plants, trees. Why with humans was the process so slow, so painful? She pitched the dead bush and plants onto a pile of decaying compost. It steamed like a dung heap.

Under the magnolia tree Mary Lou noticed a bird nest among the long brown leaves strewn on the ground. So intricate: the mud bowl, the string and grass carefully gathered. Mary Lou picked it up. It was dry and brittle. When Billy was a child she would have put it in a baggie and saved it for him to take to 'show and tell' at school. Even when he grew up she might save it to share with him.

She pitched it back onto the weepy earth.

Mary Lou's joints ached as she knelt in one of the beds to pull out dead perennials and loosen the soil. Her ankle still throbbed. All the work she and Don had done: what did it add up to, what was it worth? What was she trying to hang onto? The children, the house, the garden, the trees: everything was being swept away by time.

A light rain began but Mary Lou kept working. Then it began to come faster. The sky turned solid gray. The raindrops were like cold needles on her back. Her sweater was soaked. Still she worked the earth.

The wind rattled in the garage like a trapped lunatic. A garbage can blew over. Mary Lou's feet were sinking into the soft dirt.

Mary Lou stood up and threw her digger on the ground. She let the rain pour onto her face, mingling with her tears, fresh water and salt like river and sea.

There would be no more springs in this garden.

34

Mary Lou glanced out the kitchen window. How long had it been since she went outside? The garden was full of dock weed and "creeping Charlie." How long had it been since Helen had called? She should call her. There was no way she could get to the store, and the refrigerator was almost empty. It had a funny smell. The walls of the room were gray with grease from the stove. She couldn't remember when they had been washed or when anything had been dusted. Her knee hurt so bad, she couldn't even think of cleaning. She watched the window as the sun faded and twilight fell, then dark. She should be taking Don his dinner, but carrying the heavy tray up the stairs and down was too hard. She hadn't eaten anything herself since—when?

One day a woman from "Meals on Wheels" showed up at the door and said she would bring food so many days a week. Who had sent her? Mary Lou said no thanks and slammed the door. She didn't need anybody's help. Mrs. Wong came once with a basket in her hand but Mary Lou hid behind the kitchen door when she saw who it was. She noticed the red blinking light on the phone machine and listened to the messages: Sylvia, Helen *and* Frederick, all saying please call.

She would do it tomorrow. She trudged up the stairs to bed and crawled in next to Don. He seemed so still. Was he alive? She felt his chest. His heart still beat, slowly as an alarm clock winding down. She fell asleep.

The smell of something burning awakened her. She remembered now leaving a lit cigarette in an ashtray on the kitchen table. She went downstairs as fast as she could, holding on to the banister, not wanting to fall again. She was so afraid of falling— that was the end—and she walked much slower everywhere. Rugs and cracks in the floor, food spills: they all were traps awaiting a careless moment. When she reached the bottom of the steps, she thought, now why am I down here? Then the smell of burning cloth reminded her and she rushed into the kitchen. Mustn't run. But a fire could be even worse than a fall.

In the kitchen she found that her cigarette had dropped onto the table and had started singing the cloth, taking slow brown bites of it. Mary Lou grabbed the cloth and pitched it into the kitchen sink and ran water on it. She was too weary to deal with it further. She would take care of it tomorrow. She returned to the hall and started up the stairs to bed. Half-way up she couldn't remember if she'd turned off the water. Back down she went again. The water was off. Back up again.

The stairs seemed to go up to heaven. Her hand on the railing trembled and she felt a little dizzy.

What would she do? Couldn't drive, afraid to go out in the street. Life was that dream she had of being abandoned in the dark hospital basement, the doctor's white hair and coat disappearing into the blackness like a ghost, the elevator with no buttons.

Mary Lou sneaked back to the bedroom. From the doorway she could see that the large red numbers on the clock said midnight. Oh no. When she crossed the threshold, Don's eyes popped open and he began to stir. He shoved his covers away and started to his feet.

"What is it? Do you have to go to the bathroom?"

He said nothing, but pushed himself into a standing position, clutching the bedpost for support. His eyes were focused somewhere far away.

"Mr. Neiderhelman's got a job over in Covington," he said. The whites of Don's eyes were yellow and rheumy.

Mary Lou tried to guide him back into bed.

"Don, what are you talking about?"

"Load of flour going to the hospital." He pushed past her and reached out for his pants draped on the chair.

"Don, no," Mary Lou said. "It's midnight."

She held out her hands to urge him to sit down, but he slapped them away. "Mr. Neiderhelman called."

"Don, Mr. Neiderhelman's been dead for thirty years. That was over sixty years ago you worked for him."

Don ignored her words and grappled with his clothes, trying to dress himself.

"No," Mary Lou said.

"Get out of my way." Don's voice was harsh and ugly.

"You can't go out now." Mary Lou tried to push him back to the bed. "You're going to fall." She was no match for Don even in his condition, with the flesh falling off his bones. He pushed her hard and she went down, buckling over and onto the chair.

He staggered, about to slip onto the floor. All he needed was a broken hip, Mary Lou thought.

"Please, Don," she begged. She tried again to steer him to bed. "You go to bed now. It's dark out. You can't go to work."

Don raised his hand as if to hit her in the face. She flinched and then the crazy light in his eyes seemed to go out. He looked at his own raised fist as if it belonged to someone else and he staggered back to bed.

"I'll wait till morning, but don't try to stop me," he said. He sat on the edge of the bed.

"Don," Mary Lou said. She looked right into his eyes and took hold of his chin, made him look at her, and tried to explain to him that it had to be his illness talking and not him. He gripped her wrists until she thought they would snap.

"I'm gonna go get you a shot," she said. "Now, you sit right here and be still." She tried to draw away her hands, but he held on.

"You call Mr. Neiderhelman and tell him I'll be there," he said.

"Don." Mary Lou tried to explain again. "You're having a dream or you're seeing things. You worked for Mr. Neiderhelman over sixty years ago. He's dead. You're here at home and it's the middle of the night."

Don released her wrists and looked puzzled. She felt so terribly sorry for him. He looked like a little kid or a beaten dog.

"Now settle down and let me get what you need. Stay put now, you don't want to fall. . . ."

Mary Lou scurried to the bathroom to get an insulin shot. Her hands shook as she prepared it. She listened for him moving, hoping he was not on his feet again. Don had his moments of confusion, but not like this. This inflexible child was someone new, not her sweet man.

When she returned to the bedroom she found Don half-dressed. He was struggling with his belt buckle.

"Don, no. You can't go out." She ran over to him with the needle in her hand.

"Get away. I don't need that stuff. I'm going to work and you can come with me or not."

"It's midnight. Look out the window." She was bone tired, weak from her own sleepless nights.

The struggle took place all over again, with Mary Lou barely able to stand up. She would have bruises on her wrists tomorrow. She explained over again where they were and that he'd been sick.

"I'll call Helen. Will you listen to her?"

"No, you and Helen are in league against me."

That'll be the day, Mary Lou thought.

That crazy light was back in Don's eye and the clock was moving toward one. Was this insanity going to be permanent?

After urging and begging for another spate of time—how long she couldn't guess—Mary Lou got Don to take his pants off and lie back down on the bed. But his eyes had no sooner shut than they popped back open and he started to get up. Mary Lou threw herself against him and tried to pin him down, projecting into the future the picture of herself trying wrestle Don down—and if he became completely helpless, to get him changed and moved in bed.

"You can't tell me what to do," he muttered, insisting, after all her explanations, that Mr. Neiderhelman's wagon would be picking him up any minute.

She wanted to hold her ears and scream but decided maybe she should humor him and she went along with his ranting.

"I'll get you up in plenty of time," she said, "how will that be? You lie down and I'll pat your back."

Eventually Don, worn out and medicated, lay down, and after awhile was snoring loudly. What should she do? He was too big and strong, in spite of his illness, for her to manage any longer.

They had to be near the end.

Mary Lou went into the bathroom and rinsed her face. She was too tired to brush her teeth. As she headed cautiously toward the bed, she glanced at the clock: three-thirty. Don had been acting up for over three hours. She got only to the edge of the bed when she heard a noise in the yard.

She knew who was out there and what they were doing.

Mary Lou went to the window. There were two figures by the garage. They moved toward the steps leading to the basement. They bent over and worked on the wooden doors.

Those kids had robbed her of her neighborhood, her possessions, peace. Now they were invading the only place she felt even a little safe—all she had left, her house—

She went to the closet where she had hidden her rifle behind her suitcases. It was heavy but she lifted it and ran to the landing on the stairs, her fury giving her strength, growing as she reached the window. She opened the sash and pointed the gun toward the back yard. It felt strange against her cheek and smelled of oil.

She looked down the barrel's length and grabbed for the trigger. She must not shoot unless they entered the house. Russell said so. She heard a basement door creak open and saw the boys start down the steps.

Mary Lou shot toward them. The explosion was loud and hurt her ears.

"Jesus Christ!" she heard.

"Fuck—what was that?"

The basement door banged shut, echoing the gun shot. Mary Lou saw the boys run away from the house, toward the garage. She shot again.

She saw them disappear behind the garage. Her heart banged like someone beating on a door.

Had she gone crazy along with Don? She pulled the gun away from the window and pulled down the sash, her insides turning to water.

She trudged slowly back to the bedroom, panting with the effort of climbing the stairs. The gun was still in her hands. If those sons of bitches came back again, this time she would kill them. Or maybe she would use it on herself.

"Mary Lou?"

Oh. She stood still. Oh God, she had waked up Don. He had just quieted down and gotten to sleep. Well, of course. She had probably waked up half the neighborhood. But they'd go back to sleep. They'd heard gunshots before. . . .

"What happened?" Don sounded more like himself, not the lunatic he was earlier.

"Those no-good boys tried to break in. I scared them off." Mary Lou stood at the doorway to the bedroom.

"Where did you get the gun? Let me see it."

Mary Lou looked down at the gun in her hands. Why was she still holding it?

"Oh, not now. Tomorrow. You go back to sleep. I forgot it would wake you, but those hoodlums deserved it." She was scared now of what she had done. "I don't think I hit either one. I saw them run off I think."

"You did right. Bring it here, though."

"Don. . . ."

"I can't sleep now anyhow."

Thinking, anything to mollify him and get him back to sleep, Mary Lou held up the gun for Don's inspection. It was still warm.

"Now I'm putting it back," she said. "See?"

"No. Bring it over here. It looks like the ones we used in the army. I want to see if it is."

"Be careful. It's loaded."

Mary Lou went closer to the bed with it.

Don took hold of the gun barrel and pulled it around so it was aimed at his chest.

"Let go!" Mary Lou said.

"It's quicker than rat poison."

"Don, you're out of your mind."

"That's why I want you to pull that trigger. It's the best thing you can do for me."

"No. No."

Mary Lou tried to pull the gun away, but Don kept his grip on it.

"I tried to hurt you before, Mary Lou."

"You didn't mean to."

"You've done so much. Now one last favor. Please."

"I can't."

"You can. You'd do it for a dog."

The pleading in his eyes was like Tim's, the red membrane closing over the whites. A pleading for release, for dignity.

"It won't be as painful as poison. It won't hurt at all."

Her arms were being pulled from their sockets.

"Pull the trigger," Don said. "Do it fast."

"No."

Her hands were weakening.

"Do it. Do it! Do it!"

35

Mary Lou was watching the light coming up over the trees across the street. She heard the creak of the porch swing, and saw her feet scraping the wood floor. The floor needed painting. She noticed the tulips coming up in Mrs. Wong's yard. She loved tulips. She watched her neighbor's door open, and saw Mrs. Wong come across the street. She got bigger and bigger, until finally she was right in Mary Lou's face.

"I saw you sitting in the swing ever since I got the paper—and it's cold and I wondered. . . . Oh my God."

Mrs. Wong ran into Mary Lou's house and soon Mary Lou could hear her talking excitedly, first in Chinese then in English. She came back to the door and locked it from the inside. She was actually afraid of Mary Lou it seemed. Pretty soon two police persons arrived, Officer Debbie and the tall Puerto-Rican man who had investigated the break-in. Debbie went into the house while the man sat by Mary Lou.

"Are you OK?" he said.

Mary Lou nodded.

"Looks like a nice day," he said.

When his partner returned, he jumped up and went into the house. Debbie held out a handful of plastic bottles to Mary Lou.

"Are these all of your husband's medications?"

Mary Lou glanced at the bottles and said yes.

Debbie carefully loaded them into a plastic bag.

"You'll have to come with us Mrs. Friedman," she said.

"*Freed*man," Mary Lou said.

Officer Debbie pulled out a pair of handcuffs, but the man, who was coming out the door, stopped her. "I don't think we'll need those, do you?"

Mary Lou rode in the police car, looking out at her neighborhood through the wire mesh. It was like being a chicken in a cage. "Cluck, cluck," she murmured.

"How's that?"

The police officers took her in the back driveway of a big yellow brick building and through long halls: the jail, she supposed. They took off her blood-soaked clothes and gave her a faded blue house-dress-like thing to wear, and walked her to a cell where several women were sitting around.

"I'm going to try your daughter's number again," Debbie said. "She was out this morning. Does she work?"

"No."

The door closed behind Mary Lou. She looked around the room: a tiny high window, obscene scrawls on the wall. This was a world Mary Lou never thought to enter. It was so ugly and dark. These tough frightening women. Were they thieves or prostitutes, murderers, what? She sat on a bench and rested her head against the plaster wall. Her stomach was growling because she had not had breakfast.

The women, some reading, others watching the tv attached to the wall, turned to look at her. There was a black woman wearing a man's hat and a carved-on scowl, her face covered with dark patches and moles like tiny mushrooms, and a tall white woman with thick dyed-blonde hair. A middle-aged woman wearing a T-shirt with an image of Jesus' face on it was reading the Bible.

They took in Mary Lou's age and fragility. The blonde laughed loudly and said, "What'd you do? Rob a bank?"

The others snickered and Mary Lou turned her head away from them. They were making fun of her. Because she was old. It seemed like it was comical to be old now.

The television news came on: there was her house, her beautiful old house with its green lawn and friendly porch and old-fashioned swing. The camera showed a police ambulance taking something from the house and putting it into a van. They flashed a photograph of Mary Lou they'd taken, she supposed, from the driver's license she'd handed over to the police.

A blonde anchor woman said a man had been shot to death in the house and identified her as the "alleged perpetrator." The woman kept her face serious for a second and then said "more later on this shocking incident" and flashed her habitual smile. Mary Lou realized they were using her to keep viewers watching. The women in the cell all turned to her.

"Wow," the blonde said. She had a missing tooth.

"That you?" the black woman said. "Did you really kill your old man?"

Mary Lou could not remember. Only when the police arrived and she saw them carrying the thing out the door, did she realize something terrible had happened.

"How long was you married?"

"Sixty-nine years."

The women laughed.

"What took you so damn long?" the blonde asked. "I blew Richie away after two months."

Tears seeped from Mary Lou's clenched eyes.

"Oh now, don't cry, lover. I'm only joking."

"Um hmm," said the black woman.

She introduced herself as Vivacia and the other woman as Pearl.

"The preacher there with the Bible is Scripture Sue."

Pearl handed Mary Lou a tissue.

"They won't do nothin' to you, honey. Not a nice older lady like yourself," Vivacia said. "You got a home and relations. They'll look after you. You white."

Mary Lou shook her head.

"Me. All I did was snitch a small bottle of Wild Turkey from the deli and I'll rot in here."

"She lives on the street," Pearl said.

The commercials were over and the smiling anchor said, "More on the shooting last night on a quiet residential street in. . . ."

The prosecutor, a young man around forty with bright eager eyes, and Mary Lou thought a kind of jumpy way about him, was asked what would happen, given the age of the perpetrator and victim.

"This is murder pure and simple, and will be pursued and prosecuted like any other case."

"Oh for Christ's sake," Pearl said. "That asshole! He wants to run for some big office and doesn't care how he gets there."

The news moved on to a local saloon fire.

"You got a lawyer?" Pearl asked Mary Lou.

"No."

"I can't believe that jerk. Mary Lou here must have had a reason. . . ." Pearl said.

Mary Lou sat quietly, staring at her lap. Was the prosecutor right? She remembered struggling with Don over the rifle she had shot at the kids, but had no memory of making a decision or pulling the trigger.

Yet there was blood.

"Here honey," Pearl said. She was holding a bottle of polish she'd been applying to her fingernails. "Let me fix you up a little."

Mary Lou let Pearl take her hand, and watched as her nails grew bright purple. They looked very strange. They were still wet when a policeman came to the cell door and unlocked it and took Mary Lou by the arm.

"Come with me, Mrs. Friedman. We'll go see the judge."

"You need Solomon for this one," Pearl said.

"Good luck," Vivacia called.

The policeman escorted Mary Lou down a long hall and across a walkway through the windows of which she could see the people down in the street. Walking along free, as she was yesterday.

Mary Lou had never been in a courtroom before. It was depressing and sordid, not like the movies or tv. Instead of paneled walls and wooden jury box and judge's bench, everything was plastic made to look like wood. The light was garish and harsh. The walls were ugly, a faded greenish brown. Everyone, the judge, the man she recognized from television as the prosecutor, the several people standing around the room, were staring at her. She had not brushed her teeth for the first time she could remember. She couldn't remember if she had combed her hair. She looked down at her feet. There was a big run in one of her stockings. She tucked her legs back under her chair and tried to cover her garish fingernails with her sleeves.

The prosecutor announced that Mary Lou would be charged with murder. No one challenged him. Maybe she should have a lawyer. But she didn't really care what they did.

The judge said, "What about bail?"

"Two hundred thousand," the prosecutor said.

Mary Lou tried to speak. Where would she get such money? She wanted to go home.

"Is there something you wish to say, Mrs. Friedman?" the judge asked.

"Where's my daughter?"

"We're contacting her."

"Can I go home?"

"I don't think Mrs. Friedman is a threat to the community," the judge said. "She may leave on her own recognizance without bail."

The prosecutor jumped to his feet. "Her fingerprints were on the gun. There were bloody rags in the bathroom sink!"

"There's the question of responsibility," the judge said. He looked at Mary Lou with a kind face. "You may return to your home until further notice, Mrs. Friedman. Your daughter will be there soon. Understand you may not leave the county. Will you be all right?"

"I'll be all right," Mary Lou said. "I've lived alone—well, with my husband—for sixty-nine years."

The prosecutor scowled at her mention of Don.

They took her back across the walkway, and back to the cell she had been in before.

"Aren't I going home?" she asked.

"Soon's we get a squad car to take you."

The women gathered around Mary Lou.

"How'd it go?" "What happened?"

Mary Lou tried to describe what had taken place in the courtroom.

Vivacia said, "I tole you you would be all right. Nice white lady like you."

Pearl looked worried.

Scripture Sue grabbed Mary Lou's hand.

"Have you accepted Jesus Christ"?

Mary Lou thought a minute. The woman's hand was none too clean.

"He was a good man."

"You must believe on him to find everlasting life."

Mary Lou said nothing. She had been through just about everything that could happen to a woman. This life was what mattered to her. Any other would remain a mystery.

"Hey Sue," Pearl said, "let Mary Lou alone."

Mary Lou sat on one of the benches. Sue reminded her of Helen—that positive light in her eye. Mary Lou was sorry she could never reach Helen. She would write her a letter telling her she was sorry for the mistakes she had made and that Helen should forgive her.

Soon a policeman came and took Mary Lou out of the cell. The others waved goodbye. The policeman led her through the halls to the room where they had stored her bloody clothes. They returned her coat, which she threw over the jail uniform for the ride home.

The policeman who drove Mary Lou came into the house with her and offered to help her find fresh clothes, but Mary Lou waved him away.

"My daughter will be here soon."

"Sure you're all right?"

Mary Lou gave him her best and bravest look, the one she had worn at her mother's grave and Elaine's and Billy's funerals. The one that hid her desolation.

When the policeman left, Mary Lou sat at the kitchen table. She picked a few bread crumbs off a place mat. *Cleanliness is next to Godliness.* Her grandmother's words and her mother's dear face came back to her. She recalled Billy's grin and Elaine's tiny body when she died, her sweet smile.

She glanced around the room, at the potholders with teddy bears on them, the Mr. Coffee machine.

Don's empty chair.

She was beginning to remember what happened upstairs the night before.

Shame. . . .

She glanced down at her coat. There was dried blood on the lapel, her husband's blood. She tore the coat off and threw it away from her. There was blood on the dress underneath the coat. And underneath that, on her arms, on her hands. Nothing could be hidden. The giant shadows that hovered over her from birth were condemning, *bad, shame.*

She had done the worst thing a human being could do. It was Don's will. Her hands were his. But she was the one who took life. She was not afraid of hell, but of living with what she had done. She ran to window to water the drooping geranium, a dry red. The pot fell from her hands.

She looked at the clock. Helen would be over soon. Mary Lou got up and hurried to the stairs.

She must get to the basement before Helen came and tried to stop her, must find what Russell had left there.

The New Century

Time runs stories of the twentieth century's big events, but people remember their own stories. While he is not fond of looking back, Frederick is forced into reminiscing by his granddaughter who is probing into the family's background for an oral history project at college. He tries to think of memories for her, but gets stuck at the point where his parents died.

It has been nine years now. The notice in the paper was so ugly: "At four this morning, Mrs. Mary Lou Friedman, eighty-six, shot and killed her husband of sixty-nine years, Don Friedman. Asked his reaction the county prosecutor said, 'This is murder pure and simple and will be pursued an prosecuted like any other case.'" No recognition of his parents' age and failing health. The next day's paper brought the news of Mary Lou's death: "At her home, Mrs. Mary Lou Friedman died by ingesting rat poison." Rat poison. Did they have to say that?

Frederick hid the newspaper from his wife and daughter.

He went to Cincinnati alone for the funerals. Mary Lou and Don were cremated according to their wills. Sylvia wanted to scatter their ashes in their garden although Frederick advised her that it was illegal to do so. He refused to let her take the urns from the crematorium: but she was so vehement, and, he thought, close to hysteria, that he compromised. No one could ever say no to Sylvia; she was so flaky and spoiled. He agreed that she could take Mary Lou's ashes, and leave their father's in the urn in the crematorium. "But they should be together," Sylvia begged. Frederick stuck with his decision, annoyed that he could be pulled into so silly an argument, over his parents' remains.

Aside from his stark recall of the day they died, he has few memories of Mary Lou and Don, of his years at home; they have been covered, like most things in his life, by a kind of soft veil.

He recalls his mother as a rather sweet woman, pretty when she was young, a good cook, a gardener. Somewhat remote. He liked her apple fritters.

Where she was born or who her parents were, he has no idea. Genealogy has never interested him. He has always been interested in science and now pursues his hobby of astronomy, spending his retirement studying the heavens through his top-grade telescope. His

life has been numbers, business, bottom lines. He has always loved
skiing and still spends a month every year with his family in Aspen at
their house there. He has given up the steeper runs: too many young
showoffs on pot or alcohol right on the tail of more traditional skiers.

But about their deaths: his father was sick and his mother getting
old. Everyone gets old, though. He himself has plenty of ailments; he is
shocked at the line-up of medicine bottles in his bathroom. Still, life is
precious, more so each day.

The past is best forgotten.

Helen had dreaded the end of the century, until she began reading
books about the Rapture. She reads each volume that comes out. They
make her feel light and joyful. She feels sorry for the ignorant people
she sees around her who will not share the wonder, the humanists and
the godless media and the homosexuals. She prays that her parents will
be raised from the limbo they must be in. Why had they done the awful
things they did?

Why hadn't her mother called her if she was at the end of her
rope? Hadn't she done everything she could for her parents? If only *she
herself* had called sooner. Well, the Lord will forgive her. But how much
more suffering will she go through before she can be with Him? When
will God tell her what He has in mind for her? But maybe all this
questioning will soon be over.

She is getting closer to the age of her parents when they passed. She
composes her obituary.

She tells Russell her memories of her mother. He has heard them
all before, but loyally listens. "When we went on that trip I had this
terrible boil on my leg. It got so infected I could hardly walk, but when
I told mother about it, she just looked annoyed and said, '*It's always
something with you.*'"

"Wow," Russell says.

"Fred and I had to pay board when we worked, but they found the
money for Sylvia's big wedding, and Sylvia was wearing the diamond
pin Mother had promised *me*."

Russell shakes his head. "Yet you did everything you could for her."

Helen repeats her stories: *My mother didn't like me. She never
approved of anything I did. She always found the money for whatever Sylvia
wanted.*

Sylvia has lived in five different places in the years since she left
home for the last time: Akron for awhile, Cleveland, Steamboat

Springs (she was married to a ski instructor there), California. Her latest move was from Oakland to Venice Beach. She is well known, and business has been good since the hoopla about the millennium. She had assured her clients that the world would not end.

Sylvia believes in reincarnation and can remember many former lives. She considers being a seer her natural métier; she was always fascinated by Mary Lou's tales of her great-grandmother holding séances in her parlor over the family's mill. She thinks she came by her gifts naturally, through blood (neglecting the fact that the medium was a step parent).

Sylvia often relives the day of Helen's phone call. She rushed home as fast as she could to get there before they could bury her mother. She had to see Mary Lou one more time. She must not just disappear. But by the time she reached Cincinnati, the decision of cremation had been made by Helen and Frederick.

After their struggle over the ashes, Sylvia let Frederick leave Don's ashes at the crematorium, but she took possession of Mary Lou's to scatter in her garden. This was the strangest moment of all, taking hold of the plastic bag. In it was all that remained of a woman who had lived close to a century. For such a tiny, frail woman, her mother's ashes were surprisingly heavy.

Sylvia scattered them in the garden, over the flower beds, beneath the magnolia tree.

Sylvia went into the house. Helen and Frederic had said they wanted nothing of its contents. She was too unsettled to take any of the furniture. It would be sold. Sylvia looked through a few boxes of odds and ends. In one she found Don and Mary Lou's marriage license, their birth certificates (both born in 1904—almost a century ago). There was a bill from a finance company dated 1934, Don's discharge papers from World War II, bank statements and check stubs from years back. In a second box were some old copies of *Life*, a ration stamp, the Japanese flag Mary Lou had brought upstairs from the basement that last Thanksgiving at the house, a black Remington typewriter, a bunch of grocery store "green stamps" (she remembered those; Mary Lou got her a set of skates with them). It was like a junk heap of the twentieth century.

Sylvia left quickly. She wanted to get back to Akron. Back to her attempts to find a way of life. Away from the memories and reminders of her family. She found that people—Thor and his mother, Penny's daughter Tammy, a newspaper reporter who tracked her down—asked brutal questions of her: "What happened?" "Why do you think she did it?" "Was your mother disturbed?" All she could say was, "I was out of town," as if that excused her from responsibility.

Some years later, Sylvia tried to kill herself: she got into her car and turned on the gas in the closed garage. At the last minute, she opened the car door and ran outside: the thrill was too great, being so close to death.

Her feelings of guilt still torment her. She was closer to her mother in the days of her father's illness, but so absorbed in Thor and so devastated by Billy's death, that she had not realized what Mary Lou was going through. Whatever it was that drove her to act as she did.

Mary Lou seemed so strong. She was a good woman, a good mother. Sylvia remembers moments like Mary Lou handing her a magnolia petal instead of lecturing her about drugs, Mary Lou planning her wedding, never reproaching her for leaving Billy. Her mother wasn't demonstrative, but she gave Sylvia everything she wanted— maybe gave too much, spoiled her.

She is glad the prosecutor never got the chance to shame and punish her mother. He knew nothing about old people like her parents. But what could you expect from a first-timer?

"Murder" was the word the prosecutor used, but what did that mean? What actually happened that night? Sylvia can not imagine her mother killing. Mary Lou's act might be called desperation—insanity— mercy—an accident—or maybe even—fate.

If Sylvia had her mother back, she would smother her with kisses, and make her answer all her questions. Her attempts at reaching her through her own arts have failed. Bits and pieces are all she has of Mary Lou (the fairytale character's hat or umbrella—in the form of the grocery stamps, her birth certificate).

Sylvia dreams of standing outside a house with large glass windows. She sees her mother inside. She waves at her, taps on the glass. Mary Lou moves from room to room. Sylvia follows along. She waves again, trying to make Mary Lou look out at her. She beats on the glass, but she can not get her mother's attention.

About the Author

Dorothy Weil is the daughter of a Kentucky steamboat captain and a Cincinnati artist and writer. She has lived most of her life within view of the Ohio River, the dividing line between her two traditions, and the place her family was happiest. She has published six books: a feminist critique of America's first best-selling woman writer, a collection of poetry, a memoir, a thriller, and two comic novels, one of which was bought by Disney Productions. She has also published numerous articles for magazines and newspapers and has written regular columns of humor and art for *Cincinnati Magazine*. As writer and co-producer with the television production team TV IMAGE, INC. Weil has helped created a dozen tv documentaries, several winners of national awards. She has taught English at the University of Cincinnati and Edgecliff College. The central theme of Weil's work has been the realistic representation of women and the family drama. She has been selected as "best feminist author" twice by *Cincinnati Magazine*. When not at her computer she is painting in her studio near the riverside home she shares with her husband.